Praise for *David R. Slayton*

"Slayton crafts a setting rich in grit and grime and Americana
kitsch that's as much a character as gay warlock Adam Binder
in this, *Trailer Park Trickster*, the exciting follow-up in the
Adam Binder Novels."
—C. S. POE, AUTHOR OF THE MAGIC & STEAM SERIES

"In *Trailer Park Trickster*, David R. Slayton doubles down
on everything that made his first book great: a complicated
world, dangerous magic, a likable protagonist, dark family
secrets, and, of course, authentically painful (or is that
painfully authentic?) love. I can't wait for more!"
—GREGORY ASHE, AUTHOR OF THE HAZARD AND SOMERSET MYSTERIES

"[A] thrilling, well-crafted sequel to *White Trash Warlock*...
The interweaving of Adam's and Vic's quests builds satisfying
tension on the way to an unresolved ending that sets things
up nicely for the next installment. The result is an
emotionally rich page-turner."
—*PUBLISHERS WEEKLY*

"The complex world-building, well-shaded depictions of poverty,
emotional nuance, and thrilling action sequences make
this stand out. Slayton is sure to win plenty of fans."
—*PUBLISHERS WEEKLY* (STARRED REVIEW)

"Slayton's debut uses wry humor, alternating viewpoints, and intriguing LGBTQ+ characters that will have readers eager for more of Adam Binder's escapades."

—*BOOKLIST*

"The elves who show up would have Tolkien rolling in his grave, which is my highest endorsement, and the LGBTQIA+ rep is all around outstanding."

—*BOOKRIOT*

"A well-written story with an LGBTQ+ protagonist...Dark, haunting, lyrical, and innovative, beautiful and heartfelt, *White Trash Warlock* by David R. Slayton is crafted like something rarely seen in the world of urban fantasy: he's given the reader something unique, which is a rare and wonderful treat."

NEW YORK JOURNAL OF BOOKS

TRAILER PARK
TRICKSTER

TRAILER PARK
TRICKSTER

DAVID R. SLAYTON

**BLACK
STONE**
PUBLISHING

Printed in the United States of America

First paperback edition: 2021
ISBN 978-1-0940-6797-1
Fiction / Fantasy / Contemporary

Version 1

Blackstone Publishing
31 Mistletoe Rd.
Ashland, OR 97520

www.BlackstonePublishing.com

For Anitra,
world's best mom, friend,
and general badass.

1

ADAM

The wards were down. That was how he knew, really knew, that she was dead.

The plastic flamingos and homemade wind chimes remained, but the warmth of Sue's presence, the thing that said she'd always be there for him, that Adam had a home here, was gone.

Still, the lights were on and a television buzzed somewhere inside the trailer.

Someone was home.

Adam tasted the rain on his lips. He'd driven as fast as he could. The adrenaline that had flooded him when he'd torn out of Denver had long faded.

He'd left without a word, leaving his mom and Bobby to mourn Bobby's wife, Annie, and likely question Adam's sanity again.

Now too much gas station coffee buzzed in his veins. He should eat. But first, he had to know the details. And he had to know who was living in Sue's trailer.

He took the steps in twos, raised his fist to pound on the door, but it swung open before he could knock.

Jodi.

Adam's cousin was twenty-one, just under six feet, and pissy. They'd never gotten along.

Her black-and-purple hair was pulled into pigtails. It contrasted with the pale, thick foundation she wore to mask her pimples and acne scars. Or maybe they were crystal craters, meth sores. Either way, the sight of her made Adam glad he'd outgrown the goth look.

"What?" she demanded.

Behind her, a television flickered and boomed with some cop show. Adam's relatives probably thought it good research for getting away with crime.

"I'm here for my things," he said.

"You don't have any things here," Jodi spat.

Adam could almost hear the twang of a banjo in her drawl.

"I have clothes. Books," he argued.

"All gone," Jodi said with a dismissive shrug.

"Where did they go?" Adam demanded.

He caught a whiff of something nasty when he tried to push past her, like cat urine mixed with nail polish, but she stuck her booted foot against the door.

"Mom took everything to town," Jodi said. "Sold or pawned it."

Adam clenched his fists.

"Sue's rings? My clothes?"

"*Everything*," Jodi stressed.

Adam took a breath, let it out. He didn't trust Jodi, and he trusted her mother, Noreen, less. They were liars and cons. Sue had hated them both.

"You're lying," he said. "Let me in."

"No."

"What about Spider?"

"Who?"

"Sue's cat. Where is he?"

"That's a dumb name for a cat," Jodi muttered. "There wasn't a cat."

Adam squeezed his eyes shut. Noreen and Jodi hadn't even cared enough about Sue to know about Spider. He would take it as a blessing. Who knows what they would have done to the poor thing. Still, there was that smell.

"There had to be," Adam said. "He was old. He didn't go out."

"No cat. No books. No clothes."

"Will you at least tell me what happened to Sue?" he asked.

"Heart attack. She was old. It happens. Go cry about it somewhere else."

Jodi slammed the door in Adam's face.

He sighed. He had a key. He could try to force his way inside, and—what, physically fight off Jodi and her mom? The thing was, he didn't doubt that Noreen would have sold everything the moment Sue passed.

Noreen was Sue's daughter, so technically a cousin, but she was more like an aunt in age. She was perpetually broke and by Sue's account, addicted to any number of things, which probably explained the smell. Her habit was worth more than anything to her.

It was dark. Adam looked across the trailer park. He didn't have anything here. He didn't really know anyone either, not well enough to ask for a place to stay. He could look for Spider, not that the cat would come. Spider had only loved Sue. And yet he'd shown up in Denver, warning Adam that something was wrong before disappearing like he'd never been there.

Adam gave one of the porch posts a kick and stalked back to his car.

Climbing in, he laid his forehead on the Cutlass's steering wheel.

Noreen and Jodi.

Sue had kept her daughter and granddaughter at a distance.

She'd hated their willful ignorance, the constant begging for money she didn't have, and the visits from the sheriff's deputies asking Sue and Adam if they'd been in contact. Sue hadn't even invited them to Christmas, and Adam suspected she'd been shielding him from them.

Sometimes Adam thought being gay was a blessing. It kept him from being like his father's extended family, like most of the Binders, just like having magic had kept him from being like his mother and brother.

Noreen and Jodi would lose their minds to know Adam was dating a Mexican cop. He couldn't decide which part of Vic—Mexican, bi, or cop—they'd take more offense at.

"Dammit," Adam said, throwing his head back against the seat's headrest.

He'd left Denver without a note, without calling Vic or explaining. He'd driven straight to Guthrie like his ass was on fire.

Adam unlocked his phone, started to text or call, but he was still seething. The red in his chest was a nice contrast to the deep black and purple, the heavy surety that Sue was gone.

He didn't want to be an emotional wreck when he talked to Vic. He wasn't ready to go back to Denver, not until he found out what had happened to her, if it really had been a heart attack. Then there was Spider, poor old cat. Would he have come to Adam if magic weren't involved? Was it just concern for his mistress or something worse?

Adam squeezed his eyes shut and opened them when cold filled the air, sweeping over the car like a sleet storm. The scent of rotten blackberries and battery acid surged.

He knew this magic, knew its greasy flavor, its cloying, clinging stench.

"No," Adam said, casting about for the source.

The power pulsed once, quick. The lights across the trailer

park went out. Adam opened the Cutlass's door and was halfway out when Sue's trailer exploded.

The heat washed over him. Glass pelted the other trailers as every window blew. Smoke, black and noxious, bloomed into the air. The fire lit the night.

Adam choked, swallowed hard on the damp air, and ran for the burning trailer.

"Jodi!" he shouted. "Noreen!"

He'd almost reached the porch when a second blast went off. Adam threw up his arms, put his hands in front of his face, and felt his magic rise as it tried to shield him. The hair on the back of his hands singed.

The chemical smell of the burning trailer grew thick and acrid as the rain sizzled against the flames.

Adam circled, trying to find a way in. The trailer had burst open. Flames licked at the corner of the roof where Sue's bedroom had been.

The front door was his only option. Adam pulled his jacket over his head, gathered what magic he had, hoping it could help, and jumped inside.

The fire was everywhere, but it hadn't yet filled the living room. The television, inexplicably, remained lit. He didn't see anyone.

"Jodi!" he screamed.

No answer. Adam's heart sank and pounded at the same time. "Noreen!"

Adam choked on the smoke. It sent a wave of dizziness through him. He pressed his shirt sleeve to his mouth, breathed through that, and kept his jacket over his head.

There, some movement in the corner.

Adam kicked the coffee table aside.

Noreen lay beneath a blanket, one of Sue's crocheted afghans.

She wasn't moving, but she took a wheezing breath when Adam pulled at her arm. He lifted her as much as he could.

"Jodi!" Adam shouted.

Noreen stirred at her daughter's name. She staggered to her knees with Adam's help.

He didn't know if she was high, drunk, or just overwhelmed by the fumes.

"Come on!" Adam shouted, pulling her to her feet.

Together they staggered to the door, him coughing, Noreen wheezing.

He wasn't going to make it. He was going to pass out.

A shadow filled the doorway, a man wreathed in leather straps and a faded black hoodie. Adam couldn't make out his face through the smoke that filled the room. He held a charred skull in his open palm. Frost coated it despite the fire and the heat.

"Who are you?" Adam tried to shout, though it came out choked.

The figure didn't answer, but Adam knew. This was him, the man he'd been hunting.

Whatever he was, terrible as he was, he emitted a cold that pushed the heat back.

Adam forced himself to carry Noreen toward him, away from the licking flames and rising smoke.

They were almost to the figure. Adam spied two eyes, blue like ice, inside the hood. Adam would knock him aside if he had to.

The figure vanished as Adam stumbled into him.

Carrying Noreen, Adam fell out the door and into the rain, lungs fighting for clearer air.

He cast about, looking for the figure who'd blown up the trailer. The dark druid, the warlock who might be his father.

2

VIC

Vic grunted at the sudden pain and pressed a hand to his heart.

He'd been feeling weird all day, a combination of blue and black that said Adam was deeply upset about something. But now Adam was hurt, maybe physically, and he wasn't picking up his phone.

Vic dialed his brother.

"Baby bro!" Jesse said. "What's shaking?"

"Hey, have you heard from Adam?" Vic asked.

"He's not with you? He didn't show up for work. I figured you two were all cuddled up."

"No," Vic said, feeling himself blush as he walked toward his car. Jesse teased Vic any chance he got, especially about Adam. "Just remember that I didn't ask you to hire him."

Jesse hummed agreement. "Yeah, well, Wonder Bread is a wizard with engines."

And a wizard in other ways, Vic thought, though he didn't say it aloud. Adam was, for example, a very good kisser. He could also see spirits and astral project into their world. In their brief acquaintance, Adam had completely upended Vic's reality.

"If I see him," Vic said, "I'll tell him to call you."

"Aight." Jesse hung up.

Vic started the car and drove south.

He considered himself a patient man. He'd taken getting shot in stride. He'd dealt with the idea that Death herself had picked him to be a Grim Reaper as calmly as possible. Now he was driving across town to check on a boy who wasn't returning his calls. And damn if Adam Lee Binder didn't test Vic to the point of cursing out loud and wondering if he should stick to dating girls.

Vic didn't know what he and Adam were to each other. Boyfriends sounded immature, but Vic didn't hate the term. There was an intensity between them that Adam said was just the magic that bound them together, but Vic disagreed. It ran deeper than that, at least for him. It was all very *come here, go away*— which wasn't how Vic wanted this relationship to go.

Things were just starting to settle down.

He'd just gotten back to work, assigned to desk duty. His captain wasn't in any rush to see Vic back on the beat after his partner had put a bullet in Vic before killing himself. To make it back to active duty, Vic had to make it over a fence. He could, but wasn't supposed to be up for that yet, not so soon after being shot, so he faked it and waited.

Thinking about it still made him shudder. His entire life had changed in a day.

He'd learned magic was real. He'd become a Reaper, and he'd been saved by a frustrating boy whose ass he currently wanted to kick.

"Adam," Vic whispered, reaching for the line inside himself, the magic that connected the two of them.

It had gotten fainter as Vic had gotten better, but sometimes it still thrummed.

Right now it felt cold, not cool or distant, just . . . blue. Adam was sad, heartbroken even.

Something had happened, something bad, and Adam hadn't told Vic about it.

Vic kept his eyes on the road and tried to call Adam again.

Adam didn't answer.

Vic drove to Dr. Binder's house. If something were wrong, Adam's brother might know what.

The problem was that being a Reaper hadn't come with a manual or any kind of instructions. Vic couldn't tell if Adam was just hurting for some normal reason or if something supernatural was up.

Adam didn't feel scared or hurt, he was just grieving, deeply grieving. Vic knew it well. He'd gone through it with his dad's cancer.

He'd had his job, something fresh to throw himself into.

Now, work was work, but being back, he'd started noticing things he hadn't before, little things around the station that made him question if the force was still right for him. Vic couldn't say if it was the shock of being shot or another side effect of finding out the world wasn't what he'd thought.

At least this drive gave him something else to focus on.

Vic arrived in Highlands Ranch, a suburb he didn't spend much time in. He'd been to the house for dinner once and over for a few other things. He liked Adam's mom, probably more than Adam did.

Adam still held something against her, but Vic hadn't pried into it yet.

Vic was trying to be careful, to go slow, but he wanted something to shift soon. He wanted some sign that he wasn't alone in this. Vic hadn't been dating much before Adam, and they'd all been girls. He could definitively say that no one else had his interest right now. The problem was that Adam thought all of the intensity and intimacy was about the magic. Vic didn't agree.

Vic would normally feel like showing up unexpected was out of line, but Adam had skipped out on work. Jesse said that "Wonder Bread" was always on time like a good employee, so Vic felt justified in dropping by Dr. Binder's house. He parked on the street.

Adam's mother sat on the porch, a cigarette jabbed in her mouth, overseeing her little domain of perfect green lawn and suburban bliss like it didn't impress her much.

Tilla smiled at Vic as he came up the walk.

She bore all the marks of a hard life, like the constant Oklahoma wind had ground her down, giving her a weathered *dammit, I'm still here* look.

Tilla's hair had been dirty blond once, like Adam's, but it was mostly gray now. Her eyes were brown where Adam's were a rich blue that reminded Vic of the ocean on a sunny day. At least they did when he was happy. They darkened with anger or sorrow. Vic wondered what color they were right now.

The smoke from Tilla's cigarette hazed the air. Vic had been more aware of scents and smells since he'd been shot. He wondered if it was the near-death experience or some side effect of becoming a Reaper.

Vic wouldn't have minded having superpowers. It wasn't like his new job required him to walk around in a black cloak carrying a scythe. The Reaper part of him was a lot like his connection to Adam: nebulous, down in his blood, like a root he had to dig for. He couldn't turn it on at will.

"Mrs. Binder," he greeted.

"Vincent," she said, dropping her cigarette butt into a coffee can.

It wasn't his name, but something about Tilla Binder made Vic feel like a nervous teenager, so he didn't correct her.

"Adam didn't show up for work," Vic said, scratching the back of his head. "Have you seen him?"

He'd met plenty of girls' parents, but this was different.

Everything with Adam was different, more real, a little more intense. Vic felt something for Adam he hadn't before, and he wanted Tilla to like him.

She shook her head.

"He brought the car home to show us the new paint job. He went downstairs for a minute, then he took off, full speed, without a word."

"Do you know where he went?" Vic asked.

"That boy doesn't tell me anything," she said. Her lips pursed. She looked like she wanted another cigarette. "Not that I blame him."

"Would Doctor Binder know?"

"Robert hasn't been himself since Annie . . . disappeared."

Annie Binder had been a casualty of Mercy, the spirit who'd brought Adam to Denver, brought the Binder brothers back together, and almost killed them all. Vic had never met Adam's sister-in-law, but his older brother, Robert, had not taken the loss well.

"Did he say anything to you?" Tilla asked. "You're closer to him than us."

"No," Vic said. "He just seemed sad."

Vic wasn't certain how much Tilla knew about Adam's magic. More than she let on, he suspected, but for now he'd play it cool. He certainly wouldn't mention the bond between them, the way they could feel each other's emotions, and occasionally hear each other's thoughts.

"Is there anyone closer?" he asked. "To Adam, I mean."

"Sue, his great-aunt on his father's side. Adam lived with her in Guthrie," Tilla said, a little acid slipping into her drawl.

Vic felt it as soon as Tilla spoke. It was like a hammer against his sternum. Adam's grief had a name.

"Did something happen to her?" Vic asked. "To Sue?"

"I wouldn't know. The woman hates me." Tilla looked away.

There was something there, some bit of the complicated family history that had damaged Adam's ability to trust anyone. Now wasn't the time to pry, no matter how much Vic wanted to know, or how much he wanted to hold Adam and squeeze all those broken pieces back together, which was almost as much as Vic wanted to shake Adam and get him to talk.

"Do you have her number?" Vic asked.

"I do," Tilla said, holding out a weathered hand for Vic to hand over his phone.

He did and she dialed from memory, handing it back as it rang.

Vic put his phone on speaker and set it on the porch rail.

It rang until voicemail picked up.

"You've reached Noreen and Jodi," a voice sawed out.

Vic opened his mouth to leave a message, but Tilla reached over and hung up the call.

"Something's wrong," she said. "That was the line to Sue's trailer."

"Who's Noreen?" Vic asked.

"Adam's cousin. Sue's daughter," Tilla said. She scoffed so hard Vic thought she might spit. "She's a real piece of shit."

Tilla drew out the word until it sounded like *sheet*.

"Sue didn't want us anywhere near that side of the family," a voice said.

"Doctor Binder," Vic said, greeting the man with a nod.

Adam's brother had aged ten years since Vic had last seen him. He'd had the life sucked out of him by Mercy, which had left him unconscious for a good while. His brown hair had grayed at the temples. He needed a shave, and probably a shower. His flannel bathrobe could use a washing. A thick miasma of something hung around him. It was more than grief, a caginess—the kind of thing that Vic would question in a suspect.

"You can call me Robert," he said, offering his hand. "Or Bobby, I guess."

Vic shook it. Yeah, Robert needed a shower.

Bobby got out his phone and began typing two-handed.

"Damn," he said, lifting the screen for their inspection. "There's an obit in today's *News Leader*. Sue's dead."

Tilla looked stricken. Her face paled but hardened at the same time. She swallowed and said, "Noreen changed the voicemail at her place before she was even cold."

"The funeral's in three days," Robert said. "I'll go pack. You too, Ma."

"She hated me," Tilla said, shaking her head. "She wouldn't want me there."

"We're not going for her," Robert said firmly. "We're going for Adam."

He looked to Vic, his expression questioning, expectant.

No, Vic thought.

That was too much time in the car with Adam's family, even if Bobby cleaned up. Vic could just imagine the horror of being locked in a car with them without Adam there as a buffer.

"I'll meet you there," Vic said.

3

ADAM

The EMT hovered but didn't say anything as Adam breathed into the mask pressed to his face. At least he'd stayed conscious and hadn't ended up in the hospital again. The fire was out, the trailer ruined, and most of the gawking neighbors had returned to watching their televisions.

They'd taken Noreen away in another ambulance and left Adam sitting in the back of this one. The rain had stopped, and he hadn't sensed the druid's presence since he'd disappeared.

A man in khakis and a windbreaker walked up. Adam hadn't seen the sheriff arrive but wasn't surprised that he'd missed it. He'd spent the last hour in a daze, thinking about Sue. Grief was stupid. At least it made him stupid. Maybe it was just the smoke and chemicals.

The sheriff looked to be in his forties. Adam didn't know the man. His time with Vic had changed his perception of the police a little, but Adam still felt that clench in his gut, the instinct to smile and pretend he hadn't done anything wrong, which he hadn't. At least he didn't think so.

"Can you talk?" the sheriff asked, gesturing toward the mask.

Adam took another long draw of oxygen and nodded.

"Adam Lee, isn't it? Adam Binder? This was your aunt's place?"

"Yes, sir," Adam said.

He did not like that the man knew his name, not when Adam didn't know his.

"I came back to find out what happened to her."

"She died?" the sheriff asked.

"Heart attack. At least that's what Jodi, my cousin, said. Did they find her? Is she okay?"

"No sign of anyone but the woman you rescued."

"Noreen," Adam said quietly. "Sue's daughter."

"She's stable. At the hospital. High as a kite."

Adam shook his head.

"Jodi answered the door when I knocked," Adam explained. He nodded to the burned wreck. "She was in there."

"Neighbors saw," the sheriff said, nodding to the other trailers. "Said the two of you argued."

Adam nodded. His gut was a cold rock.

"They also saw you run inside to save Noreen," the sheriff added.

Adam shifted a little on the metal seat they'd folded out from the wall for him to sit on. That helped. He didn't *totally* look like a bad guy.

"What happened?" Adam asked.

"Not sure yet, but judging from the bottles of chemicals we found, your cousin seems to have been starting a meth lab."

"In Sue's trailer?" Adam barked, prompting another coughing fit and another deep draw from the mask.

The sheriff nodded.

"I knew your aunt," he said.

"You did?" Adam asked. He didn't recall seeing the sheriff among Sue's clients.

"I'm sorry, but I don't recognize you," Adam admitted.

"I need better reelection posters," the sheriff said. He reached out a hand. "Early West. You went to high school with my boy Duncan."

Adam blinked as he shook Early's hand, making sure his grip was firm.

He'd tried his best to forget high school, but he could remember Duncan West. He had green eyes and dark hair, quite unlike his father. Adam had crushed pretty hard on Duncan in eighth grade. Duncan had also been one of Adam's worst bullies, a total jock, in high school.

"Yeah . . ." Adam said. "How is he?"

"Up in Stillwater, studying economics," the sheriff said.

Adam blinked. He wasn't being arrested, at least he didn't think so.

"I don't suppose you know where your cousin went?" Sheriff Early asked.

Adam shook his head. "Sue didn't approve of Noreen's choices. She and Jodi weren't really around."

"Strange that your aunt left them the trailer then," Early suggested.

"I'm not sure she did," Adam said. "But maybe. Maybe she just figured I wouldn't come back from Denver."

Early cocked his head.

"I moved there a few months ago," Adam explained. "I came back when I couldn't get ahold of Sue."

"And stumbled into this." Early turned, pointing his chin at the wreck of Sue's home.

Adam nodded.

"I'm sorry about your aunt. I haven't seen her in years," Early said.

His gaze paused on the Cutlass. Adam felt a heavy relief that his car hadn't been damaged in the explosion. He'd just gotten her back together.

"Haven't seen your daddy either," Early mused. "That used to be his ride, didn't it?"

Adam flinched at the mention of the word "daddy." It did not have good connotations. He'd been slapped pretty hard for using it thanks to an old John Wayne movie and his father's notions about manhood.

Adam would not think about his mother's trailer, about its secret, about what was buried behind it.

"Yeah," Adam said. "Sue gave it to me a few years ago. I fixed it up."

"Good job," Early said. His eyes lingered on the car a moment longer before he asked the EMT, "Is he good to go?"

"Yeah," she said. "He'll be fine."

"That's it?" Adam asked.

"That's it," Early said. "For now. Get somewhere dry. You got a place to stay?"

"Yeah," Adam lied. He didn't really, but he wanted this done.

With a tip of his hat, Early walked away.

Adam looked to the Cutlass. He could sleep there, but spacious as its 1970s interior was, he didn't feel like waking up cramped and cold. He especially didn't want to sleep here, in the shadow of Sue's burned-out home.

The druid had been there. With a skull. Nothing said he couldn't come back, and Sue's wards were gone.

He hadn't attacked Adam. He hadn't even been trying to. It couldn't be about Sue. She was already dead, so why had the druid gone after Noreen and Jodi?

At least Adam's mom and Bobby were safe in Denver.

Adam drove out to Seward Road. New houses had sprouted up in the few years since he'd last been here. There was less prairie.

More homes encroached on the three acres his mom owned on the swampier side of Lake Liberty.

Things hadn't changed so much that he didn't remember the way. The Cutlass rumbled over the washboard road.

Adam pulled up to the aluminum gate. It gleamed pale in the headlights, the only sign that he'd reached his mother's property. The rest of the fence was old barbed wire, left over from his father's days. Adam climbed out. He'd forgotten how dark the country was, how loud the crickets could be.

The trailer park always buzzed with something, televisions or too loud conversations, fights, or laughter.

Vic's apartment was a lot like that—small, in a brick building where you could hear so much if the windows were cracked open.

The familiar sounds of the country night, bugs mostly, weren't a comfort.

Adam and Bobby used to run down the little hill to catch their dad as he drove home. One time, they rode on the Cutlass's hood, their dad going slow so they didn't fall off. Adam didn't try to force the memories down as he took in the night. There were no streetlights out here, just stars and endless cricket song fueled by the evening's rain.

Adam left the car running and the lights on as he opened the gate, drove in, and got out again to close it. Mom didn't even put a padlock on it, which seemed weird considering the secret she guarded.

He didn't sense any magic, not that there would be wards. His mom wasn't like him or Sue. She didn't have to worry about something slipping out from the Other Side.

Adam knew too well that there were dangerous things out there, and now the druid had shown himself.

Adam had to set a ward. It would be too thin to keep much out, but he had magic enough for an alarm, something to warn him.

He drove up the long gravel driveway and stopped, letting the headlights illuminate the trailer. It hadn't changed in his years away. Maybe the beige siding and brown trim were a little duller. The white details, like the window frames, were yellow now.

It was a long box, a single-wide, just big enough for the four of them. Then they'd become three.

Adam still thought of his dad as missing, not dead and buried in the woods behind the trailer. Bobby had killed Robert Senior when Adam was six. Mom and Bobby had buried the body, wrapped it in a tarp, and piled rocks atop it. That was why his mom would never, could never, sell the land. She'd never move to town or even to live with Bobby permanently, which probably would have been the best thing for her.

Adam circled the trailer three times, drawing a line in the mud with the toe of his boot and pouring his will into it. Some practitioners would chant, invoke the watchtowers. Others called on their gods. Adam had never bound himself to a power. What magic he had to use was just his own. Chanting was a way to focus the mind, but Adam had always felt fear and caution did a good enough job.

He pushed away the memories swimming in the air around him. His father's endless anger, his hatred, had stabbed like a knife into the heart of a too sensitive child who had no means of shielding himself from the feelings of others.

Narrowing his eyes to slits, Adam pushed his will into the ward. He wasn't that kid anymore. He could control his Sight.

But he couldn't go back to Sue's. He didn't have any money for a motel and even then, the voices and things he'd sense in a place like that would guarantee a bad night's rest. He was too tired to shut out the echoes and dreams of desperate or lonely people. Cheap motels never came without that kind of baggage and too often they were haunted.

Adam finished the warding and let himself into the trailer. He still had a key after all this time, a promise from his mom that he could come home, though he never had before. He still wasn't certain he was welcome. Things with his mother and brother were better, but still rocky.

He turned on the lights. The overhead fixture buzzed. His mom still used incandescent bulbs.

The place was tidy, but he sank a bit to see it so unchanged. Tilla hadn't moved on at all. She still lived as she had when Bobby and Adam had been there too.

The same six-sided linoleum dining room table with the tall backed chairs. The same cheap tile floor, dented and sliced from when his father had thrown the silverware sorter at it in one of his many fits of anger.

Just remembering that moment made Adam squeeze his eyes shut for a long breath.

"Geez, Mom," he said. "You could have at least painted."

Everything was the same dingy white, stained beige from decades of his mother's smoking. He'd open some windows in the morning, air the place out.

A soft meow greeted Adam from the living room.

Spider lay curled up on the couch, staring up at him with green, expectant eyes.

4

ADAM

It was a bit like that thing with the cat in the box. Spider felt alive.
He purred and curled up into Adam's lap as soon as Adam sat on
the couch. Spider was, by all appearances, the same cat who'd
taken a shit in Adam's shoes the first night he'd slept at Sue's.

He was old, but not mangy. Sue had bathed him, which he'd
somehow tolerated. He was sleek and soft to the touch.

It made no sense that he'd be here, in Tilla's locked trailer. He
had no food, no water, and no litter box.

"Mom will shoot you if you try to poop in her shoes," Adam
warned.

Spider mewed.

He gave off no magical aura, no sense of danger. Adam had
only met one thing who could cloak her nature perfectly.

"You're not Death, are you?" he asked.

Spider didn't answer.

"If you're going to eat me, get it over with already," Adam said.

Spider did not eat him.

Adam didn't want to fall asleep there, cat in his lap, still stinking
from the fire, but the day's long drive and the night's trauma piled on.

Spider's purrs lulled Adam to sleep.

Adam woke with an ache in his neck.

It was his own fault. His mother's couch was ancient, the springs long flattened. It was held together with history and a bit of duct tape.

Spider was gone, vanished by whatever means he'd come, which meant Adam's wards weren't worth the dirt he'd scratched them in. Closing his eyes, he felt for them. They remained intact, but he knew how little power he had, how easily something might blow through them.

Adam had felt the druid's magic at the trailer and knew he was outgunned. If he came for Adam, it wouldn't go well. The sooner Adam figured out the connection between them the safer he'd be. Knowledge was power, especially in magic.

And then there was that note, left for him in Denver by the druid, which had given Adam the key to defeating Mercy.

There is still time to save her, it had read. *You will know what to do.*

Adam had thought the note meant Annie, Bobby's wife. Maybe it had meant Sue. Maybe it had meant Noreen. Why would the druid leave him a helpful note then blow up the trailer?

Maybe Jodi had caused the explosion. Maybe Noreen, but it had come so close on the heels of the druid's appearance.

Stretching, Adam twisted his head side to side to loosen his neck up as he searched the house for signs of two-footed intruders.

Senses extended, feeling for anything out of the ordinary, he opened the door to the room he'd shared with Bobby and found it unchanged. Adam's back ached to see their old bunk bed still standing, taking up most of the little room.

He crossed the trailer, going to the other end. Adam didn't want to enter his mother's room, her private space, but he had to check.

The bed was made. Everything was orderly, prepped for her long sabbatical to Denver.

Bobby had taken their dad's pistol to Denver and lost it. Mom's shotgun was under the bed, loaded and ready to go.

Adam could still feel the boom of the shot that Vic had taken for him, so loud it had rattled his teeth. The thunder, the roar, still echoed in his memory. It probably always would.

Vic.

Adam should call. He should text, but he had no service when he looked at his phone.

What would he say anyway, that Sue was dead, that Adam was being haunted by her cat?

"I should have been there," he said.

She'd been there for him when no one else had. She'd taken him in without question. Adam hated to think of her dying, of her being alone in that moment. The weight of it, the sense that he'd failed her, pressed him down as he moved back to the center of the trailer into its little kitchen.

The fridge was dark and empty. His mom had unplugged it to save electricity.

Adam checked the cabinets and found a cardboard can of instant oatmeal and microwaved a coffee cup full of water.

His mother was nothing if not consistent. The oatmeal and the peanut butter he spooned into it were the store brand. It was an uninteresting breakfast, but food was food. Adam chewed, staring out the back window and tasting the bit of grit from the well water.

You could go see.

The unbidden thought didn't surprise him. Adam was curious, had been since Bobby had told him the truth.

He knew the spot, the unmarked grave where his father lay buried. He'd walked by it a hundred times, never thinking that the pile of rocks meant anything at all.

He'd climbed it once, playing king of the mountain, until his mother had yelled at him to get off of it. He'd been ten and confused at why she was shaking. Now he understood the lance of fear that he'd felt from her.

And he understood why his mother wouldn't leave these woods.

Adam understood Bobby, Robert, now. That didn't mean Adam liked his older brother, but he made a bit more sense. So many of his actions in the years since Robert Senior's disappearance slid into place now that Adam knew the truth.

Bobby was haunted by what he'd done, and he'd run as far away as he could, but it hadn't been far enough.

And then there was the druid, and Adam's binding promise to stop him. He'd never quite settled the question if the druid was his father or not. Their magic was similar, even more so now that Adam had turned warlock.

He had to go and see. He didn't want to. The idea of grimy bones did not appeal.

So he'd go in spirit.

His Sight had always been strong, almost too strong. It could come over him without warning, leave him dazed and seeing spirits. The Other Side always called to him. Never far, it lurked, whispering, tugging at his attention. Adam didn't have the power to bring his body across, but he had magic enough to send his spirit. He'd had better control of his power since the business in Denver.

Every living thing had some magic, even if they didn't know it. Most people accessed the Other Side through dreams. People with a little more power, usually from their bloodline, might have visions. Others bargained with things best left alone.

As one of his teachers, Sue had taught Adam the rules, repeating them, drilling them into him, even when he didn't want to listen. The scariest rule was not to summon what you couldn't put down.

Summonings were tricky spells, and Adam was glad he didn't have the magic to cast one.

Mostly he just had a lot of visions, so many that he had to actively work at not letting little pieces of the Other Side leak through the veil.

Sometimes the pull was too strong, and he'd exhaust himself to keep the Other Side from bleeding into his normal sight.

Adam's first love had taught him to control it, how to safely spirit walk, and how to talk to immortals and avoid their deals and traps. Sue had taught him how to sharpen his gifts, doing her best as two generations of mixing in other bloodlines had weakened the family talents. Unlike her, Adam only saw the future in flashes, in bits and images.

He opened the thin door to his and Bobby's old room. It smelled like the old moldy carpet and a bit like heated plastic, the scent of the glue that held the walls together.

Adam would ask his mother why she hadn't changed anything when he next saw her but doubted she'd give him a real answer.

Bringing his backpack, Adam climbed to the top bunk of the bed their dad had built from plywood and two-by-fours. They'd stained it dark brown, though any gloss was long worn away. Just a tiny bit of that oily tang lingered. Perhaps it and the odor of glue were just his memory.

The lines he'd scratched with a pocketknife still showed on the bed's rail.

Adam couldn't even remember what he'd meant by them, only that he'd needed to do *something*, take out what he'd felt on an object.

His dad had beaten Adam over something, a broken toy, a dropped bit of food, something small. It had always been something small that at the time had felt so important, so massive, like dropping his fork would end his world. Now he could see, with the distance of age, that his father had always been looking for an excuse. It didn't really matter what Adam did, how he messed up, or that he spent every waking moment walking on eggshells. He was going to get a beating. That had been that.

Adam sighed. It didn't matter right now. He pushed the stinging memory of his slapped face aside. Sitting cross-legged, he took his tarot cards out of the backpack. They'd been Sue's last gift to him, and though she'd left him without a home, they were the most precious thing she could have given him. Noreen would probably have just pawned them.

They were old, passed from Binder to Binder, witch to witch.

Adam shuffled. He wanted to search for the druid first, for answers, but his thoughts kept drifting to Vic and the silence he felt when he reached across the connection between them.

Adam drew a card.

Three of Wands reversed.

"Great," Adam muttered.

The card meant uncertainty, unexpected delays.

Adam had expected it, but he didn't like it.

He shuffled again, focusing on Jodi, on setting aside his dislike of her.

Three of Wands. Reversed.

Again.

This was the tarot equivalent of *file not found*.

Perhaps he was just too distracted, too worried about Vic, to get a reading.

"Fine," he said aloud. "No more putting it off."

He lay down, positioned his body like he might be walking forward, and reached out a hand to clasp the bed rail like he would hold a staff.

The Other Side was close, so close, and Adam was there almost the instant he closed his eyes.

He'd crossed often from Sue's, but never his mom's. Spirit walking had come to him at Liberty House, the asylum Bobby had sent him to in high school.

Adam was over it, mostly, but cinder block walls and menacing orderlies still lingered at the corners of his nightmares. They likely always would.

Here, the scrub oaks where Mom had set her trailer loomed around him, far taller than in the real world. He lay on its flat roof and sat up.

The usual moon, a crescent, hung low here, casting rays of green through the dark-barked branches.

Adam looked behind the trailer and saw something like a storm cloud at ground level. It moved through the air like a whirlpool, black and purple, twisting and smoky.

Adam had never seen something like it but had no trouble knowing what it marked. This was where they'd buried his dad, where his mother and brother had dragged the body and piled rocks atop it. Adam had seen death. He'd seen Mercy kill people, and shuddered to remember it, but this was new.

"What is that?" he muttered aloud.

"We call it a stain," a voice said. It didn't sound disgusted, more like the speaker was a little impressed. "It's left over from bad deeds—murder, usually. You should see a battlefield."

Adam whirled and found himself facing an elven boy he didn't know.

He lifted his defenses, pulling his will around him like armor.

"Easy, warlock," the elf said, lifting slender hands. "There's no need for that."

He was the opposite of Silver or Argent. Where they were pale, cast in shades of the metal for which they'd been named, this elf had sloe-colored hair, black with an edge of blue. His skin had a bit of that same tinge. His eyes were dark, like pools of ink. His fingernails matched them.

Adam had seen plenty of strange beings, but the crown gave him pause.

Filigree, woven of ebon wire and shards of what looked like sea glass, the crown sat tilted on the boy's head. He looked young, little more than a teenager, but appearances could be deceiving, especially when immortals were involved.

"I'm Vran," the elf said, smiling as he freely gave his name. "You must be Adam."

Adam had made himself known in Denver, and this was exactly the sort of consequence he'd wanted to avoid.

"I don't know you," Adam replied, back straightening. He could flee back to his body, retreat behind his sad little wards, but they wouldn't keep an elf out—not even a young one.

"Sure you do," Vran said, a smile teasing at his lips.

He was wearing cobalt lipstick a shade lighter than his eyes. His clothes were fine, black silk. He looked like a goth prince, the exact kind of boy Adam had idolized in his early teens. Adam's gaze flicked to the long, slender sword at the boy's hip. It wasn't metal, but some kind of bone. The hilt shimmered like the inside of a seashell. Beautiful as it was, Adam knew it was deadly. He had no weapons of his own, no way to defend himself.

"What do you want?" Adam asked.

"So hostile," Vran said, shaking his head.

Adam didn't move. He didn't know Vran, but he knew elves. He was no match for the least of them, and if Vran were royalty, then he was far too powerful for Adam to mess with.

"And so hesitant," Vran said. He sounded hurt. "So ready to run. I thought you liked my kind."

"I don't know your kind," Adam said, trying to keep his voice even, to not cause any offense.

"Liar," Vran said. He held up a finger, pointed playfully. "They've marked you, my winter cousins."

"Them, I know," Adam said. "But you're nothing like them."

"Same species," Vran said with a shrug. "Different house."

"And which house is that?" Adam asked.

"Can't you guess?"

The side of Vran's mouth rose in a smirk.

Adam could sense the murky power seeping from the boy. Argent and Silver were cold but glittering. They were winter. Air. Swords.

"I'd rather not," Adam clenched his fists. He could run. He really should run, but this couldn't be a coincidence. The maelstrom and the emo elf had to fit together somehow.

Unless Vran really had just come to taunt him. After all, if he was an elf, he was a prick. Adam considered Silver and Argent pricks and he liked *them*.

Vran pursed his lips into a pout. "If you're not going to play, Adam Binder, then I'm not going to stay."

"So go," Adam said.

Vran smiled. He had sharp teeth, like a TV vampire, like a cat.

"You sure you want that? There's a lot I could tell you about what you're facing."

"In exchange for what?" Adam asked. Nothing was free in magic, especially when immortals were involved.

"I'll have to ponder that," Vran said, looking thoughtful. "Just remember, it's always darkest right before it goes pitch black."

"What is that supposed to mean?" Adam demanded.

"It means I know what's coming," Vran said. "It means you'd be smart to have more friends."

Grinning, he stepped backward and was gone.

"Elves," Adam growled. They were drama queens with far too

much magic and time on their hands. He wondered how many wars their boredom had caused.

The scent of Vran's magic, like brine and cold blood, answered which house he hailed from.

Water, Adam thought, turning back and forth, half expecting the elf to pop up behind him. Vran's house was water. Silver was the Knight of Swords; Argent, the Queen of Swords.

So Vran was a Cup, though Adam did not know which title.

The crown meant he had one, that he was at least the page, at worst the king.

Vran might look around fifteen, but that was no measure of his true power or his true form. He could be ancient. He could be in disguise.

Adam didn't have much power but he was hard to fool. That was his specialty, flying under the radar and being able to spot the things hiding there.

He turned back toward the stain and knew instantly that approaching it from this side wasn't the best idea.

The energy leaking from it felt sickening, like the smell of rancid meat on hot asphalt. It almost flipped Adam's stomach. It felt familiar too, reminding him of the deaths he'd seen in Denver, but this wasn't the druid's magic.

Yep. The term "stain" covered it.

Adam couldn't consider what his mother and brother had done to be a bad thing. His dad had beaten Adam, again, and according to Bobby had planned to kill him.

He couldn't remember the specifics of that day, just the terror, the pain, and guilt. His and his family's emotions were tangled up inside him like a beaver dam. A lot of it, the sticky red, was his father's rage. It was always building, a pressure inside him that needed to be vented, usually on Adam, but on Bobby or Tilla too. At some point the explosion would have proved lethal to someone.

Maybe it wouldn't have happened that day, but it had been coming. Robert Senior must have never expected that he'd be the one to die.

Adam took a breath, opened his eyes, and ended the spirit walk. He lay back in the little bed, his feet sticking off the end. Usually it took time for him to recover, but he didn't feel the lag now. His power was changing, possibly growing. He'd take it. He needed any help he could get against the druid.

Well, almost any. Adam had turned down Vran's offer without a second thought.

He wrapped the tarot cards back in their bit of leather and climbed out of the bed.

He showered, scrubbed off the road funk, the sleep, and the last of the smoke from the night before.

He hadn't brought any clothes. He had the jeans he wore and a few pairs of Dickies in the trunk of the Cutlass for working at the garage.

What he had with him would have to be good enough for today, for seeing her one last time, for saying goodbye.

5

VIC

The oil in his car hadn't been a priority, not with getting shot and saving the world, but Jesse would give Vic no end of grief if he didn't change it before a road trip.

Vic drove to Jesse's shop. It was near their mom's house, and it would give him the chance to get his hands dirty and work off a little of the knot gathering between his shoulders. Walking inside, he cracked his neck.

"Jesse?" he called.

The shop was open but abandoned, with several cars on the lifts or parked in the secure spaces. It wasn't like Jesse to leave the place unattended.

A muttered curse led him to a classic bottle-green convertible and a pair of legs in greasy coveralls sticking out from under it.

"Hey," Vic called. "Jesse around?"

The mechanic wheeled out from under the car. A familiar, angular face grinned up at Vic.

"He's on the Other Side," she said, waving a wrench.

"Argent," Vic said.

He looked behind him. The sky had gone purple. Something,

a pterodactyl maybe, flew by. Vic squeezed his eyes shut for a breath. He hadn't even felt the shift, the slip from the real to the surreal, to the Other Side.

"You could have just called," he said, looking back to the elven queen in coveralls.

"This is easier," she said, standing.

"Easier, or just more dramatic?" Vic asked.

"More fun," she admitted.

Vic had to smile. He liked the elf, far more than he liked her brother, but he still knew not to trust her.

The Queen of Swords was powerful in ways Vic didn't understand and he knew better than to prod with too many questions. Adam liked her and respected her, but that came with a healthy dose of caution—and Adam was one of the bravest people Vic knew.

"You're here about Adam?" she asked, wiping her hands on an oil-soaked rag.

Vic narrowed his eyes at her, his instincts telling him to be wary.

"Basically. What do you know?"

"I know that his great-aunt died," she said, voice sad. "And I know that it must hurt him a great deal."

"I'm going to the funeral," Vic said. "I just came by to change my oil."

"It's always nice to meet another grease monkey," Argent said.

Vic raised a hand and shook it in a so-so gesture. "Jesse taught me the basics, but I'm guessing you didn't bring me across to talk about cars."

Argent's smile deepened as she balled up the rag and tossed it into a bucket.

"I'm coming with you," she announced. "Road trip."

Vic raised his eyebrows. "To Oklahoma?"

"Yes," she said. "We can take one of my cars. You like the Challenger."

Twelve hours in a car with an immortal who he knew from experience had a lead foot. That could be fun, more fun than riding with Tilla Mae and Robert or driving alone.

"Why don't you just . . ." Vic wiggled his fingers.

Argent blinked at him.

"You know? Magic yourself there."

"There are territories and rules," Argent said. "And I would like to see it from your perspective, not as the Queen of Swords."

Argent's face had gone very still.

She wasn't telling him everything, but Vic also knew he'd never get it out of her. He only had a little of Adam's experience with the immortals, but he knew they were secretive. A road trip with the queen might give him the chance to learn more.

"All right," Vic said. "Driver gets to pick the music."

"Who said I'd ever let you drive?" she asked.

Vic gave her a disapproving look. Argent tended to drive on the Other Side, where speed limits didn't apply. He'd been hoping to get a chance to see what the Challenger could really do.

"When do you want to leave?" he asked.

"I'll pick you up outside your apartment in a few hours," she said, waving him back toward the garage door.

Vic didn't like that she knew where he lived, but couldn't say he was surprised that they'd keep tabs on him. They had some interest in Adam. Maybe it was just because he was Silver's ex, but Vic's guts, what he thought of as his cop instincts, said it was something more.

He stepped through the garage door and found himself back in the real world, or at least the one he was used to. The change was instant. No more purple sky. No more pterodactyls. Vic didn't have that sense of whiplash he'd gotten the first few times it had happened. Maybe he was getting used to it, just like he was getting used to the idea of other worlds in general.

Vic made the necessary calls, citing a death in the family. His sergeant didn't hesitate to approve the PTO. Everything at work was still a little off since Vic had come back.

A weight lifted to know that he was getting to miss work and it bugged Vic that he felt that way. He'd loved graduating from the academy, had been so proud to think he'd be able to make a difference, but lately he didn't feel as welcome there, as trusted. Maybe it had something to do with the shooting, that Vic had survived and Carl hadn't.

Vic's partner had tried to kill Adam, but Vic had taken the bullet before Carl had shot himself. The surveillance footage made it clear what had happened, but the whiff of something strange remained. Carl had been a good man, a good cop, and there wasn't a way to explain his sudden change in character. It wasn't like Vic could tell everyone that Carl had been possessed by an ancient spirit trying to claw its way back to life.

Then there were the changes to Vic himself. It wouldn't do him any favors if word got out that he was dating the guy Carl had tried to kill or that he thought he was a Grim Reaper. He knew how that would sound to most people, even if he had healed far too quickly for something supernatural not to be involved.

A dog's bark brought Vic back to where he was.

"Chaos!" Jesse called.

He emerged from the garage office, chasing after his pit bull. Vic knelt to pet her.

"There you are!" Jesse called. It was weird to see Jesse in a button-up shirt and khakis. He looked like a banker, respectable even. "Did you find Adam?"

"Yeah," Vic said, making sure to get the point between Chaos's eyes. That was her favorite spot.

Her stubby tail wagged happily.

"Easy, drool monster," Vic said. He looked up as Jesse walked over. "His great-aunt died."

"Sue?" Jesse asked, face falling. "Damn."

Vic blinked. "You know about her?"

"She took Wonder Bread in when he sprung himself from the loony bin."

Vic scowled at Jesse's phrasing.

"How do you know so much?" Vic asked.

Jesse shrugged, but he wasn't fooling his brother. Jesse loved cars, his dog, and gossip.

"No wonder he bailed on work," Jesse added.

"He went back to Oklahoma," Vic said.

"And he didn't even tell you?" Jesse whistled. "That's cold."

"Yeah," Vic said. It hurt that Adam hadn't told him. Vic had thought they were moving toward something, being something real together.

"Anyway," he said, shrugging, "I'm going to the funeral."

"Did he invite you?" Jesse asked, folding his arms over his broad chest.

"Nah," Vic said. "His brother did."

"You sure you want to go chasing after him?" Jesse asked. "Missing more work and everything?"

"He needs me," Vic said, though his stomach tensed at the mention of work. "Even if he doesn't know he needs me."

"Hmm," Jesse muttered. He looked thoughtful, maybe hopeful.

"What?" Vic demanded.

"Nothing," Jesse said. "Just . . . I'm rooting for you guys."

"I'll let you know when I see him," Vic said.

Vic headed home, packed his black suit, still clean and pressed from his father's funeral, and waited. His apartment wasn't much.

A Spartan little studio in Capitol Hill, but it had a decent enough kitchen, and he did love to cook.

A car horn sounded. Vic looked out the window to see a light-silver sports car pull up to the loading zone of his building.

Argent leaned out from the driver's side window. She wore sunglasses and a bright scarf, looking more than ever like a classic movie star.

Vic grabbed his bag and ran downstairs, careful to lock his apartment.

"I thought you'd bring the Dodge," he asked. "What is this, a Mazda?"

"An RX-8," Argent said, leaning out the window. The sunglasses probably cost more than a month of Vic's rent. "But I didn't like the engine so I swapped it out."

It did not look roomy, but Vic could appreciate the utility of speed over substance. It wasn't like he'd packed heavy.

"Not very classic," he teased.

"I'd like to avoid your brothers in blue," she said. "As well as any other attention."

"So this is you being subtle?" Vic asked, waving a finger at the sports car.

"I still have my standards, Vicente," she said, popping the trunk.

"It's Vic, Your Highness," he said, moving to lay his bag in the space left beside Argent's suitcase.

It was odd that she'd pack. The purple bag could contain anything—actual clothing, a dozen clowns, or a great white shark. Magic was weird and wonderful, and Vic had so much to learn.

Grinning, he climbed into the passenger side and buckled up, checking twice that the belt was secure. He'd ridden with Argent before. And while he might be a newly minted Grim Reaper, he felt pretty certain he could still die.

Argent tore away from the curb. The acceleration pushed Vic against his seat.

"You're doing eighty in a thirty," he said, gripping the handle by the window so hard he thought he might wrench it off.

"Oh yes," she muttered. "Sometimes I forget."

The sky shifted from blue to purple streaked with bright-green clouds.

"Shortcut," she said, smiling.

"I thought you said we had to take the mortal roads."

"Once we're out of my domain," Argent countered. She gunned the engine, racing them through a version of Denver that didn't exist in Vic's world.

Downtown was hidden in a cloud, a slowly unfurling cyclone of dust, bricks, and debris.

All manner of things flew by. Birds, giant bats, and more dinosaurs. Mushrooms larger than trees sprouted in clumps. They glowed faintly blue. The highway was much the same as on the mortal side, though the lines dividing the lanes often sprouted legs and scrambled out of the Mazda's path like millipedes.

"Can all of you do that?" Vic asked. "Just leap over?"

"It isn't a gift everyone has," Argent explained, "but it can be developed depending on aptitude."

"So it's a talent," Vic said.

"And a skill. Some are naturals from birth. Others develop it."

Vic nodded. It made sense. When he'd applied to the police academy, he wasn't any good with a gun. His mom did not like them, and his dad had never taught him to shoot. Vic had worked very hard to get good enough to score high marks. It had taken him a few tries to load a clip without cutting himself on its sharp edges.

At this rate they'd be in Oklahoma in just a few hours, which was good. Vic hadn't planned for a long trip. His sergeant would eventually need him, desk duty or not. But mostly, Vic needed to see Adam, to see if he was all right.

Dammit, Adam, you have to do everything the hard way, Vic thought.

Could Adam feel his approach, his worry? He should. Vic felt it was strong enough to cross the miles.

"How long can we take this shortcut?" Vic asked.

"You'll know when the towers change," Argent said. "They mark the boundaries."

She nodded to the distance where three watchtowers marked the cardinal points. The fourth had been downtown, and its destruction had caused the storm behind them.

"Are you guys going to fix that?" Vic asked, jerking a thumb over his shoulder to indicate the tornado of dust and bricks.

"Meetings are being held with the Council of Races. Accords will be reached and a new Guardian race will be chosen for the East."

"And they don't need their queen for that?"

"You ask a lot of questions," Argent said. Her hand remained light on the steering wheel but Vic thought he detected a little crinkling about her mouth. He was prying. "But no, my brother is handling the details. He's good at that sort of thing and that is how our father prefers it."

Vic could learn to like Silver, Argent's brother, from what little he knew of the elf. The two of them had fought together against Mercy, but Adam's history with the Knight of Swords made something in Vic's belly twist, and he didn't like that.

It wasn't like Vic to get jealous of exes. He'd never been jealous of any ex before. It was just one more way in which Adam was different, how Vic felt different when it came to Adam.

He wanted to reach Oklahoma, to wrap Adam in his arms, and get the answers he needed so badly.

6

ADAM

Adam drove into town. Normally he'd take a moment to appreciate Guthrie's historic redbrick streets and beautiful architecture, but right now everything ached.

He already knew which funeral home she'd be at. Guthrie had a few, and Sue had done some trade with the owner of one, giving her free tarot readings to ensure a discount on services when the time came. She'd put aside some savings to handle the rest as to not worry him, which was so very Sue, so very practical that Adam choked up as he parked.

The home was just that, an old converted house. The wooden floor creaked beneath his feet, but Adam didn't feel any ghosts or any supernatural energy at all.

A woman came out from the back to greet him.

"Sue Binder?" Adam asked.

He didn't feel like crying now, just sunken, like everything inside him was heavier, pulling him toward the ground.

"Of course, honey," the woman said. She had tight blond curls and wore a pantsuit made from some stiff fabric. But her eyes were kind as she gestured toward a converted bedroom.

The lighting was low, and a portable stereo in the corner pumped out gospel hymns. Sue wouldn't have liked that. She hadn't had much truck with Christianity. Maybe that was why his mother had hated her so much.

Adam waffled between turning it off or asking for a different CD. He considered slipping in something she'd prefer. She'd always joked that she wanted Garth Brooks's "Friends in Low Places" playing when they lowered her into the ground. She wanted a margarita machine at the reception. He'd suggested the Chippendale dancers for pallbearers and she'd teased that he just wanted them for himself.

He smiled, almost.

Adam knew he was just trying to avoid looking where he didn't want to.

The coffin was white, metal, and so small. It sat open, with a row of plastic flowers along the lid's edge. There were vases of similar fake blooms in the room's corners.

Fake flowers. They couldn't even afford real ones.

He should have brought something. Irises were her favorite.

Adam let out a long breath and finally faced her.

She lay too pale, too still. Her hair, which had always reminded him of gravelly snowmelt, was combed and fixed too tight in a bun.

She wore a simple dress, off-white. At least Noreen had made certain she had it. Sue hadn't wanted the home to dress her, thought it would be a silly waste. This had been her final wedding gown, and she'd joked that lightning would strike her if she tried to wear pure white on yet another trip down the aisle.

The embalming was supposed to make her look restful, but she only seemed wooden to him, devoid of all the life she'd had, all the humor, and all the dry wisdom that she'd never hesitated to rain down on his head.

Adam exhaled. He had no prayers. He had no gods, and the closest things he'd met to them were jerks.

He felt strange, standing there alone. He didn't know what to say. He was sorry he hadn't been there. He was sorry he'd never get to tell her that.

————

"Sue's will was very clear," Mrs. Jenkins said. "Everything she had went to your cousin Noreen."

Adam sank back into the chair across from her. The desk was big, wooden, and covered in paperweights and pictures of smiling family members.

"When did she last change it?" he asked.

"About a year ago," Jenkins said.

She was an older woman, maybe in her fifties, with round glasses and kind eyes. Adam didn't know her. She hadn't been one of Sue's clients or one of his mother's church friends.

"On purpose," Adam muttered.

"What's that, honey?"

"She did it on purpose," he said. "Left Noreen everything."

"Noreen is her daughter," Jenkins said. "And for what it's worth, it's not much. Just the trailer, its contents, and her wedding rings."

Adam didn't say what he wanted to, that when you were poor, a little was a whole lot. Not to mention that those contents included *his* things, his clothes and paperbacks.

He didn't really care about any of it. They were just things, but the idea that Sue would leave him homeless, without somewhere to go . . .

Had she known he'd meet Vic, that he'd have reasons to stay in Denver? Had she seen it?

Sight wasn't supposed to work if you were too close to the person, and she'd loved him, hadn't she?

"Thank you for your time," Adam said, finding his feet though his legs felt wooden.

"Will I see you at the funeral?" she asked.

"You'll be there?" he asked.

"Yes," she said. "I handled all of your great-aunt's divorces you know."

"I didn't," he said, standing. "I didn't know that. Thank you."

"Of course, dear," she replied.

Outside, the day was sunny, the sky clear.

Guthrie was small, with a main drag of little shops and art galleries that came and went with the economy and all the hopes and pitfalls of a small business. It was a beautiful place, historic, and normally Adam would enjoy walking around a little.

A funeral. Sue's funeral, and Adam had nothing to wear.

He climbed back into the Cutlass and drove back toward his mother's place, passing the park with the pond and then the Beacon, the old drive-in theater.

Oklahoma was flat. The Cutlass was like a toy car on a table. Adam had never thought much about it until he'd gone to Denver. The mountains there were like a wall to the west, always in sight, always giving you a sense of direction.

Here was switchgrass and scrub oak, low trees and long stretches of yellow and ruddy clay. In Denver it was all houses and buildings with little yards. Adam knew it wasn't New York or some dense city, but still, it had been different than what he was used to.

Everything had been different than what he was used to. Vic and his family, the way he could talk about what he was thinking or feeling, the way Vic would kiss Adam like no one would care. Like them together was normal—like he was normal.

Thinking of Vic brought a warm feeling that turned blue in his gut. Adam should have called by now. He still had cell service.

Adam needed to call.

What would he say?

Hey, I'm in Oklahoma. There's a funeral. Sue . . .

Enough. He was a man, not a boy, and he cared too much about Vic to screw it up by acting like this.

Adam pulled over, unlocked his phone, and found himself dialing Bobby instead. It would work like a warm-up, help him screw up his courage to call Vic.

Voicemail.

Adam hung up.

"Just call him," Adam said.

Instead he looked at his unread texts.

Where are you?

Jesse. Shit. And Vic. Double shit.

Adam had run off, ignored everything, and now he felt that sinking feeling that said he wouldn't be able to fix it, that it was all too complicated to just type a response.

He dialed Jesse.

"Wonder Bread, you're alive!" Jesse called into the phone.

"Shit, Jesse, I'm so sorry," Adam blurted. "My aunt died and I kind of freaked out."

His drawl had kicked up with his stress. He sounded like his mom when he cussed. He took a long breath.

"Are you okay?" Jesse asked, voice calm. No anger.

Adam blinked. That was not the reaction he'd been expecting. Jesse was his boss.

"Am I fired?" Adam asked, quietly.

"No, Vic got the details from your mom and brother and filled me in, but call me next time. And you sure as shit better call him. He's worried about you."

Adam swallowed. "I will."

"How long are you going to be gone?" Jesse asked.

"I don't know," Adam said. "Things got complicated last night."

"How so?"

"There was an accident," Adam said.

Jesse's pause told Adam he wasn't going to settle for that.

"My aunt's trailer blew up," he said, cringing. "And her daughter was hurt."

"What?" Jesse demanded.

"They had a meth lab or something," Adam said. He didn't mention the druid, the magical attack.

"Way to keep it boring," Jesse said with a whistle. "You in trouble?"

Adam looked over his shoulder. He sensed nothing, no one, no thing, watching him or dogging his steps. Still, he'd only sensed the druid's magic right as he'd blown up the trailer.

"Maybe," Adam admitted.

"You'd better call Vic," Jesse said. "He's worried about you, and he could help."

Not with this he couldn't, he thought, then replied, "I will. Right now."

"Be safe," Jesse said. "And tell me when you're back in town."

He hung up.

Adam dialed Vic's number before he could find an excuse not to.

It rang and rang.

Then voicemail. He almost hung up, but let it beep.

"Hey," he said. "It's me. Sorry I bailed. I just—Just call me back. I'm sorry. I . . ."

Adam hung up and shook his head.

He felt like a moron for being bothered that Vic hadn't answered. After all, Adam had been the one to go silent. He had no right to be upset if Vic didn't want to talk to him.

Adam exhaled through gritted teeth.

He didn't want to mess things up with Vic, but what if he already had?

He couldn't do anything about it right now.

He climbed back in the Cutlass and started driving again. He could skip the funeral, go back to Denver. He'd gotten his chance to say goodbye at the funeral home.

But that meant running from the druid, leaving Noreen and Jodi to whatever he had planned. Adam didn't want to think about Noreen, but he should visit her.

Guthrie only had one hospital. Adam hadn't been there, but he knew where it was. He almost didn't turn around, but Noreen was family. And she might have some answers, some clues to the druid's attack.

Adam checked his gas and parked.

The front was brick with a long, covered porch to shelter cars dropping off patients.

He pushed through the doors with an exhale, ready to fend off the energy, the anxiety, and sticky sadness of sick and worried people.

It didn't come. The place was peaceful and his shoulders softened.

Adam even found a half-smile for the woman behind the desk.

"I'm here to see Noreen Binder," he said.

"Room 212," the woman said, nodding in that direction. "Sign in here."

She pushed a clipboard over and Adam headed that way with a quick squirt from the hand sanitizer dispenser. No one was at the nurse's station. No one questioned him.

Noreen's door was open. She lay in a hospital bed, with a ventilator tube in her nose.

She lay still, pale and pink in the light from the window. The purple and blue veins running through her thick ankles were strangely personal to Adam. He almost threw a blanket over her to hide them.

Noreen didn't stir as Adam stepped closer. He paused. He didn't want to wake her.

"She's pretty out of it," a voice said from behind him. "I don't think you need to worry about waking her."

Adam turned to see Sheriff Early standing in the doorway.

"What are you doing here?" Adam asked.

"Came to make sure she wasn't going anywhere," Early nodded to Noreen's wrist. Adam hadn't noticed the handcuffs chaining her to the bed.

"Is it like them to sleep like this?" Adam asked. "Meth users?"

"Yeah," Early said. "Coming down is rough. They crash hard."

He seemed colder than he had the night before.

"Will she get to go to the funeral?" Adam asked.

"If she wakes up, I'll bring her myself," Early said.

Adam gave a little nod, uncertain how to thank him or if he wanted Noreen there. Sue would have, wouldn't she? She'd left Noreen the trailer.

"What do you know about the satanic stuff we found at your aunt's?" Early asked, bluntly cutting into Adam's thoughts. "I was hoping to ask Noreen."

"Satanic?" Adam asked.

Early pulled out his phone and brought up pictures. Adam's old room. Painted black with glow-in-the-dark stars stuck to the walls and ceiling. It looked like something he'd have done in his goth days. Early flipped to the next pic and Adam gaped.

"Are those . . . a person?" he asked, leaning toward the phone, trying to make out the bones.

"Coroner says yes. Could be wrong. He identified a deer as a person once."

"I have no idea what they were doing with those," Adam said. "Or why they'd do that."

He stared at his old desk, now piled with human remains. There was a drill, a Dremel tool, and fishing line.

"Wait, go back to the room," Adam said.

Early thumbed the photo to the black walls again.

There. It looked like a wind chime, like the ones Sue had made to set her permanent wards. With a nod, Adam reached to expand the picture.

More bones, drilled and hung together. Symbols had been carved into them.

"What the . . ."

"You recognize it?" Early asked, eyes narrow.

"No," Adam said. "It's nothing Sue would have done."

"Neighbors say it's your old room."

"You think I did this?" Adam jerked a thumb at himself. "This is some twisted shit."

"I remember what Duncan used to say about you," Early said. "That you talked to yourself, to people who weren't there, that your brother had you taken away to an institution."

Adam ground his teeth at the mention of Liberty House.

"This is sick," Adam said, nodding to the picture. "Sue would have killed me for painting her walls black, let alone for doing any of this other crap."

Early looked Adam over.

"That's what the neighbors say too," he said. He pocketed his phone. "Said you were a good kid, liked to help people out."

Adam swallowed a frown. He wasn't a kid. But worse than that, Early had asked the neighbors about him. He had to be a suspect.

"Any sign of Jodi?" he asked. "She has to have the answers you want."

Adam wanted them too.

Using bones like that . . . it was death magic, the kind Adam didn't do, the same kind the druid did. He could be after Jodi. He could come back to finish Noreen.

Adam had no way to ward the hospital or to protect her. He might even be putting her in danger by being there.

"No," Early said. "Any ideas?"

"None," Adam admitted, and he was being honest. He didn't know his cousin, didn't like her.

"You call me if you find anything," Early stressed, eyes hard.

"I will," Adam said.

He drove back to his mom's, thinking about what Early had showed him. The bones had been carved, but he didn't know the symbols. He didn't know the magic. He'd seen the druid's work. The other warlock had tortured magical creatures to make his charms. This was similar, but Adam hadn't felt it, hadn't sensed it when he'd gone to the trailer, and he felt very certain that it had been there before the attack.

The sun was close to setting. It hadn't rained again but the air remained damp, almost chilly. It was so different than the air in Denver. Adam could breathe here, without the altitude and dryness.

He parked at the gate, went through the ritual of opening it, driving in, and closing it behind him.

By day the ivory-and-brown box he'd grown up in was more pathetic than sad.

His parents had cleared a space for it, put in a concrete slab, and installed a skirt that hid the underside. They'd had enough trees removed to make something of a yard around it, but his dad's thumb had always been black, not green, and Adam's mother wasn't very interested in gardening. All that remained of Robert's efforts was mud and switchgrass. The scrub oaks had started to encroach, reclaiming the space, and now Mom's trailer was a bit obscured.

She had a couple of sheds, neither of which Adam had any desire to open.

Those had been Dad's territory, where he'd thrown tools and anything he'd bought on a whim, like the fishing rods he thought would provide catfish for dinner, only he never caught anything and snapping turtles kept taking his bait.

Adam's memories of the lake, just a little walk through the woods, were hazy. They weren't happy, not exactly, but he'd enjoyed the trees in spring, the emerald light and birds passing through the leaves.

He wondered now how much of that had been the spirit realm, leaking into the real world through his uncontrolled Sight.

Adam let himself into the trailer.

"Spider?" he called, but the cat did not answer. There was no sign or smell to indicate that he'd ever been there.

Adam sighed. Maybe his Sight was out of control again, but he didn't think so. He wished he could have asked Early for a copy of the wind chime photo. It was important. All of his senses said so.

He could try to contact Silver, but the Knight of Swords was far too important for another lesson in how to master his powers. They were at peace . . . sort of. Adam had forgiven Silver for abandoning him, and Silver seemed to accept that Adam had moved on and found something new with Vic.

So no, Adam didn't need Silver or Sue to mentor him anymore. He'd figure out what was going on with Spider—if he saw the cat again.

For now, he had to think about the funeral. He had nothing to wear. Even if he'd been able to get his clothes from Sue's trailer, he didn't have a suit or anything appropriate. He had a few things back in Denver, at Bobby's house. But nothing Adam had with him would work, not for Sue.

He imagined Bobby tsking at him, disappointed in Adam's life choices, and lack of wardrobe.

Adam crept to the trailer's back bedroom. He hadn't been here in years, but if he was lucky, Mom would have kept Bobby's old clothes. She seemed to have kept everything else. Bobby was taller than Adam, broader shouldered. His stuff might fit a full-grown Adam.

The room was small, but it was bigger than the one he'd had at Sue's. He and Bobby had even had their own little bathroom.

It still had the dark-brown wood paneling that Adam remembered. His mom could have gotten rid of the toys or the old simple bunk beds, but from the look of things, she'd simply closed the door like her boys might return at any moment, like they might still be boys.

Adam opened the closet. There weren't many clothes. A sports jacket from Sears. Adam slipped it on. It would do if he had no other option.

Then he opened his side of the closet and found it full.

But these weren't his clothes, and they weren't all Bobby's.

He pulled out a hanger with something wrapped in a plastic garbage bag. A moth ball rattled around the bottom and gave out a whiff of ammonia. Adam pulled the bag up to reveal a brown suit.

Dad's. These clothes had been his dad's.

His mom had moved them from her closet. So she'd made one change at least.

Adam remembered them hanging in her bedroom. He'd waited for his dad to come home, never really gotten that he wouldn't.

There were fewer now. His mom had purged most signs of Robert Senior by the time Adam was in high school, but these had been nice enough that she'd kept them.

Adam dug a little farther and found another suit, this one navy, a shirt, and a tie.

Black would be best, but navy would do.

Adam didn't even have shoes. His sneakers, which he'd bought for work at the garage, would have to serve.

He shook his head.

Bobby would hate it, Adam showing up in old clothes, blue not black. Well, Bobby wouldn't be there, would he?

Adam wasn't certain how he felt about that. His feelings toward his brother remained mixed, a ball of wires he couldn't untangle. Still, facing a funeral crowd of his extended family, especially Sue's side of it—Adam could have used the backup.

7

VIC

Everything shifted from purple and green to regular blue.

"That was like dropping out of hyperspace," Vic said as Argent drove them back into the material world.

"Not exactly," she said. "We're driving the same speed. There's no shift from faster than light to sublight."

"You're no fun sometimes," Vic muttered as Argent slowed the Mazda to something legal. Still, he'd give her points for the geeky reference.

He'd never admit it, but he was ready for a slower drive and fewer hungry oddities zipping by the windows.

Vic watched a lot of sci-fi movies and shows. He played video games. They hadn't prepared him for the full-on craziness of walking houses and fields of sunflowers that grinned at the passing car with mouths full of human teeth.

He'd felt something as he stared out the window. Not quite a pull, but an instinct, the sense that part of him—the part that was neither his life nor the little piece of Adam's he'd been gifted—was at home in that strange twilight world.

Vic imagined it was like what some organ transplant recipients had described, a yearning for a beer when the recipient had never tasted it or liked it before. It was a part of him now, but he knew it hadn't come from him.

Adam had said that Reapers were a type of possession, that they lay dormant until they were called to collect a soul, but that thought begged the question: *Possessed by what?*

Was the feeling he had related to something inside him that wanted to return to the Other Side?

It was a selfish truth, but Vic's desire to find Adam and keep close to him was about more than the undeniable attraction. Vic needed answers about what had happened to him, about what he was becoming.

"What are you thinking about?" Argent asked, silver eyes narrowing.

"What makes you ask?"

"I can smell the smoke from the effort," she said.

"Adam," Vic said. "Just Adam."

"Uh-huh," she said, clearly unconvinced.

They drove on in silence for a while.

"What is this music?" Vic asked.

It sounded like jazz with a sultry soloist, a woman, singing atop it.

Argent smiled. "You're unlikely to know it. The song is 'A Guy What Takes His Time.' Mae West did it first, but this is Pearl Blue. She died in the sixties."

"You like old things," Vic said. "Cars. Music."

"I liked the singer," Argent corrected him. "But yes, we get set in our ways. Immortals. We don't handle change very well."

Vic wanted to ask her to explain but wasn't sure it was the time. Adam made it sound like even basic information was a transaction with the elves, but Vic wasn't certain Argent was like that.

He was also blunt enough to ask direct questions, without

Adam's midwestern need to beat around the bush. Vic opened his mouth to say something when he caught sight of a red streak racing through the sky.

"What is that?" he asked a second before the fireball collided with the road in front of the car.

Argent swerved and punched the gas at the same time. The car shook hard enough that Vic's teeth rattled.

The meteor—or whatever it was—sent chunks of asphalt toward them like flaming shrapnel. Something hard impacted with them. The car flew, rolling, and Vic felt Argent's hand clasp his leg. He gasped as they shifted, landing hard in the dirt on the Other Side.

Argent rolled to her feet in a single motion. A lean sword appeared in her hand. It looked Japanese but much longer, almost half Vic's height. It glittered brightly, like frozen moonlight.

Vic picked himself up, rising to his hands and knees. He'd landed hard, almost with enough force to knock the wind out of him.

He coughed and felt for damage. Nothing was broken, though he'd scraped his palms on the ground.

Patches of the real world were still visible, like holes in cloud cover showing the sky beyond. Through them he could see the burning car. It had rolled several times and sat destroyed, its windshield smashed, its panels crumpled. Smoke poured from its hood. He couldn't smell it. The air here was sweet, like honey clover on a summer day.

"My bag!" he called, seeing the burning wreck of the car.

"You can get other clothes," Argent barked.

"My gun's in there," he said. "So is my uh, scythe."

Well it was his police baton, but the one time he'd needed a scythe, it had grown from that.

Argent made a dismissive gesture and the bag dropped to the ground in front of him, undamaged. Across the veil, the car exploded. Argent made another gesture and the holes closed before any shrapnel could reach them.

"What was that?" Vic asked, checking that nothing had broken.

"Someone attacked us," Argent said calmly. She'd cocked her head to the side, like a hawk sighting prey.

"Why aren't they following up?" he asked.

"Good question," she said. "I don't think they were trying to kill us, that or they lack the means. This was a delaying tactic, to slow us down."

"Who would do that?" Vic asked. "It's a funeral."

"Another power," Argent said. "They may see this as an opportunity to weaken us."

"Why?" he asked.

Vic scanned the low hills around them and tried not to shake. He was a cop, not a soldier. He wasn't trained for combat with an unseen foe who made Argent pause. She was powerful, according to Adam, one of the most powerful creatures there were.

"My brother is undertaking some delicate negotiations. Our father had sent him to handle it."

"He's the knight, you're the queen," Vic said.

"Yes."

"So it's like chess?" Vic asked. "He's dangerous but you're more powerful?"

Argent narrowed her eyes.

"It is not the origin of the titles, but it's not an inaccurate comparison. Like I said, we all have skills. Mine are more martial than his."

"Do you know who they are, who attacked us?"

"I have my suspicions," she said, eyeing the horizon like a threat would appear at any moment.

"Tell me," Vic said.

"It would be premature," she said.

He scoffed. "You could guess."

"I could, but if I'm right, then they're bigger fools than I suspected."

"So now what?" Vic asked. "Car's wrecked. We could call Jesse, or find a rental."

"Let's walk for a while," Argent said. She opened her hand and her sword vanished, but he had no doubt she could call it back in a breath.

"That's it?" he asked. "What if they're still out there?"

"Oh they're very much still out there," she said.

"But we're just going to walk?" Vic asked. "Won't they see us, come after us again?"

He felt far too exposed, even with his gun and baton. He'd leave his bag. Hopefully Argent would find it for him again.

"Shouldn't we be more subtle?" he asked, scanning for more meteors.

"I am," she said.

Vic took in her jeans and a lavender sweater that probably cost more than he made in a month, her scarf and the expensive sunglasses. The little gems along the frame glittered.

"You sure about that?" he asked.

"What do you mean?" she said.

"I mean, shouldn't we be wearing camouflage or maybe not just walking out in the open?"

"I *am* camouflaged," she said, smile dimming as she corrected him.

Looking more closely, Vic could see that her light, the glow that always surrounded her, seemed duller. She even had a scratch on her hand from the crash.

"You're hiding your magic," he said. "Trying to pass as mortal."

"Exactly." Looking at him over the top of her sunglasses, she waved a hand at the plains and low, teal-colored grass. "Here, it's not the eyes that matter most. Walking like this, hiding my power, means I'm not broadcasting a signal. To find me, they'd literally have to see me, to look out a window. And nothing here is used to searching for threats that way. Besides, I have a secret weapon."

"You're talking about me, aren't you?" he asked.

Argent grinned, looking a bit too much like a hungry cat.

"Yes," she said.

He did not like it.

"How am I—" he started to ask.

"Shh." She cut him off. "There's smoke coming out of your ears again."

8

ADAM

Sue opened the trailer door before Adam knocked.

"I didn't know where else to go," he said.

"It's a long walk," she said, stepping back. "At least it's not raining."

"Thank you," he said, taking the empty folding chair at the cheap card table where she ate and did her meager trade in fortune-telling. He hadn't spent much time here and didn't know her that well. His mom had told him to steer clear of his dad's aunt.

Now Adam knew that magic was real, that he wasn't mentally ill, at least not like his brother and mother had thought.

"Did you know I'd come here?" he asked, glancing at the stack of tarot cards tucked to the side of the table.

Sue smiled and set a glass of iced tea in front of him.

"It's your birthday," she said. "I'd hoped."

Now, looking back on that moment, Adam put on the clip-on tie from Dad's things and remembered her face, the tea, the day Sue had taken him in without any more fuss than that.

He could have called his mother. He could have called Bobby, but neither had really been an option. They'd sent him away, made their feelings on him clear.

Adam had his Sight under control. Silver had taught him so much, but Sue taught him the tarot, working through each card with him, laying out their meanings whether right up or reversed. She taught him the different patterns and spreads.

Part of Adam had expected Bobby to show up, to try and drag him back to Liberty House or a similar place in Colorado where he lived. Then Adam realized Liberty House hadn't been about Adam's visions, his Sight, or really anything being wrong with Adam.

Bobby just hadn't wanted Adam around. He was building a new life away from Oklahoma, their family, and their shared past. Adam had been in Bobby's way, and his brother had been glad to be rid of him.

It wasn't like Adam couldn't understand. As grateful as he was to Sue, he'd felt mired in the trailer park. He hated the drawl in his voice. He hated the slow pace of the lives and people around him. He hated going to bed hungry, and never having owned a new pair of shoes.

Adam had looked around the trailer park at Sue's battered lodgings and tacky lawn decor. She'd sworn her wards protected her little lot from tornadoes, and perhaps they did. But he'd started to go stir-crazy, chafing at the neighbors, at their proximity, their petty fights and pettier crimes. The rows of trailers, their walls too thin, made privacy feel impossible. At least his mom's trailer sat on three acres, with trees and space between the Binders and other people.

"The car," Sue said one day, leaning forward in her cat-scratched, half-collapsed recliner. "Take it."

"What?" he'd asked.

She'd nodded to the end of the trailer's lot, to the tarp weighed down by cinder blocks. "It was your father's. Take it."

Sue pierced him with a stare, blue like his own eyes. She'd

look at him like that sometimes, right before she spat out an insight or truth she shouldn't have known, like telling him she knew he liked guys before he'd told her.

"The keys are on the hook by the door," she'd said. "Go and see."

So Adam had.

He'd kicked the cinder blocks aside, disturbing leaves and a thick nest of daddy longlegs.

He lifted the tarp, shifting a bit of rainwater, and shook it. Any expectation of shining steel and decent paint was quickly marred by all the dust that had worked its way beneath the plastic. The tires were long flat. Rust had settled in here and there, especially on the tailpipe.

Still, he loved it. A '77 coupe. The hood went on for days, like a bed he could stretch out on. The back seat seemed like an afterthought. The whole interior smelled of mold and old cigarettes.

Adam had run a hand over the windshield, wiped a clean swath. His dad had owned this car, had driven this car, and left it behind when he'd disappeared. Adam's memories of it were warm, riding atop the hood with Bobby as Robert Senior slowly drove the dirt road to their trailer. It had been the one thing his dad had truly loved, truly taken care of.

Now the dash had dried and cracked. The bucket seats were well worn. She wouldn't start, not without a new battery, oil, and a whole lot of other checks. She'd need tires and cleaning and who knew what else. But just the idea of fixing her up began to unwind the ball of yellow wire, the restless boredom in Adam's guts. More than a car, or the freedom it could bring, the Cutlass had been his father's. It was the only memento, the only piece of him Adam had. He'd fix her.

And it started him thinking, wondering what his life would have been like if his dad had taken Adam with him.

His mother and brother had never talked about Robert Senior. They pretended he'd never lived.

Adam had the Internet, and now he had a car. If his dad was out there, if he was someone like Adam, who might understand, Adam could find him.

Then the search led him to the dark druid, to the first of the horrible charms, a pair of cursed dice. Adam hadn't known what to do, only that they shouldn't be, shouldn't exist. He'd stolen them and destroyed them.

The search became a mission, almost an obsession, and Sue never discouraged him, never told him to stop looking. Now, as he tied the laces of his shoes and locked the trailer door, he wondered if she'd known the entire time. She'd let him search and question, doubt and drive all over, when the entire time his father was dead and buried in the woods.

———

It could have been a wedding. Rows of white folding chairs were lined up in the funeral home's chapel. The drop ceiling was water-stained in places, the hunter-green carpet flattened from an infinite number of similar services.

Adam took in the room, looking everywhere but where he had to.

The monster couldn't be Robert Senior. He was dead, but then where had the charms come from? Who'd made them? And then there was the undeniable similarity to Adam's magic.

Adam wanted to shake off the questions, to focus on Sue, on the here and now, but he couldn't. He kept his Sight open, trying to sense another attack.

Adam stood to the side as people filed in. They wore their Sunday best, or just their best clothes, and in some cases that was jeans or an ironed sweatshirt.

Most were clients of Sue's or residents of the trailer park.

Some were people he knew from town. Mrs. Jenkins wore a dark-green turtleneck and a black pantsuit. She gave Adam a small smile and muttered how sorry she was before folding him into an awkward hug.

Many others kept a polite distance. Adam felt nothing from them. They were here out of courtesy, but he still appreciated it. Sue would have appreciated it.

Adam got more than one nod from residents of the trailer park. Adam could feel their respect for Sue, but also for him. His heart almost cracked at that.

They clustered in little groups, sitting by class—the poorer people here, the middle class over there. They considered him part of their community, even though he was leaving, had already left them.

It was a small town. Most of them knew each other, some not in a good way. Exes and relatives gave each other the stink eye as Adam looked over the assembled.

Then Early arrived with Noreen. He walked with her, helping her and staying close.

She was dressed in a sweat suit, purple with white sneakers. Adam suspected Early had bought the outfit new from Walmart. She didn't have an oxygen tank. He took it as a good sign that she could breathe on her own.

Adam saw no sign of Jodi and itched to ask about her.

Ignoring Adam, Early led Noreen to the front.

Adam tried to find a seat, looking for a space at the front but away from Noreen.

The truth of it, that Sue was gone, hammered against his heart. Then he was the one who couldn't breathe.

"Adam," someone said, drawing him around.

Bobby.

His mom.

Adam opened his mouth. He didn't know what to say, didn't

have words. His whole body felt detached, almost like he was spirit walking. They were here. Adam hadn't expected that.

He didn't protest as Bobby folded him into his arms.

Adam felt so small in that moment, like a child again, but he didn't fight it, didn't protest the hug and the tightness in his throat that said he wanted to cry. It was like he was broken, couldn't *feel* what was happening. Maybe it was just too much, too much confirmation that she'd never laugh at him, roll her eyes, or teach him anything again.

"Let's sit," his mother said, breaking the stupor that he'd fallen into.

And just like that, Tilla led her sons to the front.

"Is that Early?" Tilla asked. She eyed Noreen's escort where he sat a few rows behind Noreen before turning to Sue's daughter. "She's really gone to shit."

"*Mom,*" Bobby said in a hushed voice.

"She just got out of the hospital," Adam said.

They both looked at him.

"I'll tell you later," he muttered.

Adam had to admit that Noreen did look rough. She'd aged by decades since the last time she'd come around the trailer, begging Sue for money. She looked older than Sue had, and though she sat pale and quiet, her hair limp around her head, she buzzed with a hateful energy.

"She used to threaten to sell Jodi's blood, back when the girl was little," Tilla said. "Told Sue she had no other choice. Used to sell me the same load when she came by the store."

Adam wanted to find some sympathy, even if his mother couldn't. Noreen had lost her mom. She'd nearly lost her life.

He wondered if Early had been able to ask her about the bones.

Noreen didn't even look sad, just angry and confused.

A man approached, blocked the view for a moment before taking a seat.

Tommy. Sue's son. He'd come, of course, bringing his wife and three daughters. They lived in Enid, and looked better off than the rest of the Binders, Bobby excluded.

The minister talked about Sue as a simple woman. As far as Adam knew, he'd never met her. He talked about Sue's love of her children without irony, prompting a scoff from Noreen, and her generosity as a neighbor. He looked at Adam at one point. Adam wanted to shrug but didn't.

It was a eulogy from a stranger. At least it was brief, without prayers or bible verses, which Adam knew his mother would sniff at.

Then it was mercifully over.

The music started, tinny hymns blasting from ancient blown-out speakers. People started to pass by the coffin, taking a final look. They walked a solemn line, said their silent goodbyes to the casket, and offered Tommy and Noreen their condolences.

"Adam, honey," his mom said. "Do you want to?"

He felt around inside and found himself too numb. He hadn't cried. He thought he would have cried by now. He shook his head.

The casket was closed. They'd take her to the cemetery, and that, like she would have said, would be that.

"You girls should go get those flowers," Noreen said to Tommy's daughters. "They shouldn't go to waste."

They looked to their parents. Brown-haired, rugged, Tommy was clearly related to Bobby, though the girls, all blond, took after their mother. She shook her head a little.

"Go on," Noreen said. "She doesn't need them."

Tommy put a hand to his wife's back.

"We'll see you later, Noreen," he said, leading his family toward the door.

Tommy found a sad smile for Adam as he passed.

Adam liked Tommy. He was a lot like Bobby. He'd left Guthrie, but only ran as far away as Enid. He and Sue talked pretty often. He'd even come around from time to time, checked on her.

Adam needed air. He needed light. He headed for the double glass doors.

"Where's Vincent?" his mother asked.

"Vic?" Adam blinked. "Why would he be here?"

"He was supposed to meet us," Tilla said. She gave a little sigh. "Maybe he changed his mind."

"No," Bobby said, firm. Certain. "He was coming."

Adam swallowed. He'd been so worried that Vic would be angry with him, at him. He hadn't thought Vic would figure out what was wrong and just show up. Be there.

Adam felt his eyes glisten and choked.

"You didn't think he'd come?" Bobby asked, a smile teasing the corner of his mouth. "He cares about you."

"I didn't even tell him," Adam said.

It had just been him and Sue since he'd left Liberty House. He wasn't used to relying on someone or even expecting them to care.

"Call him," Bobby said.

Adam gave a little nod.

"You!" a voice said, breaking in, disrupting the quiet, somber state.

Noreen.

She'd crept up on them, a vengeful, watery creature in purple.

Adam gaped at her. She looked enraged. He could feel it wafting off her. He was too upset to block it out. Noreen was pissed and she'd focused it on him.

She marched toward them, a finger extended toward Adam. Early stood at a distance.

"This is your fault," Noreen spat.

"What are you talking about?" Adam asked.

"The fire. The explosion! Somebody wanted you dead. Not me."

"You were building a meth lab," Adam snapped. "You were building a freaking meth lab in Sue's trailer. And what was that crap with the bones?"

"Jodi put that up to protect us," Noreen said. "After we found that bird on the door."

"Bird?" Adam asked, truly confused. And since when did Jodi know anything about wards or protections? Whatever she'd been doing it obviously hadn't worked.

"There was something on the door that morning," Noreen said. "Feathers. A lot of blood. We washed it off with the hose."

Cold fingers walked up Adam's spine.

"Did you get a picture?" he asked.

"Why, so you can brag about it?" Noreen snarled. "Post it on the Twitter and laugh at us on the Internet?"

"No, Noreen," he said, trying to sound gentle. "That's not . . . I don't know what's happening, but I'm trying to help."

Adam's heart hurt—no, not just his heart. That ached for Sue. This was his wound, his warlock wound, the bit of himself he'd maimed to appease Death and stop the spirit they'd called Mercy. It thrummed, resonating with something unseen, something looming. Something dark was coming.

"Bullshit," Noreen said. She stepped closer. "You fa—"

Noreen never got the chance to finish the slur.

The slap rang out with a crack.

"You will shut up," Tilla said, her hand still raised. She balled it into a fist. "Just shut the fuck up. And if you ever try to speak to my son that way again, I'll lay you out next to your mother, you piece of shit."

Adam's numbness, along with any remaining control over his sensitivity, shattered. Noreen's attack, his mother rising to his defense—he started to shake, the tremor moving through him.

Noreen's rage was like needles, hundreds of them, pricking his skin, but what he felt from his mother was so much worse. It was a punch to the gut.

Tilla meant it. She hated Noreen, and she'd kill to protect him. In a way, she already had. This anger meant she could tell her teenage son to kill his father with a hammer, a command Bobby had obeyed.

Tommy and his family watched in horror from where they piled into their van. Other mourners looked like they wanted to intervene, to say something. Most of them were focusing something like disappointment or anger at Adam, like he'd been the aggressive one and not Noreen. Early kept his distance, but he'd clearly decided to let it play out.

The roil of feelings that weren't his own made Adam want to vomit. He stumbled away, back toward the Cutlass. Leaning, he put his hands to the hood. The day was bright enough that the metal warmed his palms.

Adam breathed for a while, pulled himself together, pulled his defenses together, wrapping his will around himself until he was alone in his heart and head.

Fishing his phone from the suit pocket, he tried to call Vic. No answer. He texted.

> Where are you? Just check in
> with me, all right?

Adam did not type, *I need you. Please.*

He would not be that guy, though right then he really wanted to be.

His mother and Bobby walked toward him.

"Vic's not answering," Adam said.

"Do you think there's trouble?" Bobby asked.

Their mom hung back. She wore a stony expression. The rage no longer rolled off her, but Adam knew it ran deep, hid beneath the surface.

"I don't know," Adam said. "He might just be pissed at me."

"He came by the house," Tilla said. "Asking after you."

"He wasn't pissed off," Bobby said. "He was worried."

The sour mix in Adam's gut worsened, but now it had another focus.

"I'll try Jesse," Adam said. "And I'll meet you back at the house."

"I like Vincent," Tilla said, firmly.

"It's Vicente, mom," Adam said. "Though he does prefer Vic."

"Either way," she said. "Don't mess it up."

Adam gave a little nod and climbed into the Cutlass.

"Wonder Bread," Jesse answered on the second ring. "How was the funeral?"

"Fine. It just ended."

"Are you okay?"

"Yeah. I'm all right."

"You don't sound all right. Vic there? Is he scowling at you for taking off, doing that cop face of his?"

"No," Adam said. "I mean, he's not here."

The feeling creeping up the back of Adam's neck grew much worse. Vic was missing. He might be in danger.

"I called him but he hasn't answered," Adam said.

Adam could practically feel Jesse's scowl through the phone. He imagined Jesse's dark, thick eyebrows drawing together.

"That's not good. I'll try to call him too," Jesse said. "If you find him, you let me know."

"I will," Adam said. He hung up.

With a little sigh, he closed his eyes and reached down inside himself.

There was a lot going on in there. His warlock wound, his magic, but there, he found it—the thread that bound him to Vic.

Adam tugged on it.

Vic? He asked, sending the question along the line.

Nothing. The thread remained. Vic was out there, but they were cut off.

Adam wished he knew more about the connection between them. He wished he could ask someone. It was a touchy subject with Silver, who'd been offended when he'd first noticed the link between Adam and Vic.

Adam drove toward his mother's place.

As awful as Noreen was, as much as she deserved the humiliation of arrest, Adam couldn't leave her daughter to die. He needed to find Jodi before the druid did.

He parked next to Bobby, who'd driven Annie's white box of a car. Far from Adam's style, it had been purchased for safety, a mom-mobile.

Right now, he didn't mind if a few more airbags and safety features were between what remained of his family and a car crash.

Shaking his head, Adam tried to lose the black-and-green dread stewing in his gut. Bobby and his mother stood at the bottom of the steps.

"What are you staring at?" he asked.

Then Adam saw it, nailed to the door, a mess of blood and feathers.

9

VIC

"Where are we going?" Vic asked.

"Reconnaissance," Argent said.

The teal grass grew in spiral patterns like ferns. It whispered beneath Vic's feet, protesting and flattening before he could step on it. The spirit realm, the Other Side—he'd heard different names for it—usually filled Vic with awe. It was strange, bright, like a frenetic cartoon.

But right now, his skin crawled. They made their way over the plain with no boulders for cover, no trees for shade, and nowhere to hide if something attacked them.

Vic kept his eyes open, his ears cocked, and tried not to focus on his companion.

He already knew Argent wouldn't tell him who she suspected of wrecking the car, so he tried another approach.

"What lives out here?" he asked.

"Wild beasts mostly, things long dead or too strange for your world."

"More dinosaurs?" Vic asked, kind of hoping. What kid

hadn't loved dinosaurs? Then again, he didn't fancy the idea of seeing a live one in biting distance.

"Among other things," Argent said with a shrug.

"You guys are pretty territorial," Vic said. "Who's in charge around here?"

"Like someone we could report a car accident to?" she asked. "You'll have to fish better than that, Vicente. We can't blame the attack on a sovereign power. These lands aren't directly claimed."

"So it could have been anyone," he mused.

"Until we find further evidence, I'm afraid so."

"Is that what we're looking for then?" he asked, following her on into the plains. "Evidence?"

"This place is unaligned, but it's not empty. There are people we can question."

"So you do need a cop," Vic said.

"Exactly," she said, smiling.

The plain gave way to a dip. The dirt was ruddy, like old blood, but a lake filled most of the wide valley that stretched beneath them. There had been trees here once, but they lay dead, sprawled and sun-bleached. Stripped of bark they looked like bones. Maybe that's what they were.

A town floated on the lake. It looked like a series of rafts or barges, each a building or a house tethered by docks and ropes to its neighbors.

A shantytown, it drifted and bobbed atop the water like a living thing. The buildings looked hastily constructed from planks and driftwood. There were gardens of pale plants growing in nets tied beside the barges. They contrasted with the purple water.

"This isn't supposed to be here," Argent said.

"The town?" Vic asked.

"The lake," she said. "The town, Open Skies, shows up almost everywhere. It's like a watchtower, it has a presence in many worlds, but these plains are dry in both of our realms."

"Is it dangerous?" Vic asked.

Argent squinted. "It depends on whether the water is salt or fresh."

Vic wanted to press her on that, but they'd gotten close enough that he'd noticed the figures moving along the walkways. They weren't humans. A third of his height, they had purple or blue skin and long pointed ears sticking out from the sides of their heads.

"What are they?" Vic asked.

"Gnomes," Argent said.

"Adam said they lived underground."

"There are as many variations among the spirit folk as there are of humans," Argent said, her tone defensive. "Some live in caves. Some live in huts on the beach. Some are painters. Some are dancers."

"I get it," Vic said, raising his hands in apology. "I'm just trying to learn here."

Argent nodded.

"These are surface gnomes," she explained. "Those who held the Watchtower of the East, the timekeepers, dwelt in the dark."

Argent and Vic had almost reached the town, where a dock made a bridge to the land.

Vic could admit that he was uncomfortable. He was used to Argent and Silver, but Vic's contact with other magical beings was limited.

He couldn't make assumptions, and he was glad he had his gun. He was out of his depth. He might as well have time traveled.

"The past is a foreign country," he said.

Argent shot him a questioning look.

"It's something my mom says. She's a history professor."

"Your legends and stories started with us," Argent said.

"Sometimes there's even a little truth in them. They're not wrong, just often incomplete. And you're not in the past, but I suppose you could consider this a foreign country."

Vic wanted to ask if time travel was possible, but instead he focused on the when and where they were now.

"What don't I know about surface gnomes?" he asked. "Are they dangerous?"

They filled their town with industry, fishing and hawking, playing and talking, but always in motion. They were animated, and looked almost cute. They hadn't seemed to take notice of Vic or Argent.

"No," she said. "They're quite passive."

"Are they friendly?" Vic asked. He could smell the briny water. Out of place here, it marked the shore with salt.

"More or less," Argent said.

"So let's go ask what they saw," he suggested.

"Yes," she agreed, though she still sounded hesitant.

They passed gnomes wearing muddy colors, browns and reds that contrasted with their night-colored skin. About half of them had beards.

The gnomes still didn't react to Vic and Argent, but there were a lot of them.

Their numbers set Vic on edge.

"Are we safe here?" he asked.

It wasn't like he had any magic of his own, or at least not the kind he could call on willingly. And his gun would only get him so far.

The Reaper part of him slept. He had no way to call it.

Vic laid a hand to his heart. He couldn't feel his link to Adam. It slept, muted and quiet. Even if it had been awake, it was passive, and Adam didn't have the magic to play cavalry. Still, Vic missed the connection. He'd gotten used to it.

"What is it?" Argent asked.

"I can't feel Adam. Wait, are you hiding me from him?" he asked.

"Yes," she said. "I'm sorry. It's a bit one size fits all."

"What if he needs me?" Vic asked.

"We'll be quick," Argent said. "And I have my reasons. Protecting Adam is one of them."

Vic narrowed his eyes. He didn't like that she'd done it without telling him, but he trusted her enough to believe that she had Adam's safety in mind.

"He's important to you," Vic said.

"Yes. A warlock is a rare thing, and a warlock willing to harm himself but not another? That's unheard of in my experience."

Vic nodded. He'd known that Adam had hurt himself, but the particular details remained unclear, one more thing they needed to talk through, that Vic needed to understand.

"Since you're in a sharing mood," Vic said, trying to seem friendly for the gnomes, "want to explain to me just what it was he did to himself when he saved my life?"

"He should really be the one to tell you," Argent said. "You're his bonded."

"Bonded? You make it sound like we're married or something."

Facing him, Argent looked over her sunglasses and smiled.

"That is exactly what I am saying."

Vic blinked and stopped walking. He swayed with the dock.

"Come again?"

Argent sighed. "I forget how little education mortals have."

"We don't have magic," Vic said. He waved a hand at the market they'd entered. Barges lined with stalls of strange fruit and alien-looking pastries were laid out beside bright-orange flowers that could have been decoration or more produce. "We don't even know that any of this exists."

"You're right," Argent said, tapping a finger against her chin. "That was unfair of me. Perhaps it's simply that you don't have the time to learn. I mean, a century at best is almost nothing. Just the number of books you'll never have time to read—"

"Could you go back to the marriage part?" Vic asked, cutting her off.

Her eyes narrowed. She didn't like being interrupted, and Vic winced in apology. He'd forgotten her title, that she was a queen.

"Adam was ignorant of his actions when he saved your life," she continued. "His intention was noble, but he bound you together, connected you in a way that is rare, and again, in that he showed sacrifice."

"Like when he made himself a warlock," Vic said.

"Not exactly. He knew what he was doing then, knew that he would always live with the wound and the pain."

"But he did it anyway," Vic said quietly.

That was Adam. He'd saved Vic's life regardless of the consequences, even though they'd been near strangers.

Adam worried that the attraction between them was only the magic, and Vic knew for certain it was more than that, mostly because Adam was the sort of person who would bind himself to another, a stranger, to save his life.

"Does he know?" Vic asked. "What it means?"

"I explained it some time ago," Argent said.

It hurt that Adam hadn't told him, had left Vic in the dark. He was new to the intensity of his feelings for Adam. Hell, he was new to dating guys, but communication was Relationship 101. Adam had reasons for being secretive and slow to trust, but Vic was in this too.

He wanted to ask Argent if there was anything else he should know but wasn't certain he could handle it. He was already badly distracted when he should be watching for trouble. Besides, Adam should be the one to tell him.

The gnomes had made themselves scarce, leaving Vic and Argent alone on the large market barge. Only the sellers lingered. Vic tried smiling at an old woman. She wore a wool hat that looked like a cooking pot. She didn't smile back.

A trio of gnomes marched toward them. Their dark, pupil-less eyes looked serious. They wore black jackets, stiff pressed, setting them apart from the other gnomes. The old woman at the bun stall looked very satisfied at this development.

"Argent," Vic said, pointing his chin at the approaching gnomes. They carried long axes, the blades a glossy metal like unpolished steel. The weapons' length would make up for any distance in reach. "They're armed. Are these the cops?"

"Yes," she said. Her expression had not changed.

She did not look worried or afraid.

"What do we do?" Vic asked, trying to copy her relaxed posture and knowing he failed.

"We see what they want," she said. "Where they take us."

"And if it's nowhere good?"

"I'd like to know who sent them to detain us," she said. "Maybe they'll show themselves. Either way, I'll get us out of it."

She spoke with certainty, but Vic wasn't so sure.

"Trust me, Vicente," she added.

"Okay," Vic said.

He was really trying to.

10

ADAM

They stared at the bird, the mess of feathers and blood.

"What do we do?" Bobby asked.

Adam's brother had learned to trust him. Too bad Adam had no idea how to answer.

Bobby had changed since Annie's death. Up until then, Adam had always felt that his big brother was very good at pretending he was in a conversation with you. He'd pay some level of attention, nod along. It was only when you tried to make an important point, tried to say something you really wanted him to get, that you realized his mind was somewhere else. He'd trained himself to be polite, to play along at talking to people, when the whole time you were secretly monologuing without an audience.

Adam wasn't so certain that was the case anymore. His brother's grief had left him kind of raw, not empty exactly, but more receptive, more like Adam. Bobby wasn't shaking as he walked over to look more closely at the bird. He seemed more engaged.

Adam felt a little twinge, a roil of something red and sloshing in his gut. He wanted to be happy that Bobby might have changed, could see the world more like Adam did, but Adam could never celebrate because of how it happened.

He focused on the thing nailed to the trailer door. Whoever had put it there had walked through Adam's wards without him feeling anything. That could mean they had a lot of power, or it could mean their magic was close to his.

It was *wrong*, evil, a bruise on Adam's magical senses, and the exact sort of thing the druid had used in his charms. He was the best suspect.

"We should get rid of it," Adam said.

"I'll wash it off," his mother said.

"No, Mom," Adam said. "We need to *burn* it. But don't touch it, okay?"

"I have some barbecue tongs," she said. "Will that do?"

"Yeah," Adam said. "But burn them too."

She nodded and went to light the old drum barrel where she incinerated trash.

"What does it mean?" Bobby asked, voice quiet.

"I don't know," Adam said. "It's a hex or a mark. He's telling us something, that we're next probably."

The bird was white where it wasn't bloody and painted black. Tar and bog iron, he'd guess, some sort of binding paint.

"Shit," Bobby said, leaning closer. "I think it's an egret. That's an endangered species."

"Whoever did this wouldn't care," Adam said. "They're not a good person or a good *thing*."

"Who do you think it is, Adam? Is he after Mom?"

"I don't think so," Adam said. "She doesn't have any magic. Usually people without any get ignored."

Bobby stiffened.

"So it's for you?"

"Most likely. But then why did he attack Noreen?" Adam mused.

He remembered the bones, the wind chime in his old room, and what Noreen had said about Jodi trying to protect them.

"He wasn't after Noreen," Adam decided. "He was after Jodi."

"Adam . . ." Bobby said quietly, looking to where Tilla dropped the bird into the burn barrel and took a step back. "Mom is all we've got left."

He sounded afraid, the fear of losing someone else filling his voice. Adam understood. Bobby had lost Annie. Adam had lost Sue. But Mom should be fine. She'd only ever shown a hint of power, the smallest spark of magic. She'd always denied seeing anything when it came to the spirit world. Then again, there was the story Bobby had told him, how he'd heard Tilla in his mind, telling him to strike their father with the hammer.

"I'll stop him," Adam said. "I promise."

He just didn't know how he was going to do it.

"Can you?" Bobby asked. "Can you stop him?"

"I don't know," Adam said honestly.

He didn't even know who the druid was but definitely didn't have enough magic for a direct confrontation. Adam's survival up until now had been about flying under the radar. The druid had his number, knew where his mom lived.

"How can I help?" Bobby asked.

It meant a lot that he'd offer. Adam looked to the blood-stained door. Like the exterior, it was a sort of metal. Painted or enamel, he didn't know, but hopefully the mess wouldn't stick.

The Binders had the druid's attention.

The thing that Adam had avoided since he'd first driven up to Tilla's trailer gnawed at him.

It was time to answer the oldest question: Was the druid their father?

Adam let out a long breath as Tilla walked up to them.

"We need to go dig up Dad," he said.

Bobby went pale.

"What?" he asked.

"We have to know," Adam said, looking from Bobby to his mother and back. They looked sick. He got it. His own stomach was clenched like a fist. "I'm sorry, but I don't see another way."

Tilla nodded.

"I'll get some shovels," she said.

———

The shovels were not as useful as the old leather work gloves. Bobby and Adam shifted stones. Everything was muddy and cold, which at least should make the rattlesnakes sleepy if they stumbled across one. They liked to nest in crevices, holes other things had dug.

Adam's sweat had turned clammy by the time they unearthed a bit of the blue tarp. The plastic, streaked with red clay and piled with sandy dirt, hadn't decayed at all.

He braced himself. It had been fifteen years. He expected a skeleton or something grotesque, but hopefully nothing he couldn't handle. He steeled his stomach.

Bobby had gone cold, distant. Adam figured this was his doctor face, the expression he wore when he had bad news to deliver. He'd pushed his feelings down. Adam couldn't read them, but they couldn't be good.

"On three," Bobby said.

Adam nodded.

"One . . . two . . . three."

They pulled, tugging the tarp out of the cairn.

It came too easily.

It was empty.

Adam peeked inside the rock pile, brought up the flashlight on his phone.

Nothing. No body. No skeleton.

No Dad.

The three Binders exchanged glances. Bobby looked like he might throw up.

"Where?" he asked "How?"

Adam shook his head. He was as lost as his brother.

"Bring the tarp," their mother said. "We'll burn it."

"Why?" Adam asked.

"Transference," she said. "Blood. DNA."

Adam gaped at her.

"What?" she demanded. "I watch TV."

They pulled and shifted rocks until they could drag the tarp back to the trailer. It was raining a little as Tilla used a pair of heavy shears to cut it into squares.

She fed it into the old, blackened burn barrel, piece by piece. Adam and Bobby stood to the side, watching. Adam shoved his hands into his jacket pockets. The barrel, still hot from its earlier meal, sizzled when the rain hit it.

"So where is he?" Bobby asked.

"I don't know," Adam said. "Not where you left him. Are you sure he was dead?"

"I wasn't a doctor then, but I remember," Bobby said quietly. His face had taken on a distant look. "He was dead."

A shudder filled his entire body and Adam almost felt bad for asking.

"Then someone dug him up but put the rocks back," Adam said. "And they haven't bothered to come after you about it."

All of his guts were twisted up. They'd started getting that way when he and Bobby had moved the stones, but now Adam's stomach felt like a bundle of cold, writhing snakes.

It might be the stain, leaking in from the Other Side, or it might just be the messed-up situation he'd found himself in.

"At least they haven't come after us until now," Bobby said, eyeing the trailer door.

Tilla had rinsed the blood off. The door glistened, clean, but Adam could still see the poor egret. The memory wouldn't wash away.

He had to find the druid. He needed answers. He'd start with Jodi.

The grind of tires on the dirt road leading to the property drew them around.

A sheriff's car was almost to the gate.

"Shit," Tilla said. "Early."

"What does he want?" Bobby asked.

"Let's find out," Adam said, looking between them. "Calmly."

Bobby went to open the gate, to let the car in. Adam could already see the mirror shades behind the tinted windshield.

He and Bobby had a good amount of mud on their shoes and jeans. Not that it meant they were guilty of anything. There were plenty of chores Tilla could have asked them to do while they were here.

The sheriff walked back toward them, dressed all in khaki, the gun on his belt matte black in its holster.

There was nothing to worry about. They hadn't done anything to warrant attention.

"Whatcha burning?" the sheriff asked, tipping his hat.

"Garbage," Tilla said, waving away the black smoke.

"In the rain?" Early asked.

"It was starting to smell," Tilla said with a shrug. "Didn't want possums getting into it."

"I thought y'all finally got trash service out here," he said.

Tilla scoffed. "If you want to pay for it."

The sheriff gave a slow nod. Adam really hated those glasses. He couldn't get as good of a read on the man through them.

Adam opened himself up, let his senses absorb what he could feel. It wasn't his favorite move. He had spent years learning to close out other people's feelings. It would have been harder, maybe impossible, in a crowd where everything could get mixed up and Adam could get overwhelmed.

Nothing. Sheriff Early didn't seem to be feeling anything. It wasn't necessarily a good sign.

Vic could get like that. He shut a lot of feelings off to do the work. When he was in cop mode Adam often couldn't sense Vic's emotions, and they had a connection. Maybe that was why Adam couldn't sense him now. Maybe he was working, or maybe he'd shut Adam out.

"What can we do for you, Early?" Tilla asked.

She was her usual stony self, but Adam could feel the bit of something purple-black, the vein of fear, pulsing inside her. She was worried, not for herself, but for them, her boys.

Adam locked his defenses back in place.

"I wanted to talk to you about the funeral, about the blowout with Noreen," Early said.

"Did she call you out here?" Tilla asked, shaking her head. She looked like she might spit. "You heard what she said. I wasn't going to let her talk to Adam that way."

Adam cringed when his mom nodded to him. He didn't like remembering Noreen's words, her red eyes and puffy face. His mom didn't seem cowed by Early at all.

"You slapped her," the sheriff said.

"I did," Tilla said. "And I'd do it again if she ever tries to call my son that word."

"Well, you won't be needing to, Tilla Mae," Early said. "Noreen's dead."

Tilla blanched. Eyes wide, she asked, "What?"

"I took her back to the hospital after the funeral. She had a heart attack right after I dropped her off."

"My god," Tilla said, putting her hands over her mouth.

Adam swallowed hard.

A heart attack.

That was how Sue had died, at least according to Jodi.

"What about Jodi?" Adam stammered. "Have you found her?"

Bobby cocked his head at Adam.

"She needs to know," Adam said.

Early shook his head.

"Was it the meth?" Adam asked, mostly to Bobby. "Can that cause a heart attack?"

"Meth?" Bobby asked. "What are we missing here?"

Adam explained, from the beginning, from his arrival in Guthrie to seeing Noreen at the hospital. He left out the druid. Early listened, no doubt checking Adam's story for holes.

"How was Noreen cooking meth?" Tilla asked, kind of absently.

Everyone looked at her.

"We had home ec together in high school," Tilla explained. "She was too dumb to fry an egg."

"Ma," Bobby said. "She's dead."

"I'm not speaking ill," Tilla said. "Just the truth. I've seen *Breaking Bad*. I know cooking drugs takes chemistry."

Adam blinked. He couldn't imagine his mother watching anything as dark as that.

"Your brother has cable," she explained to Adam with a shrug.

Adam was glad she hadn't mentioned that her free time had come from caring for Annie. They didn't need the sheriff looking into that.

"You're not wrong, Tilla," Early said. "And we're investigating. Usually these sorts of things happen in more remote places."

He cocked his head toward the trailer.

"You want to look inside, Sheriff?" Tilla asked with a laugh. "Come in for some iced tea?"

She smiled, clearly amused as she turned toward the door.

"No, ma'am," he said. "That's not necessary."

"If it will put your mind at ease, please do," she said. "It's just me out here, after all, since the boys moved to Denver."

"Don't you get lonely?" Early asked.

"I do," she admitted. "Been thinking of selling, but where would I go? These two are grown, and I don't imagine I'd like the city."

Adam knew she was just chatting, keeping it light, but he could feel it now. She *was* lonely, sad even.

He hadn't sensed that from her in Denver. Caring for Annie had given Tilla a purpose. Maybe it was jumping the gun, but when this was over, when they'd found what had happened to Dad, maybe she could live with Bobby permanently or find a solution that would make her happy.

Bobby had been so anxious to get Adam a job at the hospital, to see him find a purpose closer to what he wanted for himself. Maybe he should have been focusing on Tilla instead, on giving her life some meaning.

"Penny for your thoughts, Adam Lee?" Early asked.

Adam could see Early thinking, but couldn't follow his feelings. Cold. Logical. He was a good cop. Vic would approve, maybe even like him.

"I was just thinking that I'd like that, Mom," Adam said, smiling. "If you came to Denver too. You know, not just to visit."

When this was over, when he'd settled all these questions—well, there was nothing for him here now, not with Sue gone, not with the trailer destroyed. Tilla too, if Robert Senior wasn't buried out back, she could move on.

"That's nice," Early said. "But I'd advise against leaving town right now."

"You think one of us caused Noreen's heart attack?" Bobby asked.

"I think something weird is happening. I've got a meth lab, an exploded trailer, and a missing girl," Early said. "So y'all stay put. All of you."

11

VIC

The gnomes spoke in a gruff chittering, kind of like angry para-
keets, as they guided Argent and Vic deeper into their floating
town. They gripped their halberds tight, clearly willing to use
them on the tall intruders.

The walls were mostly driftwood, woven together but
unpainted, simple. Vic could probably have kicked his way
through them. He could have put up a fight, but Argent went
along calmly with their capture, so Vic complied, though it often
meant bending to avoid banging his head on the low ceiling.

The gnomes led them through the bobbing building to a
room more solid-looking than the others. Built of heavy planks, it
was obviously made to hold outsiders like them. Tall enough that
Vic could stand up straight, he eyed the chains on the ceiling with
worry and grit his teeth as they took his gun and baton.

"Any idea what they want?" he asked Argent when they'd been
strung up, hands above their head.

They hadn't asked any questions or demanded anything, not
that Vic spoke their language. The gnomes had found stepladders
and gone right to the chains.

"Not yet," Argent answered.

Her own manacles made no sound as she shrugged.

"Now do you want to do some magic?" Vic asked. "Maybe get us out of this?"

Argent looked thoughtful for a moment before admitting, "I *am* rather bored."

She kicked herself off the wall and flipped, pulling the chains tight. With her feet pressed to the ceiling, Argent kicked again. The chains strained. Argent strained. Vic thought her wrists might break, but the iron gave first.

She flipped again as she fell, impossibly quick, and landed on her feet with the manacles still on her wrists. She pulled a bit of wire from her hair and began working at the locks.

"How did you do that?" Vic asked.

"I've lived many lives," she said, dropping one cuff to the floor. "And spent one as a magician's assistant. Vegas used to be a hell of a town."

She sighed wistfully and reached above him to work on his chains.

He dropped a moment later.

"I do not like this," she growled. "Something is wrong. They're not usually aggressive."

Vic rubbed his wrists. He'd be gentler when cuffing perps from now on. "Yeah, I didn't get that impression at all, not with the axes and everything."

"No, not that. We don't always get along, but they are usually peaceful. They don't know who I am, but they know I'm an elf. They're risking war by keeping us prisoner."

"Keeping us for who?" Vic asked.

"I do like that you pay attention," she said.

"You wanted the gnomes to lead us to whoever attacked us," Vic said. "Only they're not here."

"Yes," Argent said. "The gnomes are probably awaiting instructions from whoever flooded the valley."

"So is it smart to just wait here for them? We should try to get the drop on them."

"Clever," Argent conceded. "Very tactical."

"Cop," he said.

"I'm sure you'll make detective in no time."

Vic wasn't so certain, not with his creeping doubts about the force and his place in it.

"So what's next?" he asked. "We find somewhere to watch and wait?"

"No. It's tempting, but I don't think so. A confrontation will require that I reveal myself. I'd like to be certain of what we're dealing with first."

The crinkle around her eyes made him want his gun back very badly.

"You're worried," Vic said, straightening.

"Yes," she admitted.

Vic didn't know her well, but he'd never seen her show indecision. Argent was the Queen of Swords, immensely powerful, at least according to Adam. Someone that scared her was not someone Vic wanted to mess with.

"So let's get out of here then," he suggested.

Argent grinned and began fiddling with the lock on the door.

"You're enjoying this way too much," he said.

"It is nice to do something else from time to time," Argent said. The door swung open.

"You're not using magic?" Vic asked.

"Not even a spark."

She tucked the wire back into her hair.

Vic blinked and followed her into the hallway.

The barge floated beneath them, just a little bit unsteady, a small reminder that they were on a lake.

Vic checked that no one was around and whispered, "I need my things."

Argent nodded.

The building wasn't that big, just a cramped, two-story structure. Vic hunched again, minding his forehead when they passed through the doorway.

They climbed narrow stairs to the second story. They reached the roof, crouching to conceal themselves, but saw no one.

"Where are the gnomes?" he whispered.

He'd thought they'd abandoned the market to stay out of the way, but now it seemed the whole town had emptied.

Argent shook her head. "I don't know."

"So what's our plan?"

"We escape. We continue eastward on our own."

"And if we can't?" Vic asked. "If we're attacked or captured again?"

"Then we call my brother for backup," she said.

"You look perturbed by the idea," he said.

"Perturbed?" She raised an eyebrow.

"Mom used to give us vocabulary quizzes at dinner," Vic explained.

Argent smirked.

"I would prefer not to involve Silver," she said. "The destruction of the eastern watchtower occupies his time."

"You sure that's it?" Vic whispered, keeping low.

"What do you mean?"

"I mean, you're not just trying to keep him and Adam apart?"

Argent sighed. "And here I thought you were an adult, not some lovestruck teenager."

Vic flinched at the insult. It hurt a little, likely because it had landed. When it came to Adam, that's exactly how he felt. It was all weird and scary in a brand-new way.

"I'm not," he said, wishing he'd had a better retort.

He could practically hear Argent roll her eyes behind her sunglasses.

"Silver and Adam have both moved on," she said. "They're at peace, which serves everyone best."

"Is your brother dating?" Vic asked.

"I do not think that he has time," she said. She counted off the reasons on her slender fingers. "He has to negotiate the tower's reconstruction, avoid conflict among the concerned races—oh, and avoid a war should anyone protest."

"So he's not busy," Vic said.

"Not in the slightest."

"Adam said your father didn't approve of them dating. Is that why Silver is so busy and you're free to take road trips?"

Her smile twisted a little, telling Vic that he'd scored the point this time.

"Perhaps. My father likes to keep his own counsel."

So Silver wasn't over it, Vic thought, though he didn't say it.

"Wait, do you guys even have teenagers?" he asked.

She laughed quietly. It was a pleasant, musical sound.

"Not as you do. A teenaged elf, in your years, is an infant," she said. "We are considered mature around one hundred and an adult at two."

Vic whistled.

"What?" she demanded.

"That's a lot of puberty," he said. "I pity your parents."

Argent gave another quiet little laugh and he wondered which of them was charming the other, playing nice to learn more or to keep secrets. Still, he was enjoying the match.

Many of the barge houses had balconies. These were as empty

as the streets. Several of the houses floated around net gardens. The ones shaded by the taller houses grew blue and white mushrooms. It was all delicate, otherworldly, and completely deserted.

"They had to be in a rush," Vic said, nodding to the market stalls. "They didn't even close up shop. Where did they go?"

They turned back toward the stairs and Vic spied an interrupted meal. A clay mug of something green still steamed and a half-eaten fish rested on a plate. Its dead eye stood open, sad and silvery.

"An excellent question, and I doubt I'll like the answer," Argent said.

The floating building didn't bob as they descended to the first floor.

With no one around he felt safe to explore. Most of the rooms didn't even have doors. Vic couldn't tell if the nets hung on the driftwood walls were for decoration or if they were just stored there.

The gnomes certainly didn't seem too concerned with privacy. The driftwood branches had gaps he could peek through, letting light travel through the barge without impediment.

Vic found his gun and baton in one room, lying on a gnome-sized table without any precautions.

He sighed his relief and transferred the baton to his pocket and the gun to his shoulder holster.

He wouldn't shoot anyone, or rather, would do everything he could to avoid using it. He wasn't on solid ground here. The law that he followed was light-years away. Sure, the gnomes had captured Vic and Argent but hadn't hurt them.

The two of them crept outside and found the docks just as abandoned.

"What would pull everyone away?" he asked. "What would be so important?"

"Danger, or a royal decree."

"I don't see any threat," Vic said.

Then again, if it took magic to sense it, how would he know?

"I don't either," Argent agreed. Pocketing her sunglasses, she eyed the horizon and pointed to a series of tracks, so many that they made a path through the spiraling grass. "I am going to guess it was a decree. Someone has called them, all of them, and they hurried to obey."

"Who?" he asked. "Who could command an entire town to just walk away from what they were doing?"

Argent paused at the water's edge. Crouching, she dipped a fingertip and tasted a drop.

"It's salt, isn't it?" he asked.

"Yes." She shook her head. "I knew already, but wanted to be absolutely certain."

"We're going to follow them, aren't we?" he asked, nodding to the tracks.

"See?" Argent asked. "Detective in no time."

12

VIC

"What is that?" Vic asked.

It sat on the horizon, a giant sphere, taller than a skyscraper. It was like a snow globe full to bursting with dark water. Squinting, Vic could see schools of fish, but from this distance they must have been the size of minivans.

At its center he could just make out a salt-encrusted lighthouse, like an old aquarium ornament, sitting atop a pile of shipwrecks. The water and the fish almost hid it, but a golden light lit its windows.

"It is the Sea upon the Land," Argent said, her voice cold.

"It wasn't here before, right?" Vic asked, waving a finger at the sphere. "I didn't miss it?"

"No," she said. "It wasn't here."

"Is that why the gnomes left?"

"Undoubtedly." Argent narrowed her eyes. "Another clan rules over it. The Cups."

"Sea elves?" Vic mused. "They're the ones you suspected, aren't they?"

He didn't say *the ones you were worried about*. Vic didn't want to risk pissing her off, but the queen had a tell, a slight crinkling of the eyes.

She gave a little nod. "They are our cousins, and like their element, they are hard to grasp."

"But they're still elves," Vic said.

"Yes," Argent said. "And if it is them, if they attacked us, then we are looking at a civil war."

"Has it happened before?" Vic asked.

"Oh yes," she said. "When we, the North, took supremacy."

Vic tried not to picture elves dressed in blue or gray having reenactments as she nodded toward the sphere.

"Before, this was their watchtower, the seat of their power."

"The south shall rise again?" he asked.

When she shot him a confused look he said, "They're making fresh trouble?"

"It was a long time ago," Argent said. "They rattle their sabers from time to time, but we largely ignore them. Still, they have made much of the eastern watchtower's fall."

"You wanted to spy on them," Vic said, eyeing the sphere like it might do something, like roll toward them and crush the entire valley. "You didn't come for Adam at all."

"That is not true," Argent said. "If they are involved, I suspect Adam is connected to it, that they may want something from him. And regardless, he is a friend."

"Why?" Vic asked, trying not to sound demanding though it crept in. "He keeps saying he's no big deal, but you watch over him, keep him close. He's more important to you than you let on."

"Like I said, Adam is unique."

"Yeah, yeah," Vic said. "He made a warlock out of himself instead of hurting someone else."

"But do you know how few people, how few beings would make such a choice, Vicente, especially when it comes to sparing one who isn't their own kind?" Argent shook her head. "True heroism gets rarer with every age. Adam has it."

"Yeah," Vic agreed. "He does."

He got it. It was why Vic liked *Star Wars*. He liked heroes, and it had been one of the first things to draw him to Adam, that Adam was a good person. He hadn't let what he'd been through make him a bad guy. He was secretive, wary of getting hurt, and definitely slow to trust, but he was a good person.

Vic wondered if Argent pointed it out to distract him, play on his feelings to get him thinking about and missing Adam instead of asking the hard questions.

"So it's nothing more than that?" Vic pressed, insisting on not being distracted. The Sea upon the Land cast a big shadow, and Vic shivered despite his jacket. He could taste salt on the wind.

"Adam's power is slight, very slight," Argent said. "Yet he manages so much with it. He can see much that we cannot."

"His under-the-radar thing?" Vic asked. It was what Adam called it; the advantage that having so little magic sometimes gave him.

"Precisely."

"You want him to spy for you," Vic said. "To narc out other things."

"I want him to keep doing what he's doing," she said. "Looking for trouble, destroying evil when he finds it."

"What do you mean?" Vic asked.

"Once we became aware of him, in Denver, we queried the Saurians. They spoke on his behalf. And we found others. Adam has been destroying warlock artifacts, evil artifacts, on his own, for quite a while."

"He was searching for his dad," Vic said. "The druid who made them."

"Yes, but he still destroyed them. He could have kept them.

He could have sold them. They might have worked as bait, something to help his quest—but he destroyed them because they were evil. Pure and simple."

"You like him because he's good," Vic said, feeling a smile curve at the corner of his mouth. "That's what you're saying?"

"We like Adam because he does the right thing whether or not anyone is watching, without a promise of praise or reward."

"Does that make him more like you?" Vic asked, looking up at the sphere. It loomed as casual and delicate as a giant soap bubble. "Like an elf?"

"I wish more of us were as noble," she said, following Vic's eyes to the lighthouse.

"That's why you wanted to drive with me," Vic said, nodding as he put it together. "You were checking me out, making sure I'm good enough for him."

"Not exactly how I'd put it," Argent said.

"I *like* him," Vic said. "I'm not going to hurt him or anything."

"That's very endearing," she said, "but our interests aren't concerned with crushes and Valentines."

"So what do you want with him?" he asked.

She smiled.

"Only what's best for him."

"Whether he knows it or not?"

Argent's smile flattened. He was pushing his luck, he knew, but he continued, "Some might say that's a little controlling. Manipulative even."

"Perhaps," Argent agreed. "You must understand that my father never expected my brother to become so involved. He sent Silver to train Adam, to use his magic and help him survive it. We didn't understand then that Death herself had made him, combining bloodlines to get exactly the mix of an underpowered practitioner and Sight."

"She made him to be a weapon," Vic mused, feeling a chill that had nothing to do with the looming sphere.

"She made him to be a tool," Argent stressed. "One she doesn't need anymore. That's left him exposed. Other entities know about him now. So yes, despite our father's wishes, Silver and I have taken a stake in Adam's safety, whether he knows it or not. I think you'd agree that he's not exactly trusting of our kind, immortals, and I can't fault him for that."

She had a point.

"Thank you," Vic said. "For watching out for him."

Argent smiled and led him on.

They crossed low hills of the teal, spiraling grass. Vic spied lizards the size of small dogs darting among the curls. Here and there rabbits ran, only they had antlers, like deer.

"I thought we'd have caught up to the gnomes by now," Vic said.

"Better that we haven't," Argent said. "I'd prefer we go unnoticed."

True night never seemed to really fall on the Other Side, but the twilight deepened. The moon's emerald light flickered through the sphere's depths, mixing with the orange lights at its core.

Vic had read about Cherry Creek Reservoir, how if the dam was destroyed when the waterline was high enough, it could flood most of Denver.

The sphere, the Sea upon the Land, was wider than a baseball stadium at its base.

"How much water is in that thing?" he asked.

"More than enough to do whatever it is you're thinking about."

She pointed. "There."

"I still don't see them," Vic said.

"My eyes are significantly better than yours."

Vic noted that for later. After all, if he was going to be caught between warring elves, it would help to know where they had an advantage. Sadly, it looked like everywhere. If fighting broke out he'd hide behind Argent.

Still, he was here, somewhere impossible, approaching a 3D ocean on the Great Plains. Vic was thirsty but remembered Adam's warnings about eating and drinking in the spirit realm. Even if options presented themselves, he'd have to decline.

"Have you been to the ocean, Vicente?" Argent asked.

She was fishing again, but he'd nibble. He was learning a lot, so it seemed a fair trade.

"Yeah, my parents took us to Cozumel a few times."

They'd brought Emily, his high school girlfriend, that final time. He'd had fun, playing in the water, drinking the tequila his dad bought for them on the sly.

Eduardo had told Vic several times how much he liked Emily. He'd pulled Vic aside one night, said how proud he was, how happy.

Looking back, Vic had to wonder if his dad had suspected that he might like guys too. Had he seen something Vic hadn't?

Vic *had* liked Emily, had enjoyed sneaking off with her to make out on the beach. It had been his first time, furtive and awkward though they'd practiced plenty on the trip and back home in Denver.

Vic felt clueless. That trip had been like a dream, and the memories were golden, but looking back, hadn't he noticed the guys too, admired their chests and arms?

Maybe his dad had seen it. Maybe Eduardo had known.

Vic had never really thought too much about it all because he'd only seen it as a binary choice. He liked girls. He liked Emily, so he couldn't be gay.

Turns out the world wasn't that simple. Vic wasn't that simple, and he had to admit that he liked that about himself. He smiled to know he wasn't just someone so easily understood and labeled.

He hadn't spoken to Emily in years. They'd been. Then they weren't.

Vic could admit that his feelings toward her had been hot, strong, but not particularly deep. Then, he really had been a love-struck teenager, or at least lust-struck.

Would Adam like the beach? He'd be so white and pasty, likely to burn, but Vic would enjoy the chance to see him there, smiling and laughing. Adam rarely laughed, but he hadn't had much cause since they'd met.

Just the idea of kissing Adam, the sand beneath them, the ocean rolling . . . Vic knew his feelings weren't shallow here. They ran hot *and* deep.

So what was he doing here, playing supernatural spies with Argent while Adam mourned his aunt?

"How long is this going to take?" he asked.

She turned to face him and arched an eyebrow.

"I mean, shouldn't we be at the funeral, you know, be there for Adam?" he asked.

"Probably," she said. "But I cannot get us there without giving myself away, and I think that would be most unwise. I don't want to bring trouble to Adam's doorstep."

Vic followed Argent's gaze up to the sphere.

The gun was heavy in its holster.

"All right," he said. "Let's keep going."

13

ADAM

Adam sat in the Cutlass, taking in the damage. He didn't have long until the police hauled the trailer away. They'd marked it off with yellow crime scene tape. The explosion had ripped it open from the inside, letting in the rain, not that the thing was salvageable, not burnt and twisted as it was.

The explosion had erupted from Sue's room, the largest of the three bedrooms. Much of the trailer's siding had melted and curled. Sue's plastic flamingos were charred and deformed.

Reaching out, Adam couldn't detect any sign of the druid or his magic. That didn't mean he wasn't watching.

Nor could Adam sense whatever Jodi had been trying to do with the bones, at least not from here. If they had been wards or protective charms the druid had blown through them.

As much as Adam didn't want to, he was going to have to get closer and risk drawing more of Early's attention.

Adam shouldn't even be showing his face here, but the rest of the trailer park didn't come out to yell at him or confront him. Adam couldn't tell if the neighbors were afraid or angry. They stayed behind their curtains, peeking or glaring, at least where their windows weren't broken. The explosion had left more than one replaced with cardboard and duct tape.

Meth. Noreen had been cooking meth. Another hit to the Binder's sullied reputation. No wonder Tommy had rushed his family away after the funeral.

Still, Adam's mom had been right. Noreen hadn't been very smart. Where would she get the know-how? Someone else had to be behind it.

Jodi would know, not that she was around.

If Early West was any kind of sheriff, and Adam was pretty certain he was, he'd find her. Adam wanted to get there first. Early and his deputies wouldn't have any protection against the druid.

Adam wished he'd heard from Vic. The reasons were piling up, but Vic was a cop, a good one. He'd be able to talk Adam through what he knew and didn't know. It would help Adam make sense out of it all. That and Adam simply missed him.

Every aspect of his former life was gone or changed enough that he couldn't recognize it. Even the Cutlass was different since it had been smashed and he'd restored it.

At least he still had his magic, his senses. Adam reached out, let them drift over the park.

Here. There. Little shreds of magic, but nothing powerful, nothing like the elf he'd seen at his mom's place. And these bits were familiar, blessings or spells Sue had woven for her neighbors. She was gone, but enough traces of her life remained that he took comfort in it.

"Are you here?" he asked aloud. "Can you hear me?"

No answer, not that he'd expected one. Death was the end, and whatever she did with the souls she reaped, no one knew.

Adam pushed further, reached deeper, hoping to find some trace of who was responsible.

His senses tingled, just a little, at the very edge of what he could detect.

Adam knew better than to ignore those instincts. Vic said he'd make a good cop, were he to put on some muscle.

Adam smiled at that, at the memory of Vic using the comment as an excuse to touch him, to trace the center of his chest through his shirt. Adam would never admit it, but he'd started doing push-ups before bed after that. He wanted Vic to like him. He wanted Vic to want him.

"Focus, Binder," Adam muttered.

He listed off what he knew, trying to narrow in on what he couldn't—what he *didn't* know.

Sue was dead. By all accounts, it was natural. A heart attack.

But Noreen had died the same way, though meth and the fire were factors. Adam had to admit he found it hard to mourn her.

Vic was missing.

His dad's body—his dad—was missing.

Spider was missing again.

An elf he did not know from a court he'd had no dealings with had approached him.

The druid, the other warlock, had blown up the trailer, and he'd nailed charms to two doors.

It could not be a coincidence that Noreen had died after the charm had been nailed to her door. That they'd found the same hex at his mom's door was enough for Adam to convince Bobby to stay with her and keep her safe. If the charm had been a warning, then she might be next. Adam continued to hope that it was meant for him, only him.

He needed a lead. He needed information.

He could try the tarot cards again, but he was too close to his family to get real answers. They might help him find Jodi.

"What are you looking at?" a voice asked.

Startled, Adam seethed.

"What is it with elves and back seats?" he asked, eyeing Vran in the rearview mirror.

Vran's dark eyes glittered with amusement.

Adam sighed.

"I need to see something inside that trailer," Adam said, answering Vran's original question.

"Then go see it."

"That's a crime scene. That's what that yellow tape means. If I get caught I could be in trouble."

He didn't add that more suspicion thrown on his family wasn't the best thing right now, not with a long-buried body missing. More than anything, that was why Adam had come. He needed a better look at those bones.

"So let's not be seen," Vran said.

Outside the car, the rain thickened, falling hard enough that Adam could not see the trailer park beyond the curtain.

Blinking, Adam opened the door and held up a hand. Here, in the little corridor Vran had made, the rain fell normally.

"Neat trick," Adam said.

Vran smiled and Adam would have sworn his blueish skin flushed a little pink at the praise.

They approached the trailer, bending to walk beneath the police tape.

The wooden steps and little porch were slick with rain but intact. All was dark.

With a quick check that Vran's rain shield still hid them, Adam brought up the flashlight on his phone.

Despite the ruined roof, the air inside the trailer smelled of fire. The scent of cat urine rolled in sugar lingered, and Adam knew now what it was. He shouldn't be breathing this. He probably shouldn't even be walking in this air. He felt his magic itch along his skin, trying to shield him from the chemicals.

The power was out, but the holes in the ceiling let in the rain and the ambient glow from the trailer park's few streetlamps, giving a little extra light. Vran was behind him and could probably see in the dark. The elf walked silently.

Adam avoided Sue's bedroom, where they'd put the lab, and hurried to the trailer's other end, toward his room. It was strewn with paperbacks and clothes, all thrown into a corner. Jodi had lied about his stuff. No surprise there.

Adam almost tripped over a can of black paint. It had dripped down the side and onto the carpet. Sue would have hated that.

Dammit, Jodi, Adam thought.

The walls were painted black, with mystic symbols drawn like a border along the top in white chalk.

The fire hadn't marked much here. It was easy to see why the police were so interested in his old room, but Adam's old desk sat clear. The bones were gone.

"Stupid," Adam muttered. Of course the cops would take them.

Vran remained in the hall.

Adam looked for other clues.

Sparkling black dust had been scattered around the desk. Adam thought it might be glitter but shining his light closer he recognized it. Ground obsidian. There were lumps of metal too. They had a melted, dripping shape. Bog iron.

Beneath the acrid stench was something else, the taste of rotten blackberries. It filled this room, centering on the desk.

Adam stepped that way, peering closer with his Sight.

The bones were gone but they'd left something, a shadow or stain, to use Vran's expression.

Even if they'd been there, Adam had no way to identify if they were his father's but he guessed so. Adam turned toward Vran, intending to ask him what he might sense, but the elf had vanished.

Adam opened his senses further and laid a hand to the desk. Even though they were long gone from here, the sound the chimes had made—what Jodi had carved them into—still echoed in the spirit realm.

This wasn't a ward, a protection charm. It was a summons, and the scent of the magic told Adam who Jodi had been calling to.

The druid. She'd brought him here.

Adam blinked, realized a flashlight was gleaming in the hallway behind him.

"Hold it right there!" a voice commanded.

"Sheriff Early," Adam said, raising his hands. "Nice night for it."

14

ADAM

"Run it by me again," Early said.

The interrogation room was more of a little office with a plastic folding table in it, but Adam was plenty intimidated.

Vran had left him there, let him get caught. Adam did not know if the elf was malicious or just mischievous. Either way he shouldn't have let his guard down. Baby elf, baby prick.

He was probably laughing at Adam from the Other Side.

"I told you," Adam explained. "I went to see if any of my stuff was there. And it was. Lots of it."

"And I already told you that if it was, you wouldn't be getting it back, that it's tainted with who knows what," Early said. "You're lucky you didn't spend much time in there."

"I'm sorry," Adam said. "I got upset thinking about Spider."

"The cat?" Early asked.

"Sue's cat," Adam stressed.

"Does this have anything to do with the satanic shit?" Early asked. "The bones?"

Adam blanched.

"Don't play dumb," Early said. "I went to school with your

dad. I know all about his aunt and her"—he paused to make air quotes—"*psychic readings*. I showed you those pictures and you just *had* to have a closer look."

"Yeah," Adam admitted, hoping that putting a bit more of the truth into his lie would get him out of this. "I don't know what Jodi was playing at. Sue wasn't into anything like that, bones or whatever. She just read cards and tea leaves."

Adam didn't go into the difference between life and death magic, the difference between what warlocks did, subverting life, and what Sue had done, using her own magic, her life or power, to peek into the future or the past. Early would either think he was delusional, or worse, involved.

"So if we were to go through your car or get a warrant to search your mom's place, we wouldn't find anything like that?" Early asked.

"Hell no," Adam said, letting his accent out. "She invited you in. She meant it. There's nothing to see there."

"We wouldn't find walls painted black or tarot cards?" Early asked.

"Tarot cards?"

"Your cousin left some behind."

Adam hadn't seen those, but it wasn't a surprise. If Jodi were making summoning charms she probably had a Tarot deck. Early would have taken them for evidence.

Adam had to step carefully. Sue's cards, his cards, were all he had left of her. He wouldn't give them up without a fight.

"You'd find some cards," he admitted. "Sue gave them to me before I left, but they're only special because they were hers. You can buy them at any bookstore."

Early narrowed his eyes. He was clearly done playing nice.

The cards shouldn't make him suspicious of Adam. Then again, this was Guthrie. A *Dungeons & Dragons* manual might start a panic.

"Sue didn't mean anything by it," Adam said, leaning across the table between them. "She helped people."

"Conned them, you mean," Early said, his tone firm.

So that was how it was going to be. Gone were the smiles and the mirror shades, the friendly, folksy sheriff. A good bit of Early's drawl had gone away as he continued, "Plenty of people didn't look kindly on your great-aunt and her line of work. Maybe one of them had something to say about it, and maybe they were right."

"Sue told people what they needed to hear," Adam said. "Like, yes, they needed to get that cough checked out or should tell their spouse how they really felt. She helped people, and yeah, she dressed it up in a little fortune-telling."

Sue's Sight had been spot-on, but she'd been smart about it, knew when to tell people the truth and when not to. That must have been why she hadn't told Adam so many things.

"Digging up bones," Early said. "That's the kind of stuff serial killers do."

"Doesn't it work the other way?" Adam asked. The sheriff didn't look amused.

"I don't know what Noreen or Jodi were playing at," Adam said.

"You sure they weren't yours, Adam? It was your room. Like you said, your stuff was still there."

Adam knew he should keep his mouth shut, but he couldn't. He wasn't quite certain what the sheriff was accusing him of.

"And why would they be?" Adam asked. His voice was ice-cold, like Silver or Argent before they drew their blade. But they weren't here. Neither was Vic. Adam was alone, and this was not a situation he could solve with magic.

"I know you did time at Liberty House before it closed. I know what they used to say about you, that you were unstable.

Maybe Noreen said it too. Maybe she said it one too many times, and you decided you'd had enough."

"Noreen was cooking meth," Adam said. "You said it yourself, those labs explode. And are you forgetting the part where I saved her life?"

Early conceded the point with a nod.

"She got the trailer. She got everything," he said. "I think Sue was afraid of you. I think you going to Denver was the best thing that happened to her. And it would have worked out, if you'd left well enough alone, but you couldn't stand Noreen having what you didn't."

Adam laughed.

Not long ago he would have been proud to call Sue's trailer home, but he wanted more now. Maybe not what Bobby wanted, a house in the suburbs and some perfect made-up life, but he wanted . . . what, an apartment with Vic?

Adam couldn't say. He only knew that he wanted more—more than this, more than Guthrie had to offer.

"I have a life, Sheriff. A better life now. I loved Sue. I'd never hurt her daughter. I wouldn't even know how to blow up a meth lab without incinerating myself. I didn't like Noreen," Adam said calmly, "but I wouldn't try to kill her."

"Maybe not you," Early said. "After all, you're not the one who slapped her at the funeral. Rung her bell pretty good too."

"You think my mom blew up the trailer?" Adam asked. "My mom?"

He poured as much disbelief into his voice as possible. There it was, the danger, because Adam's mother had shown her temper. She'd defended Adam publicly. Now Early was trying to put together some kind of theory, build a case.

"You know my mom, Sheriff," Adam continued. "She wouldn't do something like that."

"And what about your daddy, Adam Lee?" Early asked.

Ice ran up Adam's spine.

"What about him?" he asked.

"He's been gone a long time. No one's seen him in years."

"He ran off," Adam said, dredging up the old lie. Hell, until recently he'd thought it was true. He could pretend to believe it a little longer. He let the hurt show in his eyes, the abandonment he'd felt for all those years.

Early took a long sip from his coffee mug. It said World's Best Dad.

"Funny though," he said. "These days you can find anyone, the Internet and all that. We're cops. We have search engines for everything, hunting down deadbeat dads and the like. Your father isn't anywhere we can find him."

"What are you saying, Sheriff?" Adam asked.

"I'm not saying anything. I've got nothing, Adam. I think you know that, just a bunch of odd coincidences that don't add up. But something around your family ain't right. I don't know if you're involved or not. But I think you know something you aren't saying, and I think you want to tell me what it is."

Adam leaned back in his chair. He wasn't certain how to act, what would be natural in the moment.

He could summon anger, seem pissed, not worried or panicked. He wished he could ask Vic what he should do.

Adam decided to try the truth—or at least some of it.

"I don't know," he said. "I don't know whose bones those are, but you're right, something's wrong with my family, at least my cousin. I wish I knew where she was, and if I did, I'd tell you, because I think she's the only one with any answers."

Early took another long sip from his coffee.

"I believe you," he said. "But I'd appreciate it if you stayed out of my crime scenes."

"I promise," Adam said.

"You can go, but don't leave town," Early said.

There was no worry about that. Adam had too many things to sort out.

He left the police station. Early had been kind enough to have a deputy drive the Cutlass over.

Adam growled as he adjusted the mirrors. He didn't like other people driving her, but he had other things to worry about.

Finding Jodi was the most important thing at the moment.

Adam knew where to start. Last he'd heard, she'd been working his mom's old job at the gas station.

He wondered about their inventory. If they stocked cold meds and how well they kept track of them. Jodi could have sourced some of what they'd needed for the meth lab that way.

He drove out to the gas station, but Jodi wasn't working. The man behind the counter went from surly to outright pissed when Adam asked about her.

"She hasn't shown up in two days," he said. "You see her, you tell her that's a walk out. This is an at-will state. That means no unemployment!"

Adam left; he was glad he hadn't bought any gas there.

Jodi wasn't his favorite, but the rage rolling off the man was out of proportion. It reminded Adam of his dad, the way the simplest thing could set Robert Senior off.

Adam didn't know his cousin that well, but he had a phone and was about the only person in the world without some kind of social media presence.

Jodi's stuff was all public. He didn't even have to create an account to see her posts.

Most of them were dumb memes, a lot of anti-immigrant garbage, the kind of crap Adam would have expected from Noreen's daughter.

Then he found another account, Mystic Mysteries, and suddenly understood the quick redecoration of his room.

She'd just gotten started, posting just one video of her explaining a tarot card.

She'd set her phone up to record herself leaning against the wall she'd painted black. Dressed in a lacy bra, Jodi drew the Moon and smiled into the camera.

"It's always the Moon for me," she said a little breathlessly. "So we'll start there."

She went on to give a pretty textbook explanation of the card, nothing Adam hadn't heard from Sue, but she left out that the Moon often meant what wasn't seen.

And while she didn't have a 1-800 number, she did take donations through the Internet, offering a personal reading, a blessing, and a bonus sexy pic in exchange for money.

Jodi promised more readings and signed off.

She was Sue's niece. She might have some Sight, but her interpretations of the card had felt memorized, what you'd pick up from a quick Internet search.

Adam had never talked to Sue about Jodi, about whether or not other Binders had magic. His own was so different than Sue's, a mix of bloodlines that included hers, but also his mom's and a touch of something wild that had always felt uniquely his own.

He wished he could talk to Silver about this, especially about bloodlines. More than anyone, his ex had seen Adam's magic up close, but the idea felt too intimate, especially since many of Adam's lessons with the elven prince had come with bonus make-out sessions. That, and it was never good to ask elves for favors.

"Mystic Mysteries," Adam muttered.

And Jodi had thought Spider was a dumb name for a cat.

Maybe Jodi and her mother wanted to inherit more than Sue's trailer. Maybe they wanted Sue's business, the small network of clients that despite what Adam had told Early, had kept the lights on.

Adam couldn't see that going well. Noreen wouldn't settle for helping people move past slights and old griefs. More than anything, Sue had been something of a counselor for people who couldn't afford therapy. He'd seen the similarity as soon as he'd moved in, and he'd been to enough sessions at Liberty House to know.

Noreen would try to exploit the people who would have come to Sue for help. Had Jodi called the druid to them on purpose?

It seemed like it, but it still didn't answer the matter of the bones. Adam considered the druid's eyes, blue like Sue's, blue like his. Blue like his dad's.

Adam could show the tarot video to Early, give him a lead and get him looking away from Tilla, but no, Adam needed to find more first.

He needed to find Jodi. She had answers, and worse, she had the druid's attention.

Adam kept scrolling between Jodi's posts on her other feeds. How many accounts did she have?

"Hey, guys!" she said, starting one video. "Guess who scored tickets to see Chlamydia Clown Car?"

Adam made a gagging sound at the name. He zoomed in on the tickets Jodi waved at the camera as she blew a kiss. The show was that night, at a bar called Tornadoes. The website showed that it was built out of an old double-wide trailer.

"Keep it classy, Guthrie," Adam said.

15

VIC

The water inside the sphere picked up the red of the dry ground around it, turning it purple. Vic caught glimpses of tentacles and fins as the Sea upon the Land swirled with internal currents.

Drops sprayed them as wind whipped across the sphere. The grass retreated from the salt, leaving sticky mud that made the going hard.

Vic slipped and muttered a curse while Argent walked with perfect grace. The stories had gotten that part right about elves. Or maybe she slipped and tripped and just hid it with an illusion.

They were close enough now that the sphere loomed over them. Its surface rippled with endless waves. Miles wide at its equator, it rested on the ground, like a marble on a table. Vic didn't have the math to calculate the volume. It was just what Argent called it, a Sea upon the Land.

The closer they got the more he felt the size of it. Even the tiniest roll would crush them. Vic fought the need to retreat.

The gnomes' tracks ended at the sphere's base.

"How do we get inside?" he asked. "Or can you breathe underwater?"

"I cannot," Argent said with a scowl. "I can bring air with us, but it would take magic."

"Okay, what is the plan here?" Vic asked. "We're spying on them, hoping to overhear their evil plan? Or do we just walk up and knock?"

"You are very droll today, Vicente," Argent said.

"Yeah, well, I'm hungry," he said.

It was true, but his concern for Adam gnawed at him more. Vic hadn't signed up for this and he remained kind of pissed off that Argent had roped him into it without asking him first, especially since he still didn't know why.

She'd said she had Adam's best interests at heart, but Vic didn't trust that. Elves were from another world. They lived forever. Her idea of best could be radically different from Adam's, and it might not include a future with Vic.

"What about the gnomes?" he asked, focusing on the business at hand. "Can they breathe water?"

"Good question. They cannot," she said. "Let's get closer."

Vic swallowed hard, but he followed Argent into the valley made by the sphere's weight.

A dock sat on the dry ground. It jutted into the sphere's base.

"It's a dive shop," Vic said, unable to suppress a grin.

There was a shack and racks of different sized tanks and suits just like he'd seen in Cozumel. Dozens, the smaller ones especially, were gone, but a mix remained.

"You know how to use these?" Argent asked, looking a little uncomfortable.

"I do," he said. "I can show you, but why are they here?"

"Stealth," she said. "A mundane solution for the sea elves' allies. Likely since magic might be detected."

"You said that's not supposed to be here." Vic nodded up at the sphere. "So they're planning something and they didn't want you to know about it."

"Exactly my concern," Argent said.

"That doesn't give off a lot of magic?" Vic asked, waving at the sea.

"I didn't say they were smart," Argent said.

They took turns changing in the shack, and he helped her fit a tank and goggles to her suit as he explained how to breathe.

"How do we get inside?" Vic asked. This close, it curved over him. It felt like being underground, beneath the tremendous weight of all that water.

Vic had never felt so small.

"Just step into it," Argent said. "Once we're in, keep close. You asked me what dangers lived here. Most of them can swim."

Vic shuddered, but followed as Argent touched the sphere. Her hand sank into the water as easily as it might a wave.

Vic took a long breath, adjusted his goggles, and leapt inside.

The water was cold, and he was grateful for the wet suit, though he wasn't certain how his clothes and gun were faring in the plastic bag he'd tied them in.

He swam after Argent, rising. They kept near the sphere's edge, but not too near. Vic imagined himself falling through it, tumbling to his death as they rose higher and higher.

Argent had no trouble mastering the tank. Either she was a natural or it was another elf thing. They might learn faster, take up new things faster, but that seemed to contradict their love of old things and classic cars. Vic hadn't met enough of them to decide.

The lighthouse perched atop its pile of shipwrecks. It grew colder as they swam that way, deeper, toward the core. The sunlight thinned. Vic hoped Argent remembered that his eyesight wasn't a sharp as hers.

Everything was distorted and hazy, but it all felt like someone had seen pet store aquariums and really wanted that look for their home, or their skyscraper of a fortress.

Vic took a long breath through the mask and let out a stream of bubbles. This place was whimsical, but scary too. Whoever had built this had the power to make it happen, to build an ocean in a bubble in the middle of Kansas.

They swam on, deeper and deeper into the sphere. Something blurred the last of the light behind them, like a thick cloud had passed over the sun.

Vic turned. No, not a cloud. A giant shark passed between them and the sphere's surface.

Argent went very still and Vic followed her lead, floating there, taking as few breaths as possible.

The creature was massive, bigger than most boats, than an RV.

It hadn't noticed them, but if it turned—Vic forced himself to breathe calmly into the mask. He'd seen a dragon. He was a cop, a Grim Reaper, but still, that shark could swallow him in a single bite.

Argent gave him a nod and they continued.

The tower stretched for at least twenty stories, but they swam quickly. Vic could feel the pressure tighten as Argent led him to a window near the lighthouse's peak.

She stuck her head inside, then stepped through, waving for Vic to follow.

The window was like a force field, holding back the water. Vic stepped into air. Whatever magic kept the water out, it kept all of it out. He was dry, head to toe.

The room looked like something from a theme park, but it wasn't too weird if he thought in aquarium terms. The floor was mosaic, a million little tiles of blue and teal held together by white mortar that looked a bit like toothpaste. Still, it was empty. He could hear dripping somewhere. So some water got in or it might be a feature.

"No one here either," he whispered.

"They're above us," Argent said.

He shot her a questioning look.

She pointed to her ear.

The walls were fresco, a colorful, textured plaster that was probably supposed to remind him of coral. Maybe it really *was* coral, grown here over eons. He focused on it as they shed their tanks and wet suits. Vic was glad to see the magic had dried his clothes but more importantly, his gun appeared unsoaked.

Outside, the massive shark continued its lazy swim, sunning itself on the faint beams of light passing through the sphere.

"What is that thing?" Vic asked.

"A megalodon," Argent said, appreciatively. "They're ancient, long gone in your world, but like us, our brethren of the water are preservationists. Here, they thrive."

"So they're not all bad? The sea elves, I mean," Vic asked.

"Very few people are all anything, Vicente," she mused. "Anyone can be the best or worst of persons. The greatest saints or horrors of your own kind were all human."

Vic nodded. His mother would have appreciated the thought. History said Argent's words were true.

He watched the megalodon a moment longer. Its teeth had to be as long as his fingers.

"Are we going to have to come back this way?" he asked.

"Perhaps," she said. "But it should not bother us if we don't attract its attention."

"I'll try not to look like bait," Vic said, taking in more of the room.

The ceiling wasn't quite flat, the walls not quite squared. Immortals were almost alien, and their spaces were strange. The angles weren't quite meant for human eyes.

Not that Vic was certain he was still entirely human.

He had no sense of the Reaper sleeping inside him. He didn't even know if it was part of him, or just some spirit he sublet space to. His baton was tucked into his belt. He didn't feel anything from it, any kind of tingle or sign that he or it had any special significance.

Maybe, if Adam wasn't going to tell him anything, Argent could.

"Will the sea elves know we're here?" Vic asked. "You're hiding your magic. Is that enough?"

"I have an advantage they don't know about," she said.

"The window thing, that they're not looking for you with their eyes?"

"Not just that." Argent smiled. "I have you."

"I don't get it," Vic said.

"Reapers are strange and very subtle. We've never had much chance to study one before. I suspect Death hides you the way she hides her own power. No one really knows its source or limits. She's not a god, or even an immortal as we understand ourselves. I am gambling on two things: one, that a little of her efforts to hide you will cling to me."

"And the other?"

"That if it does come to war, she wants us to win."

"I don't think she cares about politics, or whatever this is." Vic waved a hand at the coral walls and ceiling. "I think she cares about doing her job. And burritos. She said something about burritos last time."

"We don't understand her," Argent admitted. "Not really. But she showed a bit of herself in Denver. She likes balance, that life and death keep their roles. She doesn't like things that break those rules."

"Like warlocks?" he asked.

Argent stiffened.

"Very likely, though she's clearly not above using them as tools."

"Did he really have to do it, maim himself to bind the spirit?"

"This isn't the best time or place for this conversation, Vicente, but yes. Binding a spirit as old and complicated as what we've named Mercy, required a sacrifice. It was that or maim another conscious, living thing."

Vic nodded and swallowed the rest of his questions.

It wasn't just the bonding thing. There was too much Adam hadn't explained.

Spending time with Argent was starting to give Vic an idea just how much Adam was holding back, how much he hadn't said. Worse, Vic was starting to wonder if he really could trust Adam, and it put a little stitch in his heart to think that.

"So what next?" Vic asked, nodding to the shell-lined, curving hallway.

"I'm uncertain," Argent said. "I'm making it up as I go along."

"Is that smart?" he asked.

"Quite," she said. "Immortals are predictable. We like patterns. Having no plan should make it harder to anticipate what I'll do next."

"You talk like someone is watching you, watching us," Vic whispered. "I thought we were hiding."

"You can never be too cautious."

It was another lie, or at least another half-truth. Argent wasn't telling him everything. Vic didn't like it, but she was right, this wasn't the time or place to push it.

If these sea elves had been the ones to attack them, they might come for Adam too.

"After you," Argent said, gesturing Vic forward.

He took a breath, screwed up his courage, and started down the hall.

Light filtered in from great prisms of greenish sea glass. The only sound was the ocean, churning and roiling outside the windows.

"There's nobody here," Vic said. "Is that strange?"

"I don't know, but I don't like it either," Argent said.

"Do they know we're here?" he asked.

"Not so far as I can tell, but it could be a trap."

"Let's go carefully," Vic suggested as they came to a spiraling, corkscrew stairwell.

A long chain of blue glowing worms ran down its center, casting enough light for them to safely climb. Argent took the lead.

Vic felt exposed. There were too many corners, too many places for someone to get the drop on them, but he didn't see anyone climbing or descending when he leaned out past the metal rail to peek.

They'd gone up for a while when Argent jerked Vic to the side by his jacket sleeve. They pressed themselves against a wall, between two giant ceramic seahorses, waiting for someone to go by.

A group of the sea elves came up the stairs.

Vic tried to get a look without moving. They carried long tridents, and Vic imagined being skewered on one. So far this place had felt like a theme park, but now the danger got a little more real.

The sea elves were the opposite of Argent's brood. She and Silver favored grays and metallic shades, looks that brought out the glow of their pale skin and icy eyes.

The winter twins were beautiful, and these elves were no different, yet they were somehow colder. Their hair and eyes leaned toward darker shades, inky midnight, deep blues and blacks. Their skin had a blueish tint. Argent and Silver were strange, but these elves moved differently, more like birds or insects, like something predatory, something not human.

Vic wanted to ask Argent if she and Silver did that for their sakes, to fit in better with the humans they knew. He tucked the question away as the sea elves continued to climb the stairs.

Their dark hair rippled out from their helmets. Vic did not try to guess their gender. Their armor, gleaming like black beetle shells, gave no clue.

Argent waited a long while, past even when Vic would have. Only when he was starting to think she'd frozen did she move, following the soldiers up the stairs.

The light from the prisms brightened. They were nearing the lighthouse's peak.

Argent paused again, ear cocked to the side, and then hurried into the shadows. Vic followed. He crept as quickly as he could, certain the tread of his clumsier steps would give them away.

The stairwell opened onto a broad, circular space. It was a lot like an old theater, filled with velvet, ornate folding chairs and an eager audience.

Vic recognized the gnomes and sea elves, but dozens of other things sat in the theater, including a number of figures with red and purple tentacles for hair. There were shark men, with fins on their arms and heads.

Despite the crowd, the place could have sat hundreds more. It felt empty, like the sad concert of a faded legend.

Argent led Vic up to the balcony, to a private box that stood empty.

No one had been here for a long while. The carpet was dusty. The walls needed painting. Vic followed Argent's lead and crouched down near the rail, not risking a creak from the aged chairs.

Vic wanted to ask what this place had to do with Adam, but he wasn't stupid. He kept quiet and listened.

The stage was backlit by the polished disk of the lighthouse. It worked like a giant fun-house mirror, reflecting the figures sitting atop their thrones. There were four chairs, all high-backed and carved from bright-red coral, but only two were occupied.

Thankfully there was no blinding torch to light the disk, just a blue-green glow that filled the room from all directions at once. The place had a strong Vegas by way of Atlantis vibe.

Showy, Vic thought.

The man and woman occupying the largest two thrones were bickering. They made no attempt to hide their conversation, as if they didn't have hundreds of silent onlookers.

". . . he should be here," the woman said. Her voice was like a tempest, like waves crashing against the rocks.

Vic could not help but compare her to Argent, and maybe that was the point. They were different sides of the same coin, different aspects of the same thing, the same ancient power, and judging by the crown, they were both queens.

"Our guest came alone, did he not?" the man argued. Shipwrecks echoed in his voice. "Three of us should be enough."

"You are too indulgent of him," the queen argued. "You always have been."

Adam had told Vic that they only saw a fraction of the elves, of their true selves and power. Maybe that was why Vic heard tides in their voices, his brain was trying to find ways to process the magic spilling off of them.

Vic had no magic of his own, but he felt something, a pressure in the air.

Adam's magic had been a curse until Silver had taught him to control it. The emotions and sometimes even the thoughts of spirits and people had crashed into him, making it too loud in his head. He'd lost track of what was in the mortal realm and what lay on the Other Side.

Vic could understand that now. The argument happening below felt like a gathering storm. It wasn't even much of a conflict, but it washed through Vic. It could break him. He could lose himself. It was like standing on a beach as a hurricane approached.

Argent squeezed Vic's arm, and the world steadied. Vic took

several long breaths, working to keep them quiet. Argent gave him a little nod.

I'm good, he mouthed.

What had it been like for Adam, alone for so long with this in his ear? Ex or not, Vic was grateful that Silver had been there to save Adam's sanity.

A third elf entered, marching up the aisle toward the dais. She had straight black hair cut with such an edge that it could have scored glass. She wore a suit of armor, black metal plates and purple chain mail that any cosplayer would have envied. Bits of sea glass were worked into her crown of black coral, aqua and green that caught the light.

She settled into the third seat without a word of greeting to her two elders. They seemed thirtyish while she appeared around Vic's age, a woman in her middle twenties.

"Did you find him?" the first woman asked.

Queen and knight, Vic mused. The elves took their titles from the tarot suits. If the man was the king, then it was the page that they were missing and complaining about.

"He's in none of his usual haunts," the knight answered.

"I told you," the queen said, turning to the king. "He's gone to taunt his opposite. We should have chosen another."

A chime sounded. Whispers and mutters rippled through the packed chamber. They ceased when the king lifted a hand.

"It is too late to argue now," he said. His crown was something like glass, maybe crystal, but it flickered and twisted like a thing alive. It might be a whirlpool, tamed to rest upon his head. "Our guest has arrived."

A dozen sea elves marched into the chamber, walking down the broad aisle in a diamond formation.

Argent stiffened and Vic recognized the figure at the center of their march.

Silver, Argent's brother.

"Silver of the North," a guard announced. "Knight of Swords, eldest of the Pale King, Prince of the Frozen Tree, firstborn of Alfheimr, signet of the nine-realm treaty of . . ."

Vic thought he might fall asleep before the litany of titles ended. They droned on long enough that he suppressed a yawn. Even Silver looked bored before it ended.

"So?" the king asked. "Has your father considered our proposal?"

Silver wore a suit of perfect gray, with a fedora banded in black atop his head. He looked about twenty-three, with a diver's body and pale hair. Gorgeous, if you were into that, but he dressed and carried himself like an older man, like a gangster from a black-and-white movie. He stood straight, tall, and carried a cane that he didn't lean on.

"My father has heard your proposal," Silver said with an exasperated tone. "And he rejects it, again, just as he has rejected it every other time you've made the suggestion."

Vic stole a glance at Argent. She'd narrowed her eyes to slits. From her expression, Vic guessed that she hadn't known about this business.

Silver should get his head checked. Vic would not want to be the target of his sister's anger.

"The North no longer holds the sway it did," the queen in black said. "The loss of the eastern watchtower was caused by actions your sister initiated. It is time your father gave us an equal voice."

"Is it?" Silver asked. He leaned on his cane, putting both hands atop it. "I see this place, your arranged subjects, and the trappings of your former place on the council."

"The Sea remembers," the king said.

"The Sea shall rise again," the crowd responded.

Called it, Vic thought.

Silver turned his face slightly toward the crowd, but never took his gaze from the dais.

Vic wouldn't have either. The sea elves reminded Vic of eels.

"Platitudes aside," Silver said. "You do not have the votes among the Council of Races to force action."

"The council is terrified," the queen said. "The loss of the east freed many a thing, many a being better left imprisoned."

Vic felt the tremor of power moving through the room. It reinforced his idea that it was the immortal women you'd be smart not to pick fights with.

"We are dealing with the matter," Silver said coldly. "The Watchtower of the East will be rebuilt."

"Let us have it," the queen said. "Let us have a place of power again."

"It is not up to me," Silver said. "But either way, the answer is no, the council will not give two towers to the same race. That law is ancient."

"Then give us the north again," the queen snapped, the command like a rushing wave that made most of the audience flinch. "Then we'll stop the destruction at our doorstep, the pollution and murder of life."

Silver shook his head.

"You cannot drown the mortal world," he said.

"They're killing *everything*," the queen protested.

"The mortals are wrong," Silver agreed. "But wiping them back to the Stone Age is not the solution."

"So you say," the knight said calmly. She'd straightened in her seat. "We've done it before."

Silver stared her down. He was vastly outnumbered, but he did not look afraid.

"If you won't cede the tower to us, then we'll have to take it by force," the queen said.

The knight rose to her feet, her motions so quick that Vic could not follow them. From atop the dais, she loomed over Silver, a sword in her hand. It looked like a saw blade, or the nose of a swordfish, with little spines along its edges.

"We'll return your head to your father," she said. "That will show him how serious we are."

"Perhaps he'll see reason in his grief," the queen added.

Vic looked to Argent. Her eyes were narrow, her expression even. Vic could practically see the calculations moving through her mind, the exact math of how she'd kill every sea elf in the room. A cold power began to seep through the veil she'd drawn over herself.

Oh Queenie, Vic thought. He'd have backed away if he had anywhere to go. *You done fucked up.*

"Your treachery is predictable," Silver said, shaking his head.

"Then you shouldn't have come alone, Prince Silver," the queen said. The three of them were standing now. They looked like a school of sharks scenting the water, tensing to attack.

"I came in good faith, under a flag of treaty," Silver said. "And I would not see any of my people harmed by your inept attempt at a coup."

"Inept?" the knight questioned. Her sword flashed as she twisted it in the watery light.

"So you'll surrender?" the queen said, her voice dripping with bloodlust.

Vic dealt with criminals, with dealers, thieves, and plenty of addicts. He couldn't say any of them were evil. They were mostly misguided, their sense of right and wrong twisted up with their survival. Many were the heroes in the stories they told themselves.

More and more Vic was beginning to doubt if the law wasn't the problem, that he should work on untangling those stories instead of punishing people.

But these sea elves, these deep elves—they were cruel, and cruelty seemed pretty damn evil.

"I didn't say that," Silver said, his voice casual.

"There are no witnesses here who are not our vassals," the queen said. "They'll say you came to threaten us. After all, the North is known for coldness, for exactness. The council will believe *us*. We're at your mercy. You're so much stronger than us."

Silver's eyes narrowed at her mockery, and Vic knew that she'd pay for that.

"And yet the Page of Cups isn't here?" Silver asked, turning about as if the missing elf would pop up. "Did he decline to participate in this foolishness? Perhaps he will be spared from what you're about to bring down upon yourselves."

"You mean your father?" the queen said, sneering. "Aren't you a little old to threaten us with him?"

"No. No." Silver laughed. "Like I said, you're predictable, Your Highness, but you're not the only ones."

"What do you mean?" the king asked, a hint of something—not fear exactly, but a note of worry—in his voice. He cast about the room, but his gaze did not land on the box where Argent and Vic crouched.

"I mean that I'm a twin," Silver said. "And that my sister, for all her cleverness, is not quite as sneaky as she thinks."

"Now," Argent said.

She leaped to her feet, grabbed Vic about the waist, and jumped.

Her strength almost squeezed the breath out of him.

They fell in an arc.

Vic bent his knees, ready to crash into the Knight of Cups.

She lifted her spiny sword against the threat. Argent let Vic go, placing him on the ground with barely an inch to fall. She didn't even pause as she took the final step, her sword appearing in her hands.

The knight's face was a mask of concentration and panic. Vic could feel the power swirling as two storms, a blizzard and a hurricane, collided. The crowd felt it too. They gasped or cried out.

Argent's blade connected. It cleaved through the spiny sword. The Knight of Cups staggered back, her arm clearly broken, shattered by the impact with Argent's oversized blade.

The Sea Queen screamed, a deep wail of rage and agony, like she'd been the one injured.

"Time to go, I think," Silver said. Leaning toward Vic he added, "Close your eyes."

Vic obeyed as Silver tapped his cane on the ground and cold light exploded inside the reflecting dish. It burned like a frozen star, too bright even through Vic's closed lids. He pressed his arm to his face.

Then Silver's arm was around Vic's waist.

The world went very cold, like they'd stepped into a snowstorm. The air pressure changed. Vic felt snowflakes brush the back of his neck as the world fell away.

16

ADAM

The band was, to no surprise, truly awful. They didn't know how to use a microphone, or the mics were crap, because Adam could not make out a word of whatever they were screaming to the beat of the drums and the bass.

Man, I'm getting old, he thought. *I've got to stop hanging out with Bobby.*

Still, Adam sort of wished he'd brought his brother. Not that he expected Jodi to listen to either of them, but his misery would have liked the company, someone to share his complaints about the noise. The odor of ditch weed, cheap beer, and cigarettes was almost as bad.

The bar, Tornadoes, was housed in a double-wide trailer. They'd split it apart and filled the space in. It felt a bit like a barn. Maybe the music wouldn't suck so bad if it had somewhere to go.

Jodi had acted like scoring tickets to the show was some accomplishment, but Adam had simply walked up to the bar and been let right in, which told him everything he needed to know about the success of Chlamydia Clown Car.

The band was on-brand at least. They looked like diseased clowns. All clowns were scary, but these wore leather jackets and jeans. They were trying for tough but the Bozo hair, white makeup, and red noses really ruined the effect.

They launched into another song as Adam scanned the crowd for Jodi. He didn't see her.

"Backstage passes!" she'd squealed at the camera. Adam couldn't guess what constituted backstage in a dive like this.

The part they'd built in the middle had a higher ceiling, but the trailer parts were low, trapping the noise and odors. He'd start there.

Adam inched toward the restroom, following the smell of urine as much as the glow of the red light labeled *Men* in white lettering.

There was a third door there, probably a closet, but it was limned in enough light that he chanced it. Adam slipped inside quick, hoping no one saw. It was a little hall, strangely soundproofed. Adam was relieved to hear the terrible music muffled.

His guess had been right. This led to a walled-off part of what had been the trailer's living room and now doubled as a backstage and a cleaning closet.

The little room had a TV, a shelf full of bleach and other chemicals, and a mop bucket. In the middle sat a beaten leather couch and a few of those cheap folding TV tables. Graffiti tags and stickers marked everything, hiding most of the old-lady wallpaper leftover from when this had been someone's home.

The smell of weed overpowered everything else. Its smoke hung in the air like fog.

Adam shut down his nose and willed his defenses up higher, already bracing in case a contact high weakened his barriers and brought the Other Side too close. He did not have time to freak out or deal with something crossing over.

Jodi sprawled on the couch, her eyes glassy.

"Hey, cuz," she drawled. "You here to give me my birthright?"

"What are you talking about?" he asked.

"Sue's cards. They weren't in the trailer. She gave them to you, didn't she?"

Adam's first instinct was to say yes, to throw it in Jodi's face, but instead he said, "I don't know where they are."

"Liar," Jodi spat before leaning back onto the couch. She made a bitter sound that was something like a laugh and a shriek. "Mom's dead you know."

"I know. I'm sorry, Jodi."

"Liar," she repeated without any real venom.

"What happened?" Adam asked. "What was that thing you made with the bones?"

"She mixed it wrong. That's what they'll say, but it's stupid. It wasn't her. It was him. He wanted her dead."

She broke off into a fit of sobs.

"Who is he, Jodi?"

Something prickly crept up the back of Adam's neck.

"Don't know," she said, shaking her head. The motion was a little too much and she almost tipped over, but caught herself on the cushions. The leather squeaked.

"You summoned him," Adam said. "That's what the bones were for, right?"

"I thought I knew," she said.

Adam felt something gather, a bit of power.

Jodi fixed her eyes on Adam's and said, "Sue wasn't the first. Mom won't be the last. He wants something . . . us. Binders. He won't stop."

"We should get you out of here," Adam said. The music outside the little room thundered, hammering at his calm. "Get you cleaned up."

"No," Jodi protested, snapping out of her trance. She sounded angry now. "I'm having fun. Go back to Denver, Adam. Wait your turn. Go wherever you pansies go to die."

Adam took a deep breath and swallowed down her last remark.

"So what, you'll just wait for him?" he asked. "Party until he comes to kill you?"

"Might as well," Jodi said. "Can't get away. The trees will tell him where I am."

She lifted a finger to her lips and winked.

"It's the druid," he said. "You're talking about the druid."

"Yeah," Jodi rasped. She leaned forward. "Guess so."

"Why did you summon him?" Adam asked.

"I wanted my birthright," she said. "He promised he'd bring it to me."

She kept saying that, birthright, like it had real weight, but it didn't mean anything to Adam. Magic was in the blood, but it wasn't predictable.

"How did you even know where to get the bones?" Adam asked, trying to sort through what she was saying.

"Dreamt it. Saw it. Clear as day." Jodi fixed her eyes on him. "I dream all the time, Adam. All the time. Sometimes they're terrible, and sometimes they come true."

Adam swallowed. He understood. He really did.

"Don't call up what you can't put down," Jodi said quietly, her voice distant again.

Adam knew the lesson. He had no power, so he summoned nothing.

There were spirits, demons, and worse out there in the dark. They came to magic like moths hungry for light, drawn to the life of the caster.

She'd made a terrible mistake.

"Oh, Jodi," he said. "What have you done?"

"Wanted my birthright," she repeated. "I wanted what you have. It was mine. *Mine*, Adam, but she chose you. Stupid, queer, you."

"What the hell?" a voice broke in. "This guy bugging you?"

Adam turned to see one of the band, or a roadie—he wouldn't be able to tell the difference—looming in the doorway.

"I'm her cousin," Adam said. "I'm worried about her."

"He can get the eff out," Jodi slurred.

"You heard her, pasty," the guy said.

"Dude, you're wearing clown makeup," Adam said.

"Yeah, and I'll fuck you up."

The guy was massive, with arms as thick as Adam's leg.

"Valid," Adam said. "I'm not here to fight."

He had some information. Jodi wasn't worth it, but the druid would come for her, just like he had probably come for Sue and Noreen.

Adam didn't understand why though.

"Get him out of here, Billy," Jodi said. "He's killing my high."

"Jodi, it's not safe," Adam said. "I can protect you."

"How?" She laughed. "You couldn't even protect . . ."

She stiffened, trailing off.

At first Adam thought it was just the high talking, but then he felt it, a creeping cold at the edge of his senses, like the swamp in winter, chilled and slimy.

The music stopped suddenly, the last whine of a guitar trailing away.

Billy turned toward the thin wall dividing the room from the stage.

"What the hell?" he asked.

"Daddy's home," Jodi sang, low and sad.

Adam's ears had just stopped throbbing from the music when someone on the other side of the wall screamed, piercing the silence.

"Whatever you're on," he said, "it would be a really good time to sober up."

The wall between them and the stage buckled, vibrating like

a hundred tiny hands were trying to tear it down. Something poked through the plaster. A thorn. Then another. They dotted the surface, breaking through, needle by needle.

The magic felt wrong, frigid and thick like old blood and mud. Adam fought a shiver even as he shrank back from the worming, wriggling plants.

Billy looked torn between running and pissing himself.

Wide-eyed and slack-jawed, Jodi stared at the scene.

"What did you do, Jodi?" Adam asked, clenching his fists.

"I wanted my birthright," she said, voice shrill. "It was mine. Not yours!"

She had magic, but it slid around Adam, unfocused and wild. He didn't know if it was a lack of training, the state of Jodi's mind, or a combination of the two.

"Who is he, dammit?" Adam demanded.

"Your father. I called your father!"

It couldn't be. He was dead. Those were his bones. Then again, Adam had no proof that the druid was truly alive.

In Denver, Adam had promised the Guardians of the West that he'd take the druid off the board. It had been a foolish bargain. Adam didn't have the power.

The wall came down, ripped apart by the thorny, curling vines.

Adam's warlock wound ached, a rhythm that sped up until it matched his heartbeat.

The smell of the other warlock's magic, battery acid and rotten blackberries, wafted from everywhere.

The vines had ensnared most of the band. They bled from thorn pricks and scratches but fought on. Most of the patrons had fled. The bartender wielded a rusty machete and hacked at any bit of green that crept too close.

The branches rippled everywhere, growing impossibly, filling the space as if they'd had decades to consume it.

Adam recognized the canes and branches from his childhood, from the little thicket at the corner of his mother's property. He'd crawl into them, ignoring the scratches he took. It had been a refuge, a place to hide from his father's rages, but sometimes he'd go there just to watch the lights, hear the sounds of the Other Side. The blackberries he'd eaten there were dusty and sweet.

Seeing them here, used like this, made something red and sharp flush through him like a fever.

The warlock's magic was similar to his own, the best evidence he had that the druid was his father, but it was also similar enough that Adam might be able to tap into it and break the spell.

One of the clowns let out a howl. The canes whipped around him, lashing and trying to bind him. The others tried to help, rushing to his aid, and found their legs tied as the curling canes snaked over them.

They wouldn't last long. The spell was too strong. The canes grew, an endless thicket. They were overwhelming the patrons who hadn't fled.

"Adam!" Jodi screamed as the canes raced across the floor and ceiling, darting for her like a mess of snakes toward their prey.

The spell was thick, like pea soup fog. But Adam could see into it. It wasn't a wall. He could get inside its working, and maybe, just maybe, he could disrupt it enough to save these people.

Adam crouched and took a handful of the canes in his palm. He let them pierce his skin. He couldn't get inside the spell, the greasy magic, without letting a little of it inside him too.

His perspective shifted. His Sight showed him enough of the Other Side for him to see the spell. It curled all around him. At its center was a ghostly figure, the spider in its web. The druid.

Another warlock? the druid mused. *Interesting.*

He was tall, looming in a muddy, hooded sweatshirt and filthy jeans. Adam couldn't see his face. Leather belts were strapped across his body. Bones and feathers, bits of dead things, dangled from them. A rusty sickle was tucked into the belt at his waist. In his hand he held a skull. By the round hole in its side, Adam could guess whose it was.

Look at you, the warlock taunted. *Freshly blooded. Like a baby.*

"Not a baby," Adam said, squeezing his fist, weaving more of himself into the spell. "I'm all grown-up."

Give me the girl.

"No."

Adam's blood made a channel for the magic. The warlock wound beat like a drum, its rhythm synching to the spell's.

It was a constant pain, a scar on his heart and soul. It bled, forever.

And in blood, there was power.

Adam yanked at the spell empowering the canes.

It was dark, yes, he'd expected that. But it was cold too. Magic was life, and this, this absence was something else, a kind of void he'd felt before.

Do you see now? the voice asked. *What we are?*

The panicked shouts faded as the canes bound and gagged, choked off the life of the bar's patrons. The bartender went down, the thorny canes wrapped about his face. Adam hoped he kept his eyes.

"Oh, I see what you're doing," Adam said as his magic found the spell's pulse.

It was a twisted sort of death magic, pushing all of the canes' life, all of their potential, through them at once. It forced their growth and gave the druid control, but they'd die in moments.

"And I see how to stop it."

Adam wove a little more of himself into the spell. Cold as it was, it was brittle, like ice, vulnerable to any kind of light, any kind of fire or heat, any kind of life.

He poured just a spark into it, much less than when he'd done the same trick to save Vic's life.

It lit like a flame along the spell's tendrils. So delicate, they burned like a spiderweb set to a match. Adam did not have the warlock's power, but he didn't need it to disrupt the spell and break its pattern.

The druid did not wail. He did not curse as his attack dissolved into ash.

Interesting approach, he noted. *But I will have her. They are my harvest, and I will reap them all.*

The druid faded. He'd never really been here. This had been a projection. He vanished, leaving the broken bar and the dying canes behind.

Adam collapsed, chest heaving. When he'd bound himself to Vic, he'd nearly killed them both. He'd been ignorant and had poured too much into the effort. Then again, Vic had been shot. His blood had been pumping out. This wasn't on that scale, and Adam remained conscious. He'd count it as a win, even if the wound in his chest ached like he'd torn it open.

The druid had simply pushed the plants to grow unnaturally, to listen to his will. It was against their nature. Giving them a little spark of life had been enough to break his control. Still, to use them this way . . . Adam did not know any druids, but everything he understood about them was that they were supposed to serve life, not death.

"I guess that's why he's a dark druid," Adam muttered. He pulled himself to his feet. His palm was bloody, but it was nothing serious.

Around him, the remaining patrons and band members lay sprawled or sat heaving amidst the withering blackberry canes. Some groaned. Some coughed. Others weren't moving, and that was not good.

"Adam?" Jodi asked. She was still on the couch, looking terrified, her makeup a mess from the tears.

"I chased him off," Adam said. "But he'll be back. We have to figure out how to stop him."

"How?" she asked, waving an unsteady hand at the chaos and damage around them. "How do you stop something like this?"

Adam didn't really know. He knew the druid was connected to him, but the way he'd spoken wasn't with familiarity. It couldn't be Adam's dad. Dead or alive, Robert Senior would have recognized him. There would have been a reaction.

"Didn't think so," Jodi said when he didn't answer. She bowed her head, her earlier defiance cowed. She looked very young and fragile.

Adam didn't blame her. The stink of terror mixed with the magic's stench and the greasy feel of the spell. Tornadoes was closed. It should probably be burned to the ground.

"How did you find those bones?" Adam demanded without any gentleness. "You said you dreamed where they were buried?"

He was done playing, and from the look of the aftermath, neither Billy nor anyone else was in any condition to fight him. The bartender was wiping his face, but he could see.

Adam let out a breath of relief.

"Yeah. I dug them up at your mom's."

"You put some of your blood into the spell, didn't you?"

Jodi nodded.

"He tricked you," Adam said. "You gave him an in. That's how he got past Sue's wards."

Jodi blinked.

"Then you brought bones to the trailer," Adam continued. "Even if Sue hadn't been dead you'd never have been able to keep him out."

"I didn't kill grandma," she said.

"No, you didn't," Adam said. "But you handed him the gun."

It meant Jodi had magic, some level of sensitivity. She might even have Sue's Sight.

She certainly had more power than Adam had thought, maybe even more than him, but she was untrained.

Why hadn't Sue taken Jodi under her wing? She was family. She had the power; leaving her out there, untrained, was dangerous for everyone, especially for Jodi.

Another mystery for Adam's list.

There were other, more important questions.

The police would identify the remains. Early wasn't stupid, and he'd already mentioned Robert Senior. Part of Adam was still wrapping his head around the final truth. His father was truly dead.

The rest of him was trying to think. He didn't know the statute of limitations on murder, but he doubted it was seventeen years. It probably never went away.

Adam didn't know enough about the law or forensics—any of it. He needed a lawyer, probably. He needed . . .

"I wish Vic were here," he said aloud, never meaning anything more in his life.

"Then it's your lucky night," a voice said from behind him.

Adam spun to see Vic, Argent, and Silver standing at the entrance to the ruined dive bar.

The elves were arguing as Adam swallowed his heart.

"You attacked us," Argent said. "It was you!"

"I was hoping you'd investigate," Silver replied.

"You could have just asked," she said.

"I really couldn't," Silver said, his tone apologetic. "Father insisted I go alone."

"You owe me a car," Argent said. "I liked *that* car!"

The ache in Adam's chest eased.

"Want to try for something else, the lottery maybe?" Vic asked.

"Nope," Adam said. "Right now, just you. You're here? You're really here?"

"Yeah," Vic said, face pinched with worry as he stepped forward.

Adam practically leaped to close the distance between them. He crushed Vic in his arms, but his strength fled almost instantly and Vic was the one holding Adam upright.

"Easy," Vic said into Adam's hair. "You're wobbly."

"Big magic," Adam gasped, nodding to the destroyed bar.

"I'm getting that."

"We have much to talk about, and apparently, more than one problem to solve," Argent said, eyeing the chaos. "It would be best if we were not seen. There are sirens coming."

Adam couldn't hear them, but he trusted Argent's hearing over his own. He was surprised the sheriff wasn't already there. Hell, Adam was surprised Early hadn't found the same lead he had.

"Are there ambulances?" he asked Argent.

"Yes," Silver answered.

Adam exhaled.

"We can go to Mom's," he said.

17

ADAM

"I'm sorry I missed the funeral," Vic said. He reached like he might put his hand on Adam's knee, then withdrew it.

"You're here now," Adam said, being careful to drive just under the speed limit. Tonight was not the night for another encounter with the law. "That's what matters. Thank you."

Vic decided what to do with his hand, and it wasn't what Adam had wanted as he folded his arms atop the seatbelt.

"You know we've got to talk, right?" Vic asked.

"Yeah," Adam said.

"But later," Vic said, "when we're alone."

Adam gave a little nod and flicked his eyes to the rearview mirror. The back seat held three cramped passengers, none of them looking very happy.

He wasn't certain why the elves had insisted on riding this way, rather than shifting planes or driving one of Argent's many cars. It had to be one more of the many stories they all needed to tell one another.

Jodi had passed out. She slumped against Silver, and the prince did not look pleased with the contact.

Adam's and Silver's eyes met in the mirror. The elf smiled, and it looked forced, strained. Adam had never been able to read Silver's mood well, but when his eyes went distant like that, beautiful but extra cold, it was usually a sign that there was something heavy on his mind.

They were parked and inside the gate a while later.

Bobby and his mother came out to meet them.

"What's she on?" Bobby asked, looking at Jodi as Silver carried her from the car.

"I don't know," Adam said.

Bobby sighed.

"We should take her to a hospital, a detox maybe."

"She won't be safe," Adam said. "The druid came for her. I fought him off, but it was close. He's a lot stronger than me. I think I surprised him."

"Did you see him?" Tilla asked.

Adam could hear the other question, the one she wasn't asking. Maybe Robert Senior was alive, maybe they hadn't killed him all those years ago.

"No," Adam said. "Not exactly."

Tilla pursed her lips.

She turned, finding a smile for Vic as he climbed out of the car, but ignored the elves completely. She'd seen Argent once but had never met Silver. Adam thought she maybe had an out-of-sight, out-of-mind policy when it came to the supernatural beings. He had to figure out later if his mom was being rude.

"It was Jodi who took the bones," Adam explained. "She said something about her birthright. I don't really know what that means, but the druid tricked her, showed her how to lure him to her."

"Why would he need that?" Bobby asked.

"I don't know," Adam said. "Maybe some of Sue's wards were still up, keeping him out."

"What bones?" Vic asked, picking up on the one thing Adam least wanted to talk about.

He hadn't told Vic the full story, what he'd learned in Denver, that his brother and mother had killed his father to save him. Vic was a cop, and he was a good man. Adam would like to say that he didn't know how Vic would react, that he didn't want to put him in a situation that would test him, but the truth was that Adam knew exactly how Vic would handle it. He'd obey the law. He'd arrest Bobby and Tilla for murder. Since they were here and not in Denver, Vic would just turn them over to the sheriff.

And now it all had to come out.

"Let's go inside," Adam said. "I've put some wards up, but I don't think they'd keep him out if he came for us."

"They're not bad," Silver said, in that way he did when he wanted to be nice. What he really meant was that they were crap. "But they could use reinforcement. Get me some salt."

Tilla moved first, heading inside to get Silver what he needed. She was always so practical, so matter-of-fact, but Adam read the stiffness in her gait. She'd loved their dad, had a blind spot a mile wide about him. She probably would never have done anything on her own. Bobby had been the one to crunch Dad's skull with a hammer, and he'd done it to protect Adam, who didn't even remember it.

Bobby put Jodi on the couch.

"She smells awful," he said after a quick examination. "But I think she's just drunk, maybe high on weed. Her pulse is fine. She's going to have a hell of a hangover."

"Good," Tilla said, handing a cardboard can to Silver through the door. "Serves her right."

Adam couldn't argue, but he still felt a pang of sympathy for his cousin.

"She's terrified," he said. "She knew he was coming for her, said he killed Noreen."

"How did you fight him off?" Argent asked.

"His magic is strange, it's death-based." At Vic's raised eyebrow, Adam added, "Not Death, Sara Death, more like rooted in death and dying."

"That is a corruption," Argent said. "Druids are sworn to life, to nature, usually to maintaining it at any cost."

"Not this guy," Adam said.

He could still taste the spell's greasy flavor. He'd broken it, burned it, and it had left a char-like feeling in the back of his throat, but all of it tasted like blackberries. Adam would probably never be able to eat them again.

"He's the druid who made the bone charms," Adam said. "I'm certain of that much. But I don't know if he's our dad. Jodi used his bones for the summoning, so yes?"

"Not necessarily," Argent said. "Silver knows more of this sort of magic."

"His magic is a lot like mine," Adam said.

"That is an indicator," Argent said. "But not evidence."

"Either way," Adam said, "I have to stop him."

"*We* have to stop him," Bobby stressed. "He's hurting people."

Adam remembered the bar, the roadies and patrons who'd been attacked. He hoped no one had been killed.

He should have stopped to check, to do more. If they didn't get help in time—

"Adam," Vic said.

Just hearing his name stopped the spiral down into despair and worry.

Adam looked up, met Vic's gaze.

"Tell us what's going on," Vic said, calm and commanding, using his cop voice.

Adam took a long breath and started at the trailer, at the explosion. He explained about Noreen and her outburst at the

funeral and the charm nailed to the trailer door. He explained
about the bones, and the second charm, the one they'd found on
Mom's door, gesturing toward it.

"I don't understand," Vic said. "What do you mean Jodi dug
up your father's bones? I thought your dad ran out."

Adam bowed his head, not knowing what to say.

"It was me," Bobby said. "He was hurting Adam, and—I
thought he was going to kill him. There was a hammer on the
window sill."

Bobby stared that way now, like he was reliving that moment,
that day, all over again.

"I hit him," Bobby said. "Hard. He went down. I buried his
body out back."

"We," Tilla said, pausing where she'd started to make coffee.
"*We* buried his body out back."

"You knew about this?" Vic asked.

Adam nodded. "Since Bobby woke up in the hospital."

Adam felt Vic jerk away from him, the thread between them
tugged to the point of atomic thinness.

Vic's jaw clenched. Adam watched a number of feelings pass
over his face—anger, hurt—but he felt none of them. Vic had
shut him out, and Adam couldn't blame him.

Vic turned and walked out the trailer door.

Adam hesitated, staring. He'd known. He'd known how it would
go when Vic found out, and he'd kept the secret, not wanting to see
Bobby go to jail, even though he'd known it could cost him Vic.

Silver and Argent stared at the carpet like it contained the
secrets of the universe. They were royalty and they were here, in
his mother's trailer. Adam wondered if the poverty shocked them
or amused them with its novelty.

"Go after him, numbnuts," Bobby said, smacking Adam in
the back of the head. "Go talk to him."

"Oww," Adam said as he zipped up his jacket and followed Vic out into the night.

Mom had tried over the years to put in paths and some sense of order. She'd laid old roofing shingles in the mud, making a way up the slight hill. As a kid Adam had thought it steep. As a man, it was barely a rise in the landscape.

It was after midnight. The air was damp and cold, like every Oklahoma autumn Adam could remember, but he could breathe easily here. Denver's dryness made it harder.

Vic had walked to the top, to where the scrub oak thinned. Their dad had talked about building a proper house there. It had been another of his unfulfilled promises, something he'd dream about but never had the money to do, never worked hard enough to make happen. He'd talk and talk about how big it would be, how the boys would each have their own room. He'd dream out loud about a pool for the boys and flower gardens for Tilla. Even then, before his dad disappeared, Adam had learned not to trust Robert's promises.

"I don't get you at all," Vic said before Adam had even reached him. "You don't like your brother, but you protected him. He killed someone, Adam, even if it was to protect you, he killed your dad."

"I know, Vic," Adam said. His eyes were shining again, and this time he might even cry because he could no longer feel the thread between them. Vic was right there and Adam couldn't *feel* him.

"And you know I'm a cop," Vic said. "I've got to turn this in, got to turn *him* in."

"I know that too," Adam said. "And even if you didn't have to, you would. Because you're a good guy. A good man. You do the right thing."

Vic faced him.

"So why don't you?" Vic asked, stepping closer.

Adam could feel the rage bubbling off Vic but he didn't flinch or step back. Vic would never hit him.

"The whole way here, all the crap we saw, I was worried about you. But you won't tell me anything. You didn't tell me this. Why?"

"I don't know," Adam said.

"That's a shitty answer," Vic said, fists clenched at his sides. "Figure it out, Binder."

"I'd just gotten Bobby back in my life. I didn't want him to go away again, and I knew what you'd have to do, that I might lose you over it."

"So you did it anyway," Vic said.

Adam sucked on his bottom lip and nodded.

Then Adam could feel him again, could feel Vic's anger turn to hurt.

"I don't have anyone else in this," Vic said. "I had you. Just you."

Adam didn't know what to do. He wanted to take Vic's hand. He wanted to explain. He didn't know how to explain, but that word, *had*, past tense, stilled everything inside him.

"I care about you," Vic said, very quietly.

It was what Adam had wanted to hear, wanted to say. But hearing it made him tremble because he might never hear it again. This might be the end of the road.

Adam mustered all of the confidence he had, and it wasn't enough. But he had to, because if this was it, the end, he wanted to say it.

"Me too," Adam whispered. "I don't want to lose this. Us."

"So why can't you trust me?" Vic whispered. "I know we're not the same. Our families, how we grew up—"

"I'm scared," Adam said, blurting it out while he could, before he ran away from it again. "I'm so scared that any moment you're going to run away from this, from me."

"So you're running away first?" Vic asked.

"No. I mean, I don't think so?"

Vic stepped closer, so close he could have kissed Adam.

"So when were you going to tell me that we're married?" he asked, with another flash of frustration.

"What?"

"The connection between us. Argent says that means we're married."

"That's . . ." Adam paused. He wished Argent hadn't said anything. He hadn't known how to explain what the thread, their connection, meant.

He'd been waiting. He shrank a little but didn't step away from Vic. He'd been running from it, the intensity of it, since they'd met, and if he ran now, he'd never look back.

"It's for them, the immortals," Adam explained. "I didn't do it for that. I did it to save your life. I didn't know."

"You still should have told me when you found out," Vic said, jaw clenched tight. "What else aren't you telling me?"

Adam chewed his lip, casting about for what else he might know but hadn't said.

"Nothing, at least I don't think so."

"You have to think about it?" Vic demanded; the anger was back.

"No, Vic," Adam said, pulling at his hair. "I'm a little freaked out. I don't think so."

"No more murders or marriages?" Vic asked.

He was pissed and he was hurt. The potent mix slammed into Adam, not through their connection, but through his weary, weakened defenses. Adam's gut flipped. He thought he might puke.

"Let's go," Vic said, turning to walk away and not waiting for Adam. "We have to tell you what happened on the way here."

Adam watched Vic walk away, feeling like the ground between

them had opened and left a terrible chasm, a Grand Canyon–sized gulf between them. What point was any of it, their feelings, their connection, if Vic could just walk away?

Feeling like he could melt into the ground, Adam followed Vic back to his mom's trailer.

Everyone was waiting. Jodi was still asleep. Adam's gut still boiled. He didn't know where they were, what would happen, and Vic wasn't looking at him.

Bobby stood by the kitchen counter, a cup of coffee beside him.

Tilla had fired up the stove and was frying potatoes.

"Mom?" Adam asked.

"Vin—Vicente hasn't eaten since he left Denver," she said. "We could all use some food."

Adam nodded. She was taking Argent and Silver's presence in stride, like having elves in her living room was a regular occurrence. The last time Argent had come to their door she'd been more spiritous, less present in the mortal world. Now they seemed solid, almost human. Adam could sense their magic, but it wasn't the loud crash of wind and ice he usually got from them.

He wondered if they were masking it or if something had changed in his own perception.

They sat together in the old metal folding chairs his mom had used back when the ladies from her church would come by.

"We are on the verge of war," Silver announced. "We must return to Alfheimr, and Vicente must come with us."

"Wait, what?" Adam asked, looking between the elves and Vic.

"The elves of the Sea upon the Land attacked Silver," Argent said. "We must bring the news to the Council of Races, and we need him as a witness."

"Cool," Vic said calmly.

"He doesn't have any magic," Adam protested. "He won't be safe there."

Silver lifted a hand. "I will protect him, but he is the only impartial witness."

"They'll try to hurt him," Adam said. "To kill him, won't they?"

"Yes," Argent and Silver said together.

"Their wisest move would be to eliminate him, stop his testimony," Silver explained.

Vic didn't look afraid. Adam wished he was. He didn't know the powers he was dealing with, the danger—and dammit, he'd been right, so right.

Adam had left Vic ignorant.

The anger still wafted from Vic like the smoke from burning plastic, thick and acrid. And it was fair that he felt that way. Adam had screwed up. Knowledge was power, especially in magic, and Adam had put Vic in the line of fire without any defenses.

"So what are my chances here?" Vic asked.

He leaned against the wall, looking like nothing could hurt him when Adam knew that was far from the truth.

"We have to talk to Death," Adam said. "She has to protect him."

"We do not know how to summon her," Argent said, looking to Vic.

"No idea," he said with a shrug.

Adam closed his eyes, pushed his will out into the Other Side.

Are you there? he asked silently. *Are you listening? Sara. Please.*

He hoped calling her by the name he'd known her by would help, that she might take pity on him.

Nothing, just the muted presence of the elves and the lingering touch of the stain behind the trailer.

Adam opened his eyes.

"What about Vran?" he asked as his mom brought Vic a plate. Of course she'd dug up something to feed him.

Vic moved at last. He shifted to the dining room table, sat, and with a gentle thank-you to Tilla, began to eat.

Adam's own stomach grumbled but he would wait. This conversation was too important.

"One of the Sea court," Silver said. "The truant Page of Cups I suspect. He wasn't there when they made their move."

Something flashed between Silver and Argent, a flick of power. Adam felt it whenever the twins disagreed about something. He could sympathize with how Vic felt with so much happening beyond his understanding. Adam's stomach sank a little further.

"What aren't you telling me?" Adam asked. "Cards on the table, please."

"They said he'd gone to see his opposite," Vic said with a nod to the elves, potatoes speared on his fork. "They meant Adam, didn't they?"

Silver shot Vic a cold look. The prince gave good side-eye.

"Witness, remember?" Vic said before putting the food in his mouth with a bit of a stern glance at Adam as if to say *See? That's how you disclose information.*

"The Page of Cups is named Vran," Silver said. "He's quite young and known for mischief."

"But how am I his opposite?" Adam asked, not letting Silver twist the topic away from the real question. "I'm not the Page of Swords."

"Not yet," Argent said.

"We've been waiting to ask," Silver said.

Adam pressed his back against his own chair, so hard that the metal almost hurt.

"What?" he stammered, mind racing. "But I'm not an elf. I'm not an immortal."

"The title does not require either of those things," Silver said.

"Technically," Argent added. "The law is vague, never written with the possibility in mind."

"But your father makes the laws," Adam said.

"We have input," Silver said. "We want to bring you into the court, to prove that humans can be more than servants. They can be allies, friends even."

"Whose idea was this?" Adam asked.

"Mine," Silver said. "The truth is known now. Mercy was first defeated, and defeated again, by humans and elves working in cooperation. We can leverage that into true change."

"I've met your father," Adam said. "I don't see him going for it."

"Perhaps not," Silver agreed. "But I have to try, and it won't happen if we're engaged in a war with the Deep."

Adam really didn't like the idea of Vic being exposed to the King of Swords without him there as backup. Not that Adam had the power to protect Vic. The most he could do was guarantee that Vic didn't die alone if the king decided to incinerate him.

"I don't want to be your vassal," Adam said, more calmly than he thought he could have.

His worst fear, since he'd discovered the Other Side, was becoming enslaved by a power, even a power he sort of trusted.

Adam also worried that Silver had other intentions, that things weren't so settled between them. Silver had posed as Perak, the elf Adam had fallen in love with. He'd done it at his father's command, and broken it off just as quickly when the King of Swords had ordered it.

Before, in Alfheimr, Silver had been hesitant to disobey his father. Something had changed, and Adam didn't like that he didn't know what.

"That's not what we're proposing," Silver said, lifting a hand. "We know you'd never accept that, Adam. As Page you'd have a title, rights."

"And you'd have the court's protection," Argent added. "Powers know your name now. We don't think you can stay hidden, stay safe if we don't stand for you."

Adam looked to his mother and brother. They were exchanging a glance, reacting to the proposal. Adam didn't know how to explain it to them. He didn't even know what it meant or the risks involved.

But they were part of it too. With power, with Silver and Argent's protection, Adam could shield them from any fallout, anything that might come for them.

"When do I have to answer?" he asked.

"We'd like to know soon," Argent said.

"And this Vran, how did he know about me?" Adam asked. "Know that you intended to offer me the title?"

"That remains to be seen," Silver said. "We suspect they have spies among us. We certainly have our own agents in the other courts."

"That might no longer be true," Argent said, eyes narrowing. "We weren't forewarned about their clumsy coup attempt."

Adam turned to Vic.

"So you're going with them?" he asked.

He thought he'd wanted Vic to look him in the eye since they'd gotten back to the trailer, but now he wasn't so certain.

"Yeah," Vic said. "Maybe I'll learn something."

Adam wanted to step forward, wrap Vic in his arms, but the distance felt insurmountable.

"Be careful, please," Adam said.

"I promise," Vic said. He didn't smile, and it was like the sun hadn't risen. Vic always smiled. "We'll talk when I get back."

18

VIC

Things were far from all right. Bobby had killed his father. Vic knew it was to save Adam, but it wasn't like Vic could help them cover it up.

Not like how I helped with Annie, he thought.

And Vic *had* helped. He hadn't said anything about Dr. Binder's wife and her disappearance. But it was different, wasn't it? Annie Binder was long gone before they'd killed her body. Mercy had killed people, and it wasn't going to stop.

Vic hated the thought of drawing his gun. He hated that it meant he might have to shoot someone, but if it came down to saving a life, he would. He was trained for it but wasn't certain how he'd ever live with the memory.

But Adam wasn't. He wasn't an officer of the law, and Vic had stood by, helped even, while Adam put arrows into Annie's body.

Was this really different? Vic shook his head. Of course it was.

Bobby had been a teenager. He hadn't been trained. He hadn't been law enforcement. Maybe a judge would have seen it how the Binders did, but they hadn't come forward. They'd buried the guy in the backyard like a dead pet and pretended it hadn't happened. And Adam had known about it for a while now.

All the guilt and worry about his brother didn't make it okay.

Vic thought of Jesse, about how Vic would react if he'd been in that situation. He couldn't answer that, and it bugged him. Normally he was good at the hard questions.

"Dammit, Adam," Vic muttered.

"What?" Argent asked.

"Nothing," Vic said. "Just talking to myself."

They reached the top of the little hill. The trailer at the bottom was almost completely hidden by the slope and the trees. Vic wondered why they'd set it there, not moved it to the top, into the light.

Now he knew it was because they'd had something to hide.

"Hold on tight," Argent said, drawing Vic back to the moment. She offered her hand. "The transition will be hard."

"I know what to expect," Vic said. "Adam's been there. He told me about it."

"Adam was there in spirit," Silver said, offering Vic his hand as he took Argent's free one. "Not body."

"Then I guess we'll see how tough Reapers are," Vic said, taking Silver's hand.

The elves ran cool to the touch, or maybe Vic was feverish with anger and worry.

Cold white light filled the space between them, so bright that Vic closed his eyes.

A stretching feeling began, like his body was being pulled upward, into the sky, while his feet remained planted on the earth. It continued. Vic spun inside himself, losing the sense of his extremities, except for the hold the two elves had on him.

The air grew colder, chilling until it burned. Vic couldn't feel his toes, his feet on the earth. He felt stretched, in two places at once. He frayed at the edges, dissolving. It should hurt, but didn't, like the warm feeling they said you got before you froze to death.

Then something encased him, like steel left outside in winter. A different kind of cold. It wasn't the ice of the elves' magic. This was something inside Vic, rising like armor to shield him. The Reaper had stirred.

The light faded, and they were somewhere else.

Vic looked down at his hands, at his clothes. He was unchanged. Whatever the power was, whatever the Reaper was, it remained inside him but unseen. He wasn't Adam. He didn't have magic.

Thinking of Adam, Vic put a hand to his chest and felt for the thread connecting them. It was there, unbroken. Yeah, he was still pissed, but their connection was intact. Vic had closed himself off, knew that he could do that now.

He'd been honest about how he felt, his anger and how much he cared.

Adam was there too, and hearing it had filled Vic with an excited warmth that had almost pushed away the broken-glass feeling of being lied to. Still, he didn't open himself back up. He needed some time in his own head, in his own heart. He needed to deal with whatever lay ahead.

He looked up, saw where they'd brought him, and muttered, "Definitely not in Kansas anymore . . ."

"Not even close," Argent said.

Alfheimr looked like paradise, like something from a movie, not quite real.

The shift to daylight was the least of it.

Cities of white stone floated through the pure air. They drifted lazily, slowly spinning over the bluest sea. The water glittered so bright it almost hurt Vic's eyes. It was warmer here, but occasional tendrils of colder air spoke of looming winter. A flock of green-tinted birds flew in a funnel formation. The cliffs beneath them were chalky gray, marble lined with sapphire crystals.

It looked like a dream, but Vic knew his own imagination couldn't put anything this real together.

He inhaled, tasting the ocean air.

"Will I be all right here?" Vic asked.

"Eat nothing," Argent said. "Drink nothing."

"These are the Shallows," Silver said, nodding to the beach and the nearby floating city.

"He means you'll be safe here for a while," Argent explained. At his pointed look she added, "A few days at least."

"What happens if I stay longer?" Vic asked.

"Years may pass below," Silver said. "Let's not let that happen."

At the center of the drifting towers was an amphitheater, like the kind they used for plays in ancient Greece.

"You guys are big on that design," Vic said, noting the columns and pediments in the distant buildings.

"We favor the classics," Argent said.

"Too much sometimes," Silver said, sounding sad. He turned to Vic. "This place is for the Council of Races. You are the first human to stand here, ever. You may be called to address them, all those who have a say in how we rule the realms."

"What are you saying?" Vic asked.

"He's saying don't screw it up," Argent said.

"No pressure," Vic muttered.

The elves changed as they walked. Their clothing shifted from Silver's pinstripe suit and Argent's casual streetwear to something more formal, long silk jackets with high colors and perfect, platinum embroidery. They wore their swords, long and thin, on their backs.

"Do me. Do me," Vic joked.

Argent seemed to deliberate.

"Allow me," Silver said.

Stepping to Vic, he took him by the jacket and brushed as if removing lint.

Vic's clothes unwove and rewove completely, almost like a screen loading an image.

His jeans, shirt, and jacket became a black suit, with dotted lines that drew skulls and bones in a slightly darker thread.

"Damn," Vic said.

"You approve?" Silver asked, his eyebrow lifted.

"Yeah," Vic said, taking a step back as much to get a better look as to put some distance between himself and Silver.

The black silk tie was clipped with a little silver skull pin.

It wasn't his usual style, but it fit his role here, the part he was playing. He could get used to the look.

"You'll need these," Argent said, handing over her sunglasses.

"I hate to dull the sights," Vic said, looking at them.

"We don't know how much of you would survive contact with an immortal who doesn't bother with a glamor," Silver said. "Please keep them on."

"You like me," Vic teased, edging sideways to bump shoulders with the prince.

"*Adam* likes you, and he is important to us," Silver growled. "Therefore you are important to us, to proving our case."

"You like me," Vic repeated, putting the glasses on.

"Just try not to die," Silver said, walking faster to avoid contact.

"Can I keep the suit when this is over?" Vic asked.

"You really do take all of this in stride, don't you?" Argent asked.

Vic shrugged. "Maybe it's a defense mechanism. Honestly, I'm just happy, blessed, to still be here. If Adam hadn't saved me, I'd be dead."

"You are truly unique, Vicente," Argent said, smiling. She didn't

say it in a way that seemed insulting, but rather like how she compli-
mented Adam's differentness, like he surprised her in the best way
possible. Gently, she added, "As my brother said, try not to die."

"I'll give it my best," Vic said.

He had no idea what he was doing, not here, not with the
elves, and certainly not when it came to being a Reaper.

So far this trip had only brought more questions and disappointment. Thinking of Adam gave him a sinking feeling. All of
Vic's worry had morphed into something else, something heavier.

As fantastic as this place was, he didn't want to be here. Still,
if he could stop a war and save lives, then he'd testify. He hadn't
been a cop long, but he'd already had to go before a judge and give
statements. He knew how to handle that sort of procedure, and
floating towers and immortal beings aside, this was just another
type of court.

The three of them marched on. The air here was so clean, so
oxygen rich. The hills around them were coated in green heather
tipped in pale purple blooms. Vic could breathe easier.

It was beautiful.

All he could smell was the ocean and the little bit of rot that
always accompanied a beach. He decided that was beautiful too,
that if it hadn't been there, Alfheimr would be too much like a
painting. That bit of decay told him it was real.

A flock of birds took flight and there were more of them than
Vic could have counted.

The city loomed, growing slowly larger.

"You guys walk a lot more than I expected," Vic said.

"What do you mean?" Silver asked. He looked a little annoyed,
but Vic suspected that was a front. The elven prince wasn't half as
surly as he pretended to be. Perhaps he was just worried.

"I mean you like to drive," Vic said, nodding to Argent. "But
when you get there you park far away."

"It's a type of courtesy," Silver said. "We can sense each other's approach. Arriving this way announces us, shows we mean no harm."

"And it means that someone crashing the party is being extra rude," Argent said, her eyebrows lifting.

Vic was learning to pay close attention to her expressions. She was good at hiding what she was thinking or feeling, but not that she was hiding something, like how a perp would avert their gaze when they were guilty. Elves were subtle, but Vic felt like he was starting to crack the code.

"But this is your home," Vic said, nodding to the city ahead. "Isn't it?"

"She's talking about another," Silver said. He tilted his head as if listening for something he couldn't quite hear.

Vic felt it, a faint prickle on the back of his neck.

"Who is it?" he asked.

"Death," Silver said.

Yes, something inside Vic said as soon as Silver spoke her name. She was here.

"We should hurry," Argent said.

Trees lined the marble-paved path to the amphitheater's entrance. They were tight columns of silvery blue, like junipers, but their berries were a perfect black.

The amphitheater lay ahead, floating amidst the towers. The whole city turned slightly, and Vic wished Tilla had fed him something less greasy.

"Problems, Vicente?" Argent asked.

"Just getting my sea legs," he said.

She smiled and led him on.

The theater was clean, the columns and white marble benches sparkling, except the layer of fine sand beneath their feet.

The sea elves had a presence, though their numbers were

nothing close to what they'd brought to their own meeting. Vic guessed they'd packed their own hall with everyone who served them. These were just the rulers.

The gnomes too, were here, as were some of the folk Vic recognized from the attempted coup.

Everyone else was an odd mix of too beautiful humans and more alien or even monstrous things. There were lizardmen, with broad, sweeping tails. A pair of bulbous-nosed, purple-skinned giants sat politely at the back. Vic wondered how they didn't tip the platform.

He walked between Argent and Silver, who paused to speak with a delegation of antlered moose people before politely greeting a trio of crow-headed women dressed like proper Victorian ladies. There were fox people, short and unbearably cute except for their canine teeth and sharp, catlike eyes.

The sights added to the dizziness. Vic didn't know where to look or who or what he was looking at.

"I need to sit down," Vic said to Argent.

"What's the matter, Vicente?" a familiar voice asked in a southern accent.

A grinning Black woman approached him. She had spectacles and big, natural hair. Vic wanted to smile back. Her cheer was infectious. She wore a purple dress adorned with sequins that might have been actual stars. It showed every inch of her generous figure. She clutched a tall glass of iced tea in her hand.

"It's all just a bit much," Vic said, waving at the floating city. "I'll be all right."

"Glad to hear it," she said. "After all, it's all about you today."

"You're not a skeleton?" he asked, gesturing to her dress.

"I like to mix it up," she said. Her grin widened as she nudged him.

"Your presence is unexpected, ma'am," Silver said with more deference than Vic had thought the elf capable of.

"Well, I figure if you intend for Vicente to plead your case, I should be on hand to vouch for his credentials," she said.

"Word travels fast," Vic said.

"Quite," Argent said, eyes narrowing.

"Shall we get to it then?" Death said, waving a hand toward the theater's stage.

Vic nodded and followed her. It wasn't that she didn't intimidate him. Hell, she terrified him more than anyone, Argent included. It was just that with Death there, it was like having his boss working a case with him. Who else had greater authority?

Still, Vic hadn't interacted with her much. He got the sense that as long as he worked for her, was one of her Reapers, she'd have his back, but what happened if he stopped being a Reaper? Who would protect him then?

"Hey," he asked. "Ma'am?"

"Yes, Vicente?"

"Can I get some training?" he asked. "I literally have no idea how any of this is supposed to work."

She hummed understanding.

"You are special," she said. "Usually Reapers don't even know they're Reapers, but I had to make you a bit different."

"To catch Mercy?" he guessed.

"Yes," she said. "When this business is done, we'll talk about what comes next."

"But there will be a next, right?" Vic asked. Because he had to. Because she could end him in a moment if she felt like it.

Something sparked in her eye, a little light that flashed and died.

She smiled, sipped her tea, and walked toward the stage.

Silver and Argent brought Vic to the front row. They stood. Everyone stood. Well, those beings with legs stood. Some winged creatures hovered. Other things floated in the air. Some rose on their coils, their iridescent scales brilliant in the sun.

Death took the stage.

"Well," she said. "Look at all of you."

There were murmurs, whispers, one or two gasps.

"You must wonder what I'm doing here," she said.

"Yes," a voice called. It was the Sea Queen. "Why have you revealed yourself after all of this time?"

"Moments of great change require a witness," Death said, meeting the queen's gaze. "And then you lot had to go and involve one of my Reapers in this mess."

The Sea Queen flinched.

Death still smiled, but there was an unmistakable sharpness when she continued, "I came because he works for me, and what a treat it is."

"It was not my intention to involve you," Argent said, sounding apologetic. "But he was with me when we were attacked."

They weren't using his name. They were trying to keep him anonymous. His mom, Jesse—Vic had no doubt that some of the things in attendance could be nasty, and his family had no idea that the spirit world even existed.

Adam wasn't safe either, even with his magic. Vic glanced to Argent and Silver. They were right. Adam needed protection.

"Your own brother attacked you," the Sea Queen said. "You had no business infiltrating our court."

"Your vassals chained us to a wall and left us there to drown when you carried out your insane plan," Argent said. "And let's not forget your foolish attempt to murder my brother."

"You broke our knight's arm," the Sea Queen said.

"She drew first," Argent said with a shrug. Vic could taste snow. "We'd be at war if I hadn't intervened."

"We *are* at war," the Sea Queen spat. "The mortals are killing the world."

"They don't even know we're here," Argent said.

"Which is why we should drown them *now*," the queen replied. "Strike with complete surprise and begin anew."

She said it so casually. Vic knew some people thought that way, felt that way, but he'd never expected to hear someone just suggest killing billions of people like they were wiping out gophers in their backyard.

"Your single-mindedness is impressive," Silver interjected. "But it's also wrong. Just like it was wrong of you to attack an emissary who came in peace."

The Sea Queen opened her mouth to speak but bristled suddenly. The assembly fell quiet.

Vic didn't sense what shushed them. Then a rush of force, a blast of cold like a sudden northern wind rippled over the amphitheater. It ripped along the aisles and over the crowd, displacing hats, ruffling clothes and feathers, sending the flying things into a dizzy spin.

"What is it?" Vic asked into the silence.

"Father," Argent said. She looked to Silver.

The prince's face had frozen. His eyes were even colder.

19

ADAM

"So was that a job offer?" Bobby asked.

They stood side by side at the sink. Bobby loaded the dish-washer while Adam scrubbed the cast iron skillet. Adam rinsed it, feeling the grit of the trailer's well water, and set it on the stove to dry and season it.

Adam scoffed.

"So we're not going to talk about what just happened with Vic?" Adam asked. "You know, about you confessing to a murder?"

"It had to come out sometime," Bobby said. "I should have told him when I told you. I didn't mean to mess things up between you."

"It was my choice," Adam said. He dipped a folded paper towel into the Crisco can and ran it over the heated skillet.

"Do you think you can fix it, with Vic I mean?"

"I don't know," Adam said, deciding that maybe he hadn't wanted to talk about it after all.

Adam flicked the stove off. He didn't know if Vic was still his boyfriend or whatever they'd been before the night's confessions and their fight, their first fight.

"So yeah, sort of a job offer," Adam said, answering Bobby's original question and changing the subject. "I don't really know what a page does."

The only one he'd met, Vran, was a chaos monkey whose court had tried to kill Silver and was probably trying to kill Vic at this very moment. Adam wished he was there, even though he knew he had to be here, that this business with the druid had to end.

"But you aren't as afraid of them as you were," Bobby said. "Before, I mean."

Adam knew Bobby meant before Denver. Before Annie.

"No, I'm not," Adam admitted. "Maybe I'm just numb, been through too much."

"Do you trust them?" Bobby asked.

That was the million-dollar question. Once, very recently, Adam would have said hell no. That was before he and Silver had made peace, and before Argent had tried to save Annie.

Now, he might actually be considering their offer. The protection alone might be worth it.

He had no idea how to stop the druid. Adam had taken him by surprise at Tornadoes. He wasn't going to get another chance at that.

"I don't know," Adam said. "I want to, but there's a price for those sorts of alliances. But I may need their help to stop the druid."

They exchanged a look.

"Could it be him?" Bobby whispered. "Could it really be him?"

"If it is, he's a spirit," Adam said. "Jodi dug up his bones. He had a skull—dad's skull."

"How can you be sure?"

"It had the hole in it," Adam said.

"Is it even possible?" Bobby asked. "That it's dad's ghost, come back for vengeance or something?"

"I don't know that either," Adam admitted. "Magic is weird, but there's always a catch, a rule. Nature demands balance. I can't imagine Death working with him back when she did if he's some kind of ghost. She doesn't like things that break the natural rules."

"Can we ask her?" Bobby asked. "Could Vic?"

"Maybe," Adam said, swallowing, ready to change the subject.

He looked to the couch, to where Jodi still hadn't moved.

"She still breathing?" Adam asked, nodding to her.

"Yeah," Bobby said. "Think she'll bolt?"

"I give it fifty-fifty." Maybe he should have asked to borrow Vic's handcuffs.

"It's late," Bobby said. "Mom's gone to bed. You should too. I'll keep watch on Suzy Stoner over there."

Adam opened his mouth to protest, but Bobby held up a hand.

"I've pulled plenty of all-nighters at the hospital," he said. "And you fought off—well, whoever he is. Go sleep."

Adam nodded agreement, surrendering to the exhaustion.

"Thank you," he said.

He didn't quite fit in the little bunk bed, but it was all they had. It was stiff, just a flat mattress on plywood. How had he ever found this comfortable?

Kids bounce, he thought, remembering a time or two when Dad had thrown him against the wall in anger.

Adam sighed. It was not good being back here, not without Vic, but especially not without Sue.

Maybe Jodi could tell him why she'd left him nothing, left the trailer to Noreen.

A heart attack.

Adam didn't have Sue's Sight, but he had some, and he had instincts. The druid had killed her, but surely she would have seen it coming.

Maybe she'd given Adam the tarot cards and left herself blind to the attack. Or maybe she'd known and given them to him for safekeeping.

Remembering how much Jodi wanted them, Adam crept out of bed.

It might be a little paranoid, but it wasn't stupid to show caution where addicts were concerned. He'd heard enough stories from Sue about how Noreen would steal anything she could, how she'd drop by for a visit and Sue would later find knickknacks missing.

Using the little screwdriver on his pocketknife, Adam took the heating vent out of the floor. He took the tarot deck from his backpack and tucked them a full arm's length into the duct before returning the vent and making sure it was screwed on tight.

With that settled, Adam climbed back into the top bunk.

He wanted to dream of Vic, or wanted no dreams at all, but instead everything was skulls and shadows. He was driving the Cutlass through trees made of bones. Black water rose on both sides of the road as wiry branches, blackberry canes, arched overhead to seal out the red sky. It looked like blood, like when you stared at the sun through your closed eyelids. Adam knew that if they succeeded, that if he couldn't see the sky, he'd die.

He woke with a start, nearly banging his head on the low ceiling as he sat up, but threw his hands up in time. The room was lit with gray, a typical autumn day in Oklahoma.

Panting, Adam climbed down, feeling more tired than when he'd gone to bed.

At least the ache in his chest wasn't worse. Sleep usually eased it but it wasn't much better this morning.

Adam rubbed his fist across it, a growing habit.

He stumbled into the little bathroom he and Bobby had shared as kids. It had been nice, having that privacy when his brother had left for college.

Water rumbled through the pipes, telling him someone was using the trailer's only shower.

He found his mother and brother sipping coffee in the kitchen. The couch was empty.

Bobby looked tired, but not nearly as dead as Adam would have after an all-nighter, and Bobby had ten years on him.

"She's been in there half an hour," Bobby said.

"She's got a lot of funk to scrub off," Adam said. "That place was really gross, even before the attack."

"She'll be out in a moment," Tilla said.

"How do you know?" Adam asked.

"I started the dishwasher," Tilla said with a little smile.

The brothers groaned.

The trailer's sad little hot water tank could only handle so much, and the dishwasher was closer to it. Once it kicked in, the shower water went from warm to freezing. It had been Tilla's favorite way to interrupt special teenage boy alone time.

A shriek sounded from down the hall.

"I wonder what rich people do for entertainment," Adam mused.

"Probably something to do with lawsuits or yachts," Bobby answered.

Jodi emerged a few moments later wearing an old pair of sweatpants and an Oklahoma University hoodie.

"Where are my clothes?" she demanded.

"Washing machine," Tilla said. "They stank so bad, I should have just burned them."

Jodi stiffened, but Bobby cleared his throat.

"Everyone settle down. No one wants a fight before breakfast."

"I kinda do," Adam said. Anger was easier than hurting, than thinking about Sue or his fight with Vic. "What in the literal hells did you do, Jodi?"

"I told you, I think," she said, pausing to blink. Her eyes were bloodshot, but her head seemed clear . . . well, clearer than she'd been the night before. "I summoned him. I used his bones to call him."

"Our dad?" Bobby asked, voice steady.

"And he came to you in a dream?" Adam demanded.

"Yeah," she said. "I recognized him. He said I needed his bones."

"What did he look like?" Adam asked.

"Just like how I remembered him. He said he was dead, but he could come to me, teach me, if I made the charm for him."

She said it so eagerly. Adam could believe she'd fallen for it. His own Sight and visions had overwhelmed him. If someone, some thing, had appeared in a dream with a recipe for relief, Adam would have taken any offer. He'd never been so grateful that he'd had Silver for a teacher. He'd gotten his heart broken, but Silver hadn't taken advantage of his naivete. Jodi had lost her grandmother and her mom.

"What's this birthright you keep talking about?" Adam asked.

"Sue told me. When I was a little girl, she said I had a birthright. I didn't think anything of it until Mom and I took that trip to Galveston last summer. There's a great witchcraft shop there. The psychic who read my cards said I had a birthright, that it was tied to magic." Jodi lifted a finger, pointed it at Adam, and on a dime turned surly again. "And I think you know what it is. I think it's those tarot cards. You took them."

"Sue gave them to me," Adam said. "And they're safe in Denver."

"Bullshit," Jodi spat.

Adam turned to pour a cup of coffee and gather his patience.

He couldn't argue that the cards had something of the Binder family in them. They'd been passed from witch to witch, magician to magician, then from Sue to Adam. They were all he had left of her, and he'd be damned before Jodi, or anyone else, got ahold of them.

Jodi's smile turned wicked, sly.

"I have more power than you thought, huh?" she asked.

"Yep," Adam said, taking a sip of his coffee. "And it's about to get you killed. Good for you."

"Jodi," Bobby tried. "He's going to come after you again, real soon. Do you want to face him alone?"

"You can't stop him," she said, her eyes showing some of the previous night's desperation. "He killed Mom. He probably killed Grandma. What can *you* idiots do?"

"I stopped him last night, remember?" Adam said.

Jodi scoffed.

But she wasn't wrong. Adam didn't have the power, not on his own, but the more he knew, the more of a chance he had.

"Fine," Adam said. "Take your clothes when they're dry and go. We'll settle this without you."

Jodi looked like she was considering it.

Tilla looked like she was about to say something meaner.

"I don't want to die," Jodi said.

"Then help us figure this out," Adam pleaded.

Jodi considered it. "He said he's going to kill us all."

"No," Adam said. "That wasn't it. He said *they are my harvest and I will reap them all.*"

Bobby and Jodi looked at him.

"Well that's downright creepy," Bobby said.

"I don't think it's Dad," Adam said. "He didn't recognize me."

"You were six when he died, Adam," Bobby said.

Adam carefully did not look at Jodi in case she was putting together why those bones had been buried behind the trailer.

"Still, I don't think it's him," he said.

"This man, this druid," Tilla said. "He has magic?"

"A lot of it," Adam said.

"Robert didn't," Tilla said.

"How do you know?"

It was the closest Adam had ever come to directly asking his mother if she had any Sight herself.

"Your father would have used it," she said, "to get money or something like that."

"Could it have activated when he died?" Bobby asked.

"No," Adam said. "I don't think so. Magic tends to cling to life. Someone like that, with that much magic, would have had to be pretty powerful when they were alive."

"Could he have stolen it?" Bobby asked.

"I don't think so," Adam said. "I mean, it's tied to the person. It can't be given away."

Bobby's eyes dropped to his coffee cup.

"Yeah," he said. "Yeah, it can."

Adam blinked.

"In the hospital, in Denver," Bobby said. "That's how I woke up."

Adam squeezed his mouth shut. They'd already given Jodi enough ammunition to use against them, but Adam understood. Bobby had told him that Annie had come to him, said goodbye. He saw it now, looking at his brother with his Sight. It was like a transplant, a bit of life and power fused to Bobby's own. Annie had put back what Mercy had stolen, and maybe, if not for that, she might have survived.

"If it can be given . . ." Bobby said.

"Then it can be stolen," Adam finished.

"But it's not Robert," Tilla said, her own sorrow rising, her last hope crushed.

"No," Adam said.

"It can skip generations," Jodi said. "Mom didn't have any either, or not very much."

"What about Tommy?" Adam asked. "Sue's other kid?"

"Other *kids*," Tilla stressed. "She had another son."

Adam blinked. "What?"

Tilla left her kitchen chair and fetched her Bible from the living room.

"I kept the family tree on your father's side," she said, laying it on the table and opening it. "See?"

She pointed to a branch written in her spidery handwriting as they crowded around her.

"James Jr. Jimmy."

"I've never heard of him," Adam said.

It hurt, really hurt. He was Sue's son, and she'd never mentioned him. She hadn't been big on photographs, but Adam couldn't remember any hint of a Jimmy. It felt like another illusion, like Liberty House, like someone was messing with his head.

"I'm not surprised Sue didn't talk about him," Tilla said, and for once she mentioned her nemesis without disapproval. "We went to high school together. All of us. He disappeared after I dropped out to have you, Bobby."

"What do you mean 'disappeared'?" Adam asked.

Tilla shook her head. "They say he ran away. I don't remember anything else. Early might. They were in the same class."

Adam was still reeling. He should have asked Sue more about her life. He'd been selfish, too preoccupied with his own things. His heart was like a rock, cold and heavy in his chest.

"We should talk to Tommy," Bobby suggested.

"I think Jimmy used to do auto repair," Tilla said. "You share that with him, Adam."

"That's not all you shared," Jodi said. She made a rude gesture with her fist and her tongue in her cheek.

Tilla's eyes narrowed.

"You can leave anytime, Jodi," she said coldly. "Go back to whatever hole Adam dug you out of."

Adam held up a hand, gesturing for peace. He wished he had decent cell service or Internet out here. It was hard to believe there were still places where you couldn't get it.

It was even harder to believe that Sue's son had been gay. That's what Jodi was crudely indicating.

Sue had never mentioned that either.

There was so much family history Adam didn't have, didn't know, and—shit. This was exactly how Vic must feel.

I'm sorry, Adam thought along their connection, knowing it wouldn't go through. *You were so right, and I'm sorry.*

Tilla had said that Jimmy disappeared. They were related, and if Jimmy were like Adam, then maybe that explained the similarity in their magic.

"Why didn't I know about this?" Adam asked. "About him?"

"It was before you were born," Tilla said. "We never knew what happened to him. He was Sue's baby, her youngest. It broke her heart."

That might explain why there'd been no pictures, no mementos. Still, Sue had hidden Jimmy from Adam completely. She'd hidden her broken heart, and it stung.

"Mom hated him," Jodi said with a shrug. "That's all I know."

"Jimmy's grandfather doted on him," Tilla said. "I remember Robert saying that. Sue didn't like it."

"Why?" Adam asked.

"It was inappropriate. No, not like that," Tilla said in response to Adam's expression. "Sue didn't want them spending time together, but she never really said why."

"Sue's Sight was really strong," Adam said. "If her instincts were telling her something was wrong, something was wrong."

"Then Jimmy disappeared. Sue was devastated. Tommy and Noreen had already moved out. That's when Sue left James Senior."

"I always thought he left her," Adam said.

"No," Tilla said. "She walked out. Got a divorce from that Jenkins woman. It happened, not as much as it does now, but it happened. She went from man to man after that."

The note of distaste in his mother's voice told Adam what Tilla thought of that. She'd only ever been with their father. Adam knew she was old-fashioned, and to be honest, he wasn't much different. He wasn't prone to spending time with guys he didn't really like, not that there had been many between Silver and Vic.

Still, he smiled. Sue had been a bit wild in her day, and Adam admired that she'd done her own thing, what she'd wanted, and hadn't tried to fit into what Guthrie thought a woman should be.

"I think she went a little crazy then," Tilla mused. "Losing Jimmy."

"What about great-grandpa?" Bobby asked, face pinching with thought. "I remember him. A little."

"He died. Your dad always wanted to buy the old place, but it went to James Senior and his kids. It might be yours now, Jodi."

"Uncle Tommy has the deed," Jodi said. "Won't sell it and wouldn't give it to Mom. Said he promised his grandpa he'd keep it in the family, but he's never done anything with it. Says he doesn't have the money."

The way she said it told Adam everything he needed to know about why Noreen and Jodi had been so quick to move into Sue's trailer. They thought they deserved it, that it was *owed* to them.

"I think we should talk to Tommy," Adam said. "See if he can tell us where to find Jimmy."

"What are you thinking?" Bobby asked.

"Nothing solid, but I'm starting to think that Jodi's right about some kind of legacy, and I'm starting to think it's not anything good."

20

VIC

Even with Argent's glasses, Vic couldn't look directly at the King of Swords.

About nine feet tall, the elf loomed over his children like a frozen tree. He had slender limbs and narrow shoulders. His hair gleamed like wet ice. His skin was the same tone, just a bit more animate, like slow churning water on the verge of freezing.

The sword he carried was comically oversized, with a broad blade forged of bone or ivory, some pale, blue-veined substance.

The king's presence felt like an ancient glacier, some place humans should never go and wouldn't long survive.

"There you are," Death said casually, making it clear that she did not fear this primal force any more than she feared Vic.

"Would you care to weigh in?" she asked, waving a hand to the packed amphitheater. "We've all been waiting."

The king glowered at her, at them. Not much of a talker, Silver and Argent's dad.

"Okay then," Death said. "I'll lay it out for you. On the one hand, the Sea upon the Land has a point. The humans are breeding like rats and overstretching their limits. They're extinguishing all other life."

"So do something," the Sea Queen snapped. "You're Death. Kill them. Reap them. Then the ocean can heal. The earth and winter can heal. Support our claim to the tower."

"It's not that simple," Death mused. Pausing, she took a long sip of her iced tea. "I am bound by rules."

Vic clenched his jaw tight. He could not decide which scared him more, the absolute seriousness of the Sea Elves, that they were considering genocide, or that Death herself had no stronger protest than that she simply wasn't supposed to agree to it.

"You interfered in Denver," the queen said, pointing to Vic. "You used him to reap the spirit there."

Did everyone know about that?

So much for anonymity.

Death gave him a little smile, and he wondered if she'd guessed his thoughts, if this was why she'd kept her Reapers a secret all these years.

"The spirit was an anomaly that had to be removed." Her voice went cold, all the life and vibrancy draining away.

Vic shivered as the Reaper in him stirred. It wasn't hungry, or anxious, just ready to do its duty.

"But there are a myriad of reasons life is not ruled by me," Death continued. "And there is the other hand. The Sea attempted to kill Silver, Knight of Swords, and blah, blah, blah. My Reaper was a witness. My presence here is not to intervene, but to protect what's mine."

She made a come-here gesture, waving for Vic to step to her. He swallowed hard and went to stand on her right.

Stay right there now, Death said in his mind. He heard her and knew the others could not. *Don't move.*

"The Sea is right," the King of Swords announced in a booming voice.

The crowd went silent. Only the breeze and the faint buzz of wings followed in the wake of that statement. Vic froze.

"The mortals are destroying life itself," the king continued.

Vic felt the air freeze. He knew, as a mortal, it should have iced him to the core, maybe shattered him, but standing in her shadow, Vic was protected, shielded.

"My son knows this," the king continued. "And he knows my will. We are to end them. It is the only way."

The king's rage echoed through Vic as the crowd gasped and murmured.

Silver had lied. He'd told the Sea Elves that his father disagreed with their plan.

They gloated now, their grins spiny and cruel, as though they'd won a game, as though they weren't talking about extinguishing all life on earth.

The wind grew harsher, like the worst of sleet, the kind that cut bare skin. Vic took another step toward Death and felt himself steady.

She watched the exchange with a neutral expression. She was waiting for something.

"What's happening?" Vic whispered.

"Old tools can be best," she said, gently, almost a little sadly. "Built to last, but sometimes they outlive their usefulness, and it is time for them to retire."

"So that's how it goes?" Vic asked. "You just use us and throw us away?"

"No, Vicente," she said, sounding sympathetic. He thought that maybe she even meant it. "But all things must die."

"Except you," he said.

"Except me," she agreed. "I will remain until the last living thing has passed into my hands."

"The mortals must die," the king said with perfect finality.

Vic looked from Death to him.

"All of them, Father?" Argent asked. "Has it finally come to that for you?"

"It has," he said. "Silver knows this. We will keep the North, but we will ally with the Sea upon the Land to end the mortal stain."

Silver stood frozen, like a man carved of marble.

"No," he said, lifting his chin. "You are wrong, Father. As you are wrong about so many things."

He spoke with power too, the strength of a blizzard, but it wasn't nearly enough to counter an immovable glacier.

Vic could feel the King of Swords' magic meshing with the Sea Queen's, the tilt of tides and darkness. The world would freeze and drown. The light would retreat and maybe never come again.

Billions would die, and Vic would watch, powerless against these titans. Still, he had to try.

Vic tensed, ready to step forward, but Death threw up an arm, doing the soccer mom block.

When he looked at her, he saw something deep in her eyes, the end of starlight in a black hole. She shook her head, and Vic did not fight her, no matter how much he wanted to.

"You overstep, my son," the king said, his voice icy. "I shall punish you for not bringing my will to the Sea. I shall cast you into the lowest pit and never free you. You will languish there, forgotten."

"Father!" Argent protested.

"For not drowning the Earth?" Silver asked. "For not freezing it and killing all life upon it?"

"Just so."

The crowd remained fixed in place, silent. They were wide-eyed, entranced by their shock.

Silver turned to the assembled races.

"We are the stewards of life, yet he condones this. Do the rest of you agree?" he asked.

Some of them stirred, shuffled in their seats, but no one protested. Vic hung his head.

"They will not contest my will," the king said, narrowing a wintry eye at them. "I am the King of Swords. I have spoken."

In the midst of all the ice and blue, there was a bit of fire. Perhaps it was cold, but it lit his eyes with a white gleam. Alien or not, ancient or not, he was, Vic decided, utterly insane.

"This is a council, Father," Silver said, his tone as sharp as a razor.

"Mine is the only voice that matters," the king said. "I am king."

"Then we need a new one," Silver said calmly.

"You would challenge me?" the king raged.

Vic could see his madness, but he also thought he saw a fleck of pride at Silver's defiance.

"I am," Silver said. "I do."

The king lifted his sword, wielding it in a single hand. Silver looked too slender and slight against it, far from enough, far from anyone who could win this fight.

Vic considered leaping between them.

"No," Death said.

"We're not going to do anything?" Vic asked her. He kept his eyes on the impending duel, felt the winter power gather and coalesce around the king, around his blade. Silver did not move. He did not draw his sword.

"This is their way, their law," she said.

"But—" Vic tried to protest.

"You are far from your jurisdiction, my Reaper," Death said, cutting him off.

"You will not relent?" Silver asked.

"No," his father said. "Let them drown."

"So be it," Silver said.

He reached into his jacket, drew Vic's gun, and shot his father.

Three booms.

Three gunshots echoing in a place a gun had never been and should never be.

Silver's aim was perfect. He put two bullets into his father's heart and a third between his eyes. The king fell back. His sword clattered to the amphitheater's stone floor, and all hell broke loose among the council.

Their silence turned to shouts, in voices and tongues Vic couldn't understand. It was like the entire UN shouting all at once. The winter cold fell away.

Vic shook. He felt for his jacket pocket but found it empty. At some point Silver had pickpocketed his gun.

Vic looked at the prince. Silver's head dipped and he offered the weapon to Vic, holding it out in his open palm. Vic took it, unloaded it, and pocketed it.

The king lay sprawled. Liquid light leaked from him, pooling beneath him. It was like ice with the sun gleaming through it. The crowd fell silent again. All eyes were on Silver, and Vic could taste their apprehension and fear in the too clean air.

"The king is dead," Argent whispered, quieter than Vic thought she was capable of. Still, it echoed over the shocked amphitheater.

"Long live the king," Silver said.

Vic took a step back toward Death. Somewhere in the depth of her eyes a spark had lit. Pale and bright like a single star—it glowed once then faded.

He held his breath, felt the king's soul or spirit pass through her. That was why she'd come, to reap the King of Swords herself.

A faint smile crossed her face as Vic stared at her. Like she was proud of him for figuring it out, like he was a puppy who'd performed a trick.

The assembled races began to calm. They hadn't moved, hadn't approached the scene. They weren't human, Vic had to remind himself. They did not react as humans would react.

Silver faced them.

"The North does not side with the Sea," he proclaimed, voice loud and steely. "The mortals shall not drown. Any who disobey this edict will meet the same fate as my late father."

The Sea Elves looked too shocked to speak. Even their queen said nothing.

"This council is adjourned," Silver declared.

Most of the beings vanished, fading away in a shadow or a faint sparkling of light.

The Sea Elves remained.

"You would be wise to go now," Silver told them.

The wind gathered, cold and icy. Vic had felt the elf's power before, but now it cascaded off of him, not as unbridled as his father's had been, but a live current Vic wouldn't have risked approaching.

The Sea Queen looked like she might say something, offer some challenge. She opened her mouth, but the Sea King took her arm. They vanished in an inky cloud.

Argent pressed her hands over her mouth.

"Oh, brother, what have you done?" she asked.

"What I had to," Silver said, kneeling. Tears streaked his face.

Was this how it was for immortal creatures? They killed their fathers?

Vic had lost his own to cancer, quick and awful, and there

were days when he'd trade anything to have Eduardo, to have his dad, back. For Silver or Robert Binder—they just did what they needed to.

It couldn't be right.

But billions of lives . . .

Vic's mother. Jesse.

Or Adam's life, a little boy's life.

Vic reeled. His stomach soured at the idea of doing the same thing. Could he even? Would he? If he had to, could Vic have killed his father?

These weren't questions he should ever have to ask himself. Robert and Silver had found their answer, and a large part of Vic was happy that he'd never have to know.

21

ADAM

"Another funeral," Tommy said, ducking his head so his trucker cap shaded his eyes. He wiped away the tears. "I'm the only one left."

Cousin Tommy, Sue's oldest, was Tilla's age.

He had brown hair, brown eyes. You could see the resemblance between him and Bobby. They were the same height, with broader shoulders than Adam. He'd always felt a little smaller, a little slighter around the other Binder men.

They sat in Tommy's living room. It was a nice house, brick, in the better part of Enid. Bobby had to approve of Tommy's middle-class life.

Not that their cousin felt blessed at the moment.

They'd never been close, mostly from the age difference, but Sue had liked her eldest son far more than she'd liked her daughter.

Tommy shook his head.

"Noreen and I didn't get along, but she deserved better," he said. "I just wish she'd had a different life."

Bobby nodded, looking sympathetic, and Adam doubted he was acting. He'd wanted a different life for Adam. They hadn't talked about it for a while. Adam didn't know if his brother had let it go or if he was just distracted by his grief.

"We wanted to tell you in person that we're so sorry," Bobby said. The years he'd added since losing Annie had closed the distance between him and Tommy. They didn't look so far apart in age anymore.

"I'm the only one left," Tommy repeated, looking to the stone fireplace and its mantle full of framed photos.

Adam took his coffee cup and went to look.

There were pictures, a group of kids and their smiling mother, a much, much younger Sue. The dad was always out of frame, taking the photos instead of being in them.

"Is that Jimmy?" Adam asked.

The boy was blond. He wore a yellow polo shirt and brown corduroy pants. Tommy was obvious in a red sweater and jeans. They were clustered around Noreen, who sat on a tricycle.

"Yeah." Tommy's eyes dropped to his cup.

"She never talked about him," Adam said.

"I don't think she ever got over it," Tommy said. "It broke her heart when he disappeared."

Tilla had said the same thing.

"And you never heard from him?" Adam asked.

Tommy shook his head.

"I sometimes wonder," Tommy said, "if she hadn't taken you in because of him, because of the gay thing, you know? Dad was a monster about it. I don't think Jimmy would have run off if he'd not said the things he did. And Mom . . .she was just done with our dad after that."

"Jodi said Noreen hated Jimmy," Adam said coolly. It made his stomach flip to think Sue hadn't really cared about him for his own sake, that it might be because of Jimmy, of some mistake she couldn't fix or some hole she was trying to fill in her life.

"Noreen blamed him for breaking up our parents, for coming out," Tommy said, shaking his head. "But that's not how it works. It wasn't Jimmy's fault."

He sunk into the couch, staring into space, lost in memories.

"We'll let you rest," Bobby said, standing. "Thank you for the coffee."

"If you need anything . . ." Tommy said quietly.

"Same," Bobby said, pressing a hand to Tommy's shoulder and giving it a squeeze.

Adam moved the small distance to the kitchen and deposited his cup in the sink.

They shuffled outside, keeping quiet until they were back in the Cutlass.

"Get anything?" Bobby asked.

Adam shook his head. "There's no magic here, at least none I can sense. It really does skip around."

"I feel bad for him," Bobby said as Adam pulled onto the road.

"Me too," Adam said.

It was an hour drive back to Guthrie. Adam was ready for it. He needed time to think.

Tommy had lost his mother and his sister. That had to be hard.

"He was wrong you know," Bobby said. "Sue loved you. It wasn't about Jimmy."

"You don't know that," Adam said.

There wasn't any way to be certain, and now he'd never get the chance to ask.

"Where to next?" Bobby asked after several miles of prairie had rolled by.

"Somewhere we can get a signal," Adam said, glancing at his phone. "Spend some time on the Internet. The library, maybe the newspaper to search obituaries."

"Should we be going into town?" Bobby asked.

"I don't know," Adam said. "The sheriff isn't thrilled with me, but I don't think he's got a reason to arrest me."

"I'm more worried about Mom," Bobby said.

"I'd be more worried about what she'll do if Jodi gets on her nerves," Adam said.

He realized he'd made a bit of a murder joke and gripped the steering wheel, but Bobby chuckled.

"Do you think Jimmy's the druid?" Bobby asked.

"I don't know," Adam said, sifting through his feelings on their missing cousin. "I'm honestly clutching at straws here. I thought it was Dad, until you told me what you told me."

Bobby nodded. More prairie, more grass, and half-collapsed barns rolled by.

"We can pick up some food for Mom too," Bobby said, clearly ready to change the subject. "She didn't get much yesterday."

"Yeah," Adam said. She'd been kind enough to feed them, and Vic, but he didn't want to think about Vic just then.

Be safe, Adam thought, willing it out through their connection. *Please.*

Guthrie was an anachronism, a little bit of history stuck in modern times. Redbrick streets, Victorian houses, and the big Masonic temple with all the rumors that swirled around it. Adam loved this town. Despite his need for more, he still felt a little pride in being from here.

Maybe, he thought, *when this is over, I can show Vic around.*

Adam had no idea whether or not Vic would appreciate it. The used bookstore, sure, but Adam wasn't certain about so many things when it came to Vic's interests.

They needed to date, to spend time together, and instead they'd been thrown into a deep connection without preamble. It was like an arranged marriage, only Adam hadn't meant to arrange it.

Now Vic was stuck with him and Adam had no idea where things lay.

Too much was unsettled. It made his heart hurt.

Adam rubbed his chest with his fist and parked on the street.

"I'm going to try the library," he said.

"I'll get the groceries," Bobby remarked. "See you in about an hour?"

Adam nodded and headed inside.

The building wasn't very large. Adam had used it from time to time, reading for free when he didn't have the money for paperbacks or when the used shop didn't have part two in a series. He wanted to give audiobooks a try but needed a better phone.

Thankfully, he did have a card, and they had computers.

He opted for that, rather than tap out his sad data plan.

Adam paused. He hadn't even thought of that. With Sue gone, he'd need a new contract for his phone. They were bound to shut it down at some point. He'd always just given her cash to pay his part, and she'd been kind enough to not keep him to strict dates. One more reason to go back to Denver and work for Jesse. A steady job was a new thing and Adam liked it. He especially liked having some money in his pocket for once.

Sue would have been proud of him, and her loss hit him like a punch to the chest. She hadn't told him so much. Maybe she *had* taken Adam in so he wouldn't vanish like Jimmy, but she'd loved him.

Adam had checked out of Liberty House on his eighteenth birthday. He'd walked away, dead broke and with just a worn-out backpack full of threadbare clothes.

He'd gone to Sue's, hiked there, though it had taken all day.

She'd taken him in. She hadn't had much and she'd shared it with Adam.

He pushed his doubts aside.

He wished he could show her the Cutlass, the work he'd done on it, not that there wasn't a ton more to do when this was over.

Adam almost texted Jesse right then to say he was sorry again, to make sure he still had a job, but it could wait. Right now, he needed to find out what happened to Jimmy. Maybe he could put his cousin to rest, and maybe somewhere out there, Sue would know about it.

The library archives had the local paper, the *Guthrie News Leader*, on file for decades. They'd digitized most of it. Adam smiled. The building was small. Its hard drives weren't.

It only took a moment to confirm that James Binder Jr. had gone to high school with Adam's parents and Early West. He'd been on the high school football team. There was even a picture of him after a game.

Jimmy had pale blond hair that covered his ears and a nervous smile that Adam understood all too well.

"Your cousin?" a voice asked. The sheriff. He'd crept up without Adam hearing.

Adam blinked but tried not to look surprised. Early kept popping up. Maybe it was nothing. His office was close. He might have seen the Cutlass.

"That's a sad story." Early nodded to the monitor.

"Yeah, he wasn't at the funeral," Adam said. "I thought I'd look him up."

"He disappeared one day," Early said.

"But you remember him?" Adam asked.

"Of course. It's a small town, a small high school. We didn't have hardly any crime back then. We just figured he'd run off to California to be himself, to be queer out west, you know?"

Adam bristled at the *q* word. He knew a lot of people were using it now, had reclaimed it from being a slur, but in his ears, it still had echoes of the schoolyard, of the boys who'd chased him, bloodied his lip, and given him more than one black eye. Adam didn't know how Sheriff Early meant it, but he wasn't quite ready to give the man the benefit of the doubt.

"No one's heard from him in years," Adam said. "Sue never really talked about him. As far as I know he never came back."

He looked away from the sheriff, back to the screen, to the broad-shouldered, corn-fed boy who'd been his predecessor.

"We just figured he died of AIDS," Early said.

He lifted his hands in a gesture of peace at Adam's expression.

"I didn't mean anything. There was a lot of that then, Adam," Early said.

"Times change," Adam said. Even Guthrie changed, though maybe not enough, not so much that Adam wanted to show Vic around after all. Adam looked up at Early and asked, "Can I help you with something, Sheriff?"

"As a matter of fact," he said. "I wanted to talk to you about your mother."

Early shifted a little and his drawl deepened when he said, "I was wondering if she was seeing anyone."

"You mean, like a psychiatrist?" Adam asked.

Early chuckled. "I mean romantically, like dating, hooking up—whatever you kids call it now."

He scratched the back of his head.

Well, holy shit, Adam thought. *I did not see that coming.*

So much for his Sight.

"Um, I don't think so," Adam said honestly. "But please don't say hooking up. It doesn't mean what I think you think it means."

The whole idea of his mother dating had thrown him off balance. He could picture it, though he'd never pictured it before. There were whole avenues open to his mom that hadn't been there before. She didn't have to stay in Guthrie. She didn't have to live alone in the woods. She could date, or whatever, if she wanted to.

Looking a bit bashful, Early nodded to the screen. "I had such a crush on her back in the day. But she liked the bad boys, guys like your dad. But he's been gone a long time, and Duncan's mother left a while back."

"I could ask her?" Adam stammered. He'd known that his mother had a soft spot for his dad, had loved him regardless of his temper and his laziness, but bad boys? Adam wasn't ready to think of her like that.

"Or better, *you* could ask her," Adam decided.

"You're probably right," Early said bashfully.

With a nod, he retreated, leaving Adam alone.

The whole thing might be cute if it weren't so scary. What if Early knew exactly what had happened to Jimmy? What if he only wanted to talk to Tilla to get closer, to find out what happened to Robert Senior?

Adam knew he was likely being paranoid, but his encounter with the sheriff at the station hadn't been so cordial. Early hadn't mentioned the bones. Had they identified them?

Adam turned back to the screen, to the picture.

"What really happened to you, Jimmy?" he asked. "Where did you go?"

22

ADAM

They ate breakfast at the little table in the trailer's kitchen. Mom had cooked burgers, thick patties of ground beef she'd mixed chopped green pepper and onion into. It was dinner food, but so much better than stale oatmeal.

Jodi, looking resentful, had three. At least she kept any shitty remarks to herself.

The night had passed, quiet and tense. Adam and Bobby slept in their old bed, neither of them fitting, neither of them sleeping well. Adam found the low ceiling too close. It had been a comfort when he was little, like he was safe there, though of course he hadn't been. His dad had pulled him out by the ankle once, dangling him and spanking him in midair.

Eating, Adam tried to push aside thoughts of Robert Senior.

"There wasn't anything at the library," he said. He waffled on telling them about the sheriff's visit but decided he'd had enough with holding back. It had cost him too much already.

"I ran into Early again," he said. "I think he's keeping tabs on us."

"You can't really blame him," Bobby said.

He and Adam exchanged a look. Early had to suspect the bones had been their dad's, even if he didn't have a connection between them and the trailer or to their mom.

"I think we should check out the old property," Adam said. "The homestead."

"I haven't been out there since you were little, Bobby," Tilla said. She looked to the back window. "Your dad loved that place. Said it was some of the only happy memories he had."

Bobby reached to pat her arm.

Adam didn't know what to say. She always talked about their father with a bit of fondness, like the terror he'd brought into their lives or the fact that Bobby had been forced to murder him hadn't happened. It was like there were two versions of Robert Binder Senior, the man she loved and held in her memory, and the one Adam best remembered, the one Bobby had killed.

Then again, if what Early had said was true, and his mother had liked his dad because he was a bad boy, maybe she'd known the whole time. Maybe she could ignore the way he was because she'd loved him, even long after she should have stopped.

"There's nothing to do here," Jodi said, dropping her fork on her plate. She nodded to Tilla. "She doesn't even have Internet."

"So?" Adam asked, though he could sympathize with the complaint about the Wi-Fi.

"So you have to take me with you," Jodi said.

Adam thought about it.

The druid was after Jodi. Taking her away from here might be the best thing for Tilla's safety.

"Another pair of eyes can't hurt," Bobby suggested.

"Sure," Adam said.

And Jodi did have the Sight. She might spot something he didn't, or might let slip something useful. Adam felt certain there was more to her story.

"Just stay inside the house," Adam said to his mother.

Tilla tsked.

"I've got my shotgun and my Bible," she said.

"Please, Ma. For me?" Adam asked.

"Fine."

———

Bobby rode shotgun as Adam drove. Jodi sat in the back, applying too much makeup from her purse and occasionally giving directions.

"Does anyone live there?" Adam asked.

"Not for years," Jodi said. "Mom said it's full of rattlesnakes."

It was well outside of town, out where the grass went on forever. Bits of rusted barbed wire on old posts, many homemade from trees, separated one acreage from another.

At least the sky was clear and the wind, a near constant, was low today.

They found it after driving for a while. Adam knew how sneaky the plains could be, how you could get lost out here among the endless grass and flat landscape. In Denver the mountains were always to the west. Here, there were no landmarks, nothing most people could use.

Adam didn't have that problem. He could peek into the Other Side, use the watchtowers to tell him the cardinal directions, though he'd never get used to the missing tower in the east.

The old house had two stories, with a beaten windmill to pull well water.

The paint had been scoured away by the constant wind.

The barn out back was half-collapsed.

Adam frowned. This had been someone's dream, someone in his family's dream. He sank a little to see it fallen into ruin.

Adam parked. His stomach fell, a sense of dread washing over him like an inky wave.

"We shouldn't be here," Jodi said.

"You feel it too?" Bobby asked.

"It's a curse," Adam said. "A ward to keep people out. Give me a sec."

He closed his eyes, took a breath, and focused. Usually he'd assume a position, but he didn't have the space or a dance partner to invoke the Four of Wands. Instead Adam visualized it, concentrating.

"What's he doing?" Jodi asked.

"I think he's spirit walking," Bobby whispered.

Adam practically felt Jodi roll her eyes as she scoffed.

She said she wanted her birthright, but clearly she had little interest in actually learning.

Ignoring her, Adam sank into himself, down through his body, and out of the car. He opened his eyes.

The scent of blackberries and battery acid filled Adam's mind as the curse came into view.

A fence of spectral, thorny snakes ran around the property, more solid to Adam's Sight than the half-fallen, rusted barbed wire. They coiled and hissed, warning him away.

The spell was powerful, but not particularly thick. Adam tested a bit of his will against it. The snakes parted for him. It wasn't a solid defense, just a deterrent.

"I can make a hole for us," he said aloud, slipping back into his body and opening his eyes.

He was getting good at the transition, at coming and going between the two.

With a deep breath, he opened the car door.

The weeds and grass were knee-high, and the day was warm. It was a good place to step on a rattlesnake.

"Jodi," he said, nodding for her to stand beside him.

"What?" she said, shutting the Cutlass's door with more force than he appreciated.

"Come here. I want to show you something."

She sighed, but listened.

"Can you see the curse?" he asked.

"No," she said, squinting.

Adam didn't know if she was really trying or not.

"Hold up your hand," he said, doing the same. He pressed against the boundary, the edge of where the snakes coiled. They weren't real, and it didn't hurt, just tingled as they hissed and rattled, trying to make him afraid, trying to get him to turn away. "Can you feel that?"

"Yeah," she said, nodding.

"Good," Adam said. "Now concentrate, try to push it back, to make a hole."

The curse gave against her will. With practice and focus, she could be powerful. Adam could teach her, maybe not as well as Silver might, but Vic had been right. Adam should share what he knew, and if what Jodi had hinted at in the bar was true, that her Sight haunted her dreams, he could try to help with that.

Adam added his will to hers, sweeping the spectral snakes aside and gesturing for Jodi and Bobby to follow him onto the property.

"That feels better," Bobby said, rubbing his stomach.

"It's not that strong," Adam said. "Just intended to scare people away."

"It's doing its job," Bobby said, nodding to the house and the barn. "It doesn't look like anyone's been here. No graffiti. No squatters."

"It probably doesn't work on snakes," Adam said, nodding to the tall grass and the sunny sky. "Watch out for them."

"Graffiti or not, it's a shithole," Jodi said, though she shuddered at the ruin. "Creepy though."

Adam had to agree with both sentiments. Several boards had come loose from the wooden siding. The house had been large for its day, a sprawling first story and a second, smaller one. Dead weeds and grass jutted everywhere. Despite all the recent rain, the place was dry, like it had never recovered from the Dust Bowl.

"It reminds me of Liberty House," Adam said.

"No," Bobby said, voice sounding distant. "It wasn't this bad."

"What are you talking about?" Adam asked, a little of the old anger and hurt rising. He'd forgiven Bobby. Mostly. He tried to tamp it down. "It was a lot like this."

Adam waved a hand to indicate the cracked window panes and the roof with its missing shingles.

"No," Bobby said softly.

Adam tried not to glare at his brother.

"But it was," Bobby said, eyes dipping to the ground. "Wasn't it?"

"Yeah," Adam said with a nod.

"Death wanted me there," he said. "She wanted me to hate you, but also how to learn to control my magic. She hid what it was from you."

Adam was trying to let it go. He really was.

Bobby had seen Liberty House as one thing. Adam had seen another, its true form. He knew he shouldn't resent his brother for being fooled, for not having the magic to pierce the illusion, but he still did.

"Wait—" Jodi said. "Death is a she?"

"Yep," Adam said.

"Badass."

"She's been screwing with the Binders for a long time," Bobby added. "Our family is just a tool to her."

"So she's evil?" Jodi asked.

"Yes," Bobby said.

"Not exactly," Adam countered.

The brothers exchanged a look.

"She's more like a natural force," Adam said.

"I don't buy that," Bobby said. "Not after what she did to us. She could have found another way."

Adam had to nod agreement.

If Bobby blamed Sara for Annie, for her possession and death, well, he had every right to.

"Either way," Adam said as they approached the house along the driveway's muddy path, "the druid has worked for her before. She used him to break the seal and set Mercy free."

"Who's Mercy?" Jodi asked.

"I'll explain it, most of it," Adam said with a pointed glance at his brother, hoping that he successfully conveyed that he'd leave Annie out of it. "If we live through this."

"Great," Jodi snarled.

The glass in the front door and the windows was broken but not boarded up. The switchgrass had encroached, coming right up to the walls. Adam tensed, listening for rattles.

He pushed the front door open and found only dried leaves, dust, and shadows.

Bobby shuddered. He froze in the doorway.

"Place like this, big and empty," Jodi said. "I should tell Billy about it."

"I'm not sure that's a good idea," Adam said.

Even if Jodi's stoner clown of a boyfriend could get through the curse, the place couldn't be safe. Adam just couldn't say why.

He sensed something, old and lingering, though he couldn't name it.

The unlocked front door swung open onto a dusty, weathered

entryway. The house's interior smelled a bit like mold, but was otherwise lifeless. The air tasted of dust and too much time gone by.

The floor was broken, split with the now-familiar blackberry canes. They'd climbed the walls to make a prickly, indoor bramble. Thin and reedy, dug into the wallpaper, they shouldn't be so ominous, but Adam kept his distance. They reminded him of skeletons, of fingers reaching from the ground. A rattle sounded, out of sight, but close enough for the hair to prickle along the back of Adam's neck.

"That doesn't look natural," Bobby said, eyeing the growth.

"It's not," Adam agreed, inhaling.

He almost had it, felt certain it was the trace of an old spell, a great expenditure of magic. It coated the walls like fine dust, invisible, but there.

"Let's stay together," Adam said, leading them past the little foyer into the house's parlor.

The place was that old, to have a parlor instead of a living room. The furniture was wooden, spindly and cracked with age. Tilla would have tsked at the sight.

A rug crunched beneath their feet. It had a bit of green to it, long faded but enough color remained to tell Adam it had once matched the pattern of the time-bleached, peeling wallpaper.

"Someone should turn this into a haunted house," Jodi said.

"Somebody already has," Adam replied, certain of it.

A spirit circled them. It was faint, just a bit of mist on the Other Side. Adam opened his Sight further, risked being seen in order to see more himself, but the ghost, whoever it was, was too faded, too far gone for Adam to recognize them.

They weren't familiar, but the flavor of their murder was. It matched the stain behind his mom's trailer.

Whoever they'd been, however they'd died, they'd met a nasty end.

Adam didn't want it to be Jimmy, the only other gay family member he knew about. He moved on, into the kitchen.

It looked like it hadn't been touched since the 1950s. The refrigerator was the ancient kind, heavy, avocado green, and tiny by modern standards.

The stove was cast iron. Despite the dread creeping up Adam's spine, he could see Jodi's point. If the curse hadn't been keeping people away the place would surely have been looted by now. The stove alone would probably go for a few hundred in an antiques shop.

The wallpaper in here had been darkened by the smoke from the stove. Squinting, Adam could make out cutesy chickens in wire cages and roosters, a bit of faded whimsy. Someone had loved this place. Someone had called it home.

He peered out the window. Some of the glass remained, though it had gone wavy with time. Then there was the land. If Sue had owned this, why hadn't she sold it? Maybe she hadn't wanted to live here, but she could have used the money.

Adam sort of wished his mom had come. She might have been able to shed some light. The place was old, like turn-of-the-last-century old, but his grandparents had been in their prime in the '60s and '70s. It had stayed in the family a long time.

"I don't get it," Adam said. "Why didn't we come out here when we were kids?"

"Huh?" Bobby perked up from where he'd been searching the cabinets, looking at the old dishes and boxes of cereal or canned goods, their contents or labels completely nibbled away by mice and age.

"Wait," Adam said. "Where's Jodi?"

"In here," she called from down the hall.

Adam found her in a bedroom.

A massive bed had once stood in the middle. Its posts were collapsed now, its mattress rotted away. In its center was a tangle of blackberry canes, all dried and dead, but they'd decayed into a long, oblong shape. It looked like a nest, or a cocoon.

Adam scowled at it.

"What does it mean?" Jodi asked.

"I don't know," Adam admitted. "The druid's magic comes from nature. He'd bonded to it, but he's a warlock too. He's maimed magical creatures to make charms."

Adam had felt something in his own wound during their fight at the bar, but the druid didn't have a wound. There was something about what Adam had done to himself that he didn't understand. He needed Argent or Silver, someone who could explain.

This was the center of the spell he'd detected, whatever lingered on the walls.

"We need to figure out what happened to Jimmy," Adam said.

"You think this was him?" Bobby asked, nodding to the bed.

"I don't know," Adam said, and he was getting really tired of saying that.

If Jimmy was the warlock it made a kind of sense that he'd kill Noreen. Maybe he'd hated her as much as she'd hated him. But why wait so long, and why kill Sue?

Adam grimaced at the thought of a spell that could look like a heart attack.

But maybe it wasn't just murder. Maybe Jimmy was collecting all the Binder trading cards, stealing their magic for some purpose.

"No books or anything," Bobby said, completing a look around the room. "Nothing useful. No clues."

Jimmy hadn't lived here. Adam would have liked to see his room. That might have provided some clues.

This whole place *felt* wrong. The curse kept its distance, lining only the fence, but the queasy taste of the stain had thickened.

Adam turned to Jodi.

"Did your mom have anything of Jimmy's?" Adam asked. "Did she tell you anything else about him?"

"No," Jodi said, shaking her head. "Like I said, she hated him."

"And Sue didn't have anything?" Bobby asked, peeking into the closet.

"No," Adam said. "It was a small trailer. I would have seen it."

He still didn't understand why Sue had erased her youngest son so completely. Maybe it had hurt too much, but he wondered if it was a clue. Maybe Jimmy had gone bad and that had been the thing that had broken Sue's heart.

"Let's try the rest of the rooms," Adam said.

He brought up the flashlight app on his phone and led them down the narrow hall. Long rugs remained, just as dirty as everything else. Something rattled the metal furnace grate.

Fantastic, Adam thought.

There was a crawlspace. That was somewhere he never wanted to peek.

The back part of the house had been added on. Or maybe it was older, the original part. Either way, the ceiling pressed close. The rooms here were smaller, like the house was shrinking. The floor was uneven, like something had given away between where they stood.

Adam stepped carefully into a tiny bedroom.

It held a desk and a typewriter.

Jodi practically leapt forward. She opened the desk drawers, riffling through them.

"There has to be something," she said.

"What are you hoping to find?" Adam asked.

"My birthright," she stressed, like they should know.

"Why is this so important to you?" Bobby asked. "What does it even mean?"

"We got *nothing*," Jodi said. "Sue gave us nothing. Mom didn't even want me."

Jodi kicked the wall.

"Is that why you were doing those tarot videos?" Adam asked. "Trying to get Sue's clients?"

"I have the Sight," Jodi snarled. "What good is it if it can't pay the rent?"

"It's not," Adam said, shaking his head. "Not any good, most of the time."

Adam should know. His Sight and magic had been more of a curse than a blessing. He traded a look with Bobby and knew his brother was thinking it too.

"There's nothing here," Bobby said, trying to assure Jodi.

Rust and dust, Adam mused. That was all the Binder legacy had to offer, the only birthright any of them had gotten.

"There's always the barn," Bobby suggested, looking out the window. "Let's check there."

They were out the back door, halfway to it when the windmill creaked, not quite turning. It was rusted and missing too many blades to pump water.

"It's the well," Adam said, feeling it in every bone, every cell. His Sight wasn't like Sue's, but when it came on like this, Adam knew he was right, dead right.

Bobby and Jodi did not argue. As one, they moved that way, off the tilted concrete pavers of the porch.

The stain got worse the closer they came, pressing in, thick and greasy. The land had been something once, someone's hope for a farm, but now it felt infected, sick and dying.

The grass whispered in the wind. The sun was bright when Adam would have preferred frost. It would have provided less cover, which meant less chance of snakes. He thought he heard rattles, but it might just be the wind mixing with his imagination and the yellow sour feeling in his guts.

The well was a cement ring capped with boards, thick planks nailed together.

A row of cottonwoods, a line someone must have hoped would break up the sheer flatness, stood dead nearby. The wind had stripped their bark, leaving them gray and pale like the grasping bone trees of Adam's recent dream.

Like everything else about the homestead, the well's cap had seen better days. Maybe once it had been colorful. A few traces of John Deere Green remained.

With a nod, Adam and Bobby took opposite sides and hefted off the cap. A gust of something foul, mold, old rot, and the unmistakable odor of something long dead washed over them. Adam gagged as Jodi leaned forward with her phone's flashlight, the lip of her T-shirt pulled up over her mouth and nose.

Adam held his breath and peered into the well.

A long bundle, bedsheets and a blanket tied with rope, was submerged in murky water. A body.

Adam and Bobby staggered back. Jodi kept looking.

"Jimmy?" Bobby asked. "Or someone else?"

"We need the sheriff," Adam said. But he wasn't certain how they'd deal with the curse.

A cold breeze rose from the well.

The familiar scent of battery acid and rotting blackberries came in bits.

The rattle of a snake sounded, closer than ever.

Adam tensed, every muscle going rigid, torn between fight or flight. He looked to Bobby and Jodi. They'd felt it too.

"Run," Adam said.

The three of them took off across the grass.

They'd almost reached the Cutlass and found snakes curled, blocking their path.

Adam skidded to a stop.

The grass on either side of the driveway rippled. More rattlers, dozens, maybe hundreds, slithered toward the three Binders.

They piled together, wriggling and rising.

"Where's my cigarette lighter?" Jodi asked, rummaging in her purse as the snakes began to circle, forming a ring around them.

"You're going to smoke a joint?" Bobby demanded. "Now?"

"I've got hairspray, dipshit," Jodi said, wielding a can and shaking it. "Southern girl's flamethrower."

"I don't think it will help," Adam said, reaching for his magic as the snakes made a writhing, slithering wall.

The three of them pressed together, back to back as the diseased magic filled the air. It mixed with the snakes' musk, so thick that Adam gagged.

"Dammit," Adam said.

"How's he doing this?" Bobby asked as the ring around them began to tighten.

"He's a druid," Adam said. "Animals come with the territory."

"Let's break through," Bobby said, eyeing the wall of tails and fangs.

The rattles grew louder.

"Not a good idea," Adam said.

"Can you do what you did last time?" Jodi asked.

"No," Adam said.

The druid was smart. His control over the snakes wasn't made of death magic. It wasn't like the blackberries, a single spell. It was dozens of little spells, cast in waves.

Adam simply didn't have the magic.

Extinguishing them, countering them the way he had before, would kill him.

He raised his defenses, drew a circle with his mind, and made a sphere. Adam poured his will into it. The effort made his knees buckle, but the squirming ring stopped its advance.

"I felt that," Jodi said with a gasp. "How are you doing that?"

The snakes were a storm and the three Binders were its eye. The writhing bodies piled higher and higher, ankle-deep against the dome Adam had constructed.

The druid appeared. He moved like the snakes, jerking, pulled toward them.

Had he risen from the well?

Adam still couldn't see his face inside the hood, still could not say if it were Jimmy or someone else.

Either way the druid still clutched the skull, Robert's skull, in one hand. In the other, he held the rusty sickle.

"That would be cool if we weren't about to die," Jodi said.

"What do you want?" Bobby railed at the figure.

Adam had to keep his concentration. He had to keep the sphere around them, keep the snakes away. It would only take one moment, one lapse, and they'd drown in fangs and venom.

Birthright, the druid mocked, pointing his sickle out toward Jodi. *Blood calls blood.*

"It's another projection," Adam said through gritted teeth. "He's not really here."

The well had been booby-trapped. They'd triggered it when they'd moved the cap.

The snakes were real. Nests of them were common enough in grass fields like these.

"Who cares, he can still kill us!" Jodi shrieked.

"Stay behind me," Adam said.

"There's nowhere else to go!" Jodi shouted. "Can you stop it?"

Adam ignored her and focused on the druid. This was their chance, maybe their only chance, for answers.

"What birthright?" Adam asked, eyes flicking from Jodi to the druid. "Why do you two keep mentioning that?"

Binders. Binder blood. My harvest. The druid pointed to Bobby and called in a gravelly, deep voice, *Robert Jr., Bobby Jack.*

"Who are you?" Bobby demanded.

Adam's defenses were cracking. He could feel Jodi's terror and Bobby's desperation.

The snakes swarmed, closer and higher, breaking against the sphere. Adam could feel them wriggling into the earth, trying to get through that way. There were hundreds of them now, maybe thousands.

Adam felt the strain, the push of the snakes, the spell driving them to attack.

"Why are you killing Binders?" he demanded, desperately trying to find a way out.

My blood. My harvest.

"Life," Adam said. "He wants life."

The druid was stealing magic.

Mercy had done something like that, drained practitioners of life, trying to rebuild itself from the bits of power it stole. The spirit had been ancient, birthed long before the rules of life and death had been set in place, that was why Death had wanted it off the board so badly.

But the druid had to work inside the rules. He couldn't take from just anyone.

"His descendants," Adam said quietly. That was why the stain here was so much worse, sunk so much deeper into the land. It had started here. It had gone on here for a while.

"He can't be Dad. Or Jimmy," Adam continued. "He's much older than that. He's been killing a long time. Haven't you?"

The druid didn't answer, but he grinned inside his hood.

The tide of snakes was chest high now. They bit and hissed, their rattling incessant. The pressure increased. Adam felt something in his head snap. A sharp pain and blood trickled from his nose.

The sphere around them held, but Adam felt his life draining away. He poured everything into it, his love for Vic, the forever pain in his chest. It was like giving blood, too much, too fast. He bobbed, ready to collapse.

"Adam?" Bobby asked, worried.

"I have an idea," he said, handing him the keys to the Cutlass. "Get ready to run."

Just that motion almost cost Adam the sphere. He was shaking, like he'd run miles on an empty stomach.

Adam contracted the shield, all of his magic, all of his life. The snakes swarmed closer, almost to them.

"What are you doing?" Bobby demanded, panicking.

"Just run, Bobby. I'm going to make you an opening."

"What about you?"

"I'll see you on the Other Side," Adam said, wishing it were true.

He squeezed the rest of his will, the rest of his magic and life into a ball and pushed it outward all at once, detonating it like a grenade. It ripped through the snakes, breaking the druid's control. The swarm broke and fled, their concentrated will dissolving into confusion.

"Go!" Adam shouted. It would be the last thing he said.

He fell to his knees. The world went black.

23

VIC

"There wasn't another way?" Vic demanded.

"Not that Silver saw," Argent said. "And not one I can see either."

They sat beside each other on a bench, in the now-empty amphitheater.

The Queen of Swords remained regal, still powerful, but she'd sunk into herself a little.

Vic had been there. He hadn't known how to process his father's death. Unlike her, it hadn't snuck up on him. The cancer had announced itself pretty loudly.

Nor was Vic's father supposed to live forever, not to mention he hadn't been murdered by Vic's brother.

Death had departed, leaving Vic behind without a word or a promise to stay in touch. She'd been there, then she wasn't. That seemed to be her way.

The city was quiet, subdued. The other elves seemed shocked, uncertain about how to react. That or they were terrified of their new, unpredictable king.

Vic could understand. He could. Billions of lives, the animals and trees, that had been what the Sea Elves had wanted to drown.

"He was insane," Vic said, eyeing the blood staining the dais. Blue, it shone like ice, like tears. "Wasn't he?"

Elves in white had taken the body. They'd wrapped him in cloth and carried him away. No one had come to clean the blood, and Vic wondered why.

As he watched, it changed, morphing into flowers, a pool of pale-blue blooms with perfect white leaves.

Argent watched them rustle in the breeze. Her pale eyes picked up their color.

"Not exactly," she said. "He was old. Older than your civilizations. He still saw everything through that lens, that time when we ruled alone."

Vic did not want to argue with her. She'd just lost her father, and he knew how that felt.

But he'd also heard too many times how racist people were always given the excuse that they'd grown up in another time. People who beat their kids came from somewhere else so it should be excused, right?

Vic had some uncles like that. He had aunts who made the excuses for them and wondered if he'd ever get that old, so stuck in his ways. If humans could become so rigid, how much older and beyond growth was a king from the dawn of time?

And being immortal didn't excuse his plans, what he'd condoned.

Dammit, Vic thought, *Silver had been right to stop him.*

"Could it still happen?" Vic asked. "Could the Sea Elves still drown the world?"

"Without our support?" Argent pondered. "Or with the guarantee of war if they tried? No."

They sat a while longer, watching the flowers, watching the sky slowly spin by.

"Whatever he was thinking, whatever he'd meant to do," Vic said. "He was still your father, and I'm sorry for your loss."

"Thank you," Argent whispered.

Silver approached them. He still wore his robes and long hair, but he'd added an edge. A weight had settled onto his shoulders, and he looked more like the gangster he often dressed as.

That unseen shadow contrasted to the perfect blue sky and the occasional bird, the paradise of the floating city. This beautiful place had its own darkness, and it resided in its people.

"You used me," Vic said to Silver. "You used me to get a gun in here. My gun."

Vic clenched his fists so hard they hurt, but he didn't stand. He knew he could not strike Silver, not here, not ever. Reaper or not, the elf had powers Vic could never match.

"Yes," Silver admitted. He seemed so young and so old in that moment. An ancient being and just a boy. "He would have been prepared for a sword. I would not have won on his terms."

"You killed your father," Vic said.

Silver turned to Vic. He was crying again.

"Yes," he repeated. "I fought with him about this, privately of course. I pleaded. I begged. But he would see no reason. He saw the Sea's plan as noble, the righteous way to save the Earth from your kind."

"Did you know?" Vic asked Argent. "Did you know he'd do this?"

She shook her head. For once she seemed speechless, struck silent by her grief.

"He wanted me to succeed him," Silver said. "But he was never going to give me the throne. That is how it is among our kind. We wait forever for change, but it never comes naturally."

"You sound like he wanted you to kill him," Vic said. "Like he expected it of you."

"In some ways, he did," Silver said. "And in some ways I don't think he could ever have let go. He would have struck me down first."

Vic couldn't understand. He just couldn't. A healthy man, an immortal, had longed for death because change was scarier than dying.

Life was precious, that was what the elves endlessly preached. They went on and on about it. So how could they just let that go? How could Silver just snuff it out?

Vic swallowed and admitted that his feelings weren't entirely about the shooting.

"How long have you planned this?" Argent asked, bringing Vic back to the moment.

"Long enough," Silver said. "I imagined it would come to this someday, but I never thought he'd go so far so quickly."

"You killed your father," Vic repeated.

How many times could he say it? When would the truth of it sink in?

"Yes," Silver said. "I did. He pushed me to it, but I pulled the trigger. And I'll live with it forever, as long as I reign, until I become so rigid in my thinking that someone must kill me in turn."

Vic shook his head. This other world was beautiful, fantastic, but it was not *better*.

He understood Adam's cynicism now, how he always talked about the elves in a jaded tone.

For all their morals and charm, the elves were no better than humans, than the people Vic dealt with every day. They were just as capable of crime and murder.

Death had said these were their laws, not Vic's. He didn't belong here. Even if he could somehow change how they did things, he didn't have any right to.

And what about Adam? What about his brother killing their father?

The Binders were bound by the same laws, the same system as Vic. They weren't alien elves with duels and ancient customs who'd never seen a gun.

That was the real question, the one Vic had been putting off since they'd brought him here.

Where did things stand between him and Adam?

Could he fix them, and did he want to if it meant setting the law aside?

"Vicente?" Argent asked softly, looking to him.

She'd sensed his withdraw, that he'd reached some conclusion. She'd straightened, but kept her distance on the bench. Her eyes were still pale, still sad, but some of it was for him now, for the innocence he'd lost today.

"I think I'm ready to go home," he said.

"Back to Oklahoma?" she asked.

"No," Vic said, shaking his head. "Home."

24

ADAM

"Why aren't I dead?" Adam groaned as he opened his eyes.

"I don't know," Vran said, looking down at him. "Are all mortals such drama queens?"

Adam lay in a warm puddle of faintly glowing water. It was raised, like a shallow bathtub, and cushioned with damp seaweed. Maybe this is what Sea Elves used for a bed.

Vran leaned against the cavern wall, his black crown askew. The elf retained his emo prince look: jet hair, dark eyes, and slightly blue, perfect skin.

The room itself was strange, like the inside of a sandcastle, like the walls had been dripped into place.

There were things scattered around it, video game systems, an old blender, rocks, and a ball of mud with feathers stuck in it.

"Is this your room?" Adam asked, groaning as he shifted.

"No," Vran said. "It's somewhere I go."

"To think?" Adam asked. "To get away?"

Vran nodded.

"I get that," Adam said.

For him it had been the blackberry bushes. He'd liked to hide there and imagine his father's anger would never find him.

The stupid druid had ruined blackberries for him.

Adam stretched, forced himself to sit up. He felt dry, lifeless, every nerved burned like he'd been lying in a tanning bed for a week.

"Why am I here?" Adam asked, looking around the cave.

"That's not very nice," Vran said, crossing his arms over his chest. "I saved your life."

"Great. Thanks," Adam said. Debts to immortals were his worst nightmare. He already had one and no idea how to pay it. "Where's my brother? My cousin?"

"They were driving off as I snatched you away."

The glowing water rushed around them in little streams, dripping from the walls. Adam could feel the life in it trying to fill the emptiness he'd created when he'd stopped the snakes.

Adam's clothes were soaked, but he was too bone weary to care.

"I was supposed to kill you," Vran said quietly.

Adam blinked.

"Is that what you meant when you said I had no idea what was coming?" he asked.

"That was another thing, but it's not going to happen now," Vran assured him.

"Okay," Adam said. "Are you still going to kill me? If so, saving my life seems like a real waste of your time."

Vran nibbled his lip.

"Why did you save her?" he asked. "She was your enemy."

"Who?" Adam asked.

"The woman in the box, in the trailer."

"Noreen?" Adam asked. "She was in trouble. She needed help."

"I've been watching. She wasn't nice. She was your enemy."

"I wouldn't go that far," Adam said with a shrug that he immediately regretted. "But no, she wasn't nice."

"I'm supposed to kill you," Vran repeated.

"Why exactly?" Adam asked.

"Because you're my opposite. Because you're *human*." Vran said it like it was something shameful.

He seemed to be on the fence about the killing part.

Adam hoped this wasn't a cat and mouse situation. Spider had caught mice and brought them to Sue from time to time. He'd treated them a bit like pets, but his method of playing with them meant that Adam had eventually had to take them outside and put them out of their misery. He'd brought a lizard in once. It had dropped its tail and run loose. Adam didn't have a tail, so it wasn't a trick he could manage.

"I haven't said yes," Adam said. "To being the Page of Swords I mean."

"I don't even know why we're enemies," Vran said, rolling his eyes. "The Winter Elves are our kin."

"I'm not good at politics, but family is complicated," Adam said. "And thank you, for saving my life."

Vran nodded.

"That was an interesting trick, expending all your magic at once," he said.

"Did it hurt the druid?" Adam asked.

"No, but I think you surprised him again. You're two for two with him. That has to really piss him off. Plus, you broke that spell. He must have spent years setting that up."

Vran smirked, looking impressed by Adam's act of magical vandalism.

Adam liked this kid, not that he'd ever admit it. It would cost him any cool points he'd just earned.

"Well, he did start it," Adam said. "Leaving me a note and all."

He still didn't understand that part.

There's still time to save her, it had lied.

Any her—Sue, Noreen, or Annie—had all died. It might mean Tilla or Jodi, but why warn Adam if the druid was the one killing the Binders?

The trip to the homestead indicated that the druid was too old to be Jimmy, and that left the question of the body in the well.

My harvest, the druid kept saying. *My blood.*

If he was stealing magic, killing Binders to get it, why hadn't he come after Adam? He had more than Noreen or Jodi.

Adam didn't look like his brother or cousin Tommy. Their hair was all brown, and his was dirty blond, like his mother's. Adam had blue eyes, but so had Robert Senior.

Maybe, just maybe, Adam's father wasn't really his father.

That might have been the source of Robert Senior's hatred, why he'd beaten Adam so often and so badly.

And Adam's magic wasn't like Sue's. He had Sight, but not the same.

Maybe Adam wasn't really a Binder.

"What are you thinking about?" Vran asked.

"Bloodlines and birthrights," Adam said. He stretched again. "So what now, am I your prisoner?"

Vran considered the question.

"No."

"Are you sure?" Adam asked. "Your family tried to murder Silver."

"They're not my family," Vran said, voice going cold. "They're my court."

"All right," Adam said, lifting his hands.

Vran sighed.

"And they're all drama queens too," he said. "I just wanted to make certain you're all right."

"Why?" Adam asked.

"I don't need a reason."

"You're an elf," Adam said. "Elves are, in my usual experience, pricks. You must want something, Vran."

"I want to *understand*," Vran said. "You keep sacrificing yourself. To save the cop, to stop the spirit, and now to save people you don't even like. Like that woman. The box was on fire, but you ran into it. It's like you want to die."

Adam cocked his head.

"I really don't," he said. And he meant it. He wanted to live, if only to see what he and Vic might become. "But I can't let them suffer."

"You have so little life," Vran protested. "You should hoard it like dragons hoard shiny things, but instead you risk throwing it away for anybody."

"Not just anybody," Adam argued.

This was starting to sound like a conversation he'd had with Vic more than once, the idea that Adam was some kind of hero. He never planned it like that. Someone needed help, so he helped, usually without thinking it through, like when he'd saved Vic. If anything, he was more of a spontaneous idiot.

"And yeah, you can play it safe, stay home, never go outside, try to live as long as you can, but I'm not sure that's actually living," Adam said.

"Would you risk yourself for me?" Vran asked, his voice quiet.

Adam wondered what had happened to Vran's family, how he'd become the Page of Cups, and why he seemed so shocked at the idea of basic kindness. It was something Adam could understand not understanding. He must be looking at Vran the way Vic looked at him sometimes, not with pity, but a sort of sympathetic confusion.

"Probably," Adam admitted. "If the druid came for you, or something like that. If you weren't hurting anyone. Silver said you weren't there when they tried to kill him."

Vran scoffed. "They want to drown the mortal world. You lot are already working on that. It's your plane of existence. Kill it if you want."

"That's not very elven of you," Adam said.

Another scoff.

"How old are you?" Adam asked.

"I'm two hundred," Vran snapped, a little defensively.

So he *was* a teenager.

"I need to go back," Adam said. "Will you let me go?"

Vran pondered it.

"Say please," Vran teased with just an edge of seriousness.

"Please," Adam said.

The elf nibbled his lip.

"What about the druid, are you going to try to save him too?" Vran asked.

"I don't think I can," Adam said. "Whoever he is, he's pretty gone. He's killed people. He wants to kill more. He wants to kill my family."

Once he said it, he realized it was true. Family or not, how did you get forgiven for what the druid had done? Just becoming a warlock the way he had made the druid irredeemable in the elves' opinion, and, he supposed, in Adam's too. Even if Adam wasn't sworn to take him out, the druid could not continue.

"Your family is like your court," Vran said. "You're stuck with them but you don't like them."

"Not always," Adam said. "But that's family. Wait—Do you know who he is?"

"Maybe," Vran said.

The pool Adam sat in rushed up and swallowed him. He fell through dark water, and landed in the mud outside his mom's trailer, soaking wet and sputtering. What had been warm was quickly cold.

"Elves," Adam muttered, though there was no bite in it.

Still, the kid had answers he wasn't sharing.

Picking himself up, Adam glared at the mud puddle.

"Brat," he said, hoping Vran heard it.

Bobby and Tilla leaped up when Adam stumbled through the door.

"Are you okay?" Bobby asked, wrapping Adam in a hug. "We thought you were dead."

A mix of feelings flooded Adam, just like at the funeral, only he wasn't so numb now. He could feel Bobby's concern for him, his love, and it felt good, dammit.

"Yeah, a friend got me out," he said.

Adam still wasn't certain how he'd survived. Vran or no Vran, he'd pushed all of his magic out in one go. It should have killed him. And he wasn't quite certain he should call Vran a friend.

He needed backup, Silver or Argent. He needed Vic—but they had their own thing to deal with and it was selfish to want them here. What they had on their plate was so much bigger.

Jodi didn't look happy or sad to see Adam. She just looked pissed, which he decided was her usual state.

His mom didn't rush to hug him, but she hovered nearby, nibbling her lip, a sign that she'd been worried. Adam felt a tug in his heart, a nice change from the ache of the warlock wound.

"Did you learn anything?" Tilla asked.

Adam looked to Bobby.

"We didn't tell her," he said. "We waited for you."

"There's a body in the well," Adam said. "I don't know who it is. We need that answer first."

"How?" Bobby asked. "How do we find out?"

"The curse is broken," Adam said. "We can get the sheriff out there. But first, I think we should have another look at Mom's bible."

Tilla reached for the book and opened the cover to the family tree.

Even Jodi leaned in as they circled the dining table.

Adam traced the line from James Jr. with his finger, following it upward.

"What do we know about great-grandpa John?" he asked.

"He died in the mid-nineties." Tilla took a breath. "Your dad loved him. Like Jimmy, they were close. He doted on the boys. He built that house up, settled that land. He inherited it from your great-great-grandparents. It was supposed to be a farm, before the Dust Bowl came."

"It killed the farm, didn't it?" Adam asked.

"It killed *everything*," Tilla said. "Our grandparents were kids then. A lot of people headed for California. Lots of my family did. You boys still have cousins out there, and in Oregon."

Every kid in Oklahoma learned about the Dust Bowl, the terrible drought, an environmental catastrophe that turned the Great Plains from prairie to dry, dead land. Massive dust storms had choked out what life remained.

Tilla ran a hand over the family tree, like she was smoothing the page, not that it was wrinkled.

"But the Binders stayed," she said. "John didn't want to give up the land. It was worthless then. Probably still is."

"Yeah," Adam said distantly. "It's not much to look at. Just snakes and grass."

"Adam, do you think it's him?" Bobby asked, face going pale. "Our great-grandfather?"

Adam swallowed. He took another sip of the iced tea his mom had made. It was sweet. A full pitcher in the old brown Tupperware she'd had his entire life. Five bags of Lipton, two cups of sugar. Ice.

Adam could have made it in his sleep. He took a long breath, another sip. He knew he had to say it, the thing that he'd put together during the attack.

"Yes. I think he's been farming his family, using his descendants to keep himself alive. I think he killed Jimmy because he had no reason to let him live."

"Why?" Tilla asked.

"Jimmy was gay. He wasn't going to perpetuate the bloodline."

"So my birthright . . ." Jodi said, horror creeping into her voice.

Adam nodded. "Is to provide him with more Binders."

"You said his family," Bobby said, voice low. "Not *our* family."

"Both times I've faced him, he hasn't recognized me," Adam said. He fixed his eyes on Tilla. "He keeps saying them, not you, not me."

"What are you saying, Adam?" Bobby asked.

Adam swallowed hard and looked his mother in the eye.

"Am I a Binder, Mom?"

25

VIC

"You don't want to stay for the coronation?" Argent teased, a bit of her usual spirit showing through.

Vic scoffed. "Do you?"

She shook her head a little, but said, "My place is here."

"Will you have a funeral first?" Vic asked.

"I don't think so." Argent reached out and traced a circle on the stone bench with a finger. "Death is so rare among our kind. And Father—well it will take us a while to imagine a world without him in it."

Vic wondered what a while meant to them. Decades? Centuries?

"I'm sorry," Vic said.

He'd lost his own father, and some days it still hit him hard, out of nowhere, like a truck. He didn't know how to comfort someone whose father was never meant to die.

"It had to happen," she said, reading his expression. "I know you don't understand, but it is the law. Silver was in his rights. He didn't do anything illegal."

"I understand," Vic said. "But illegal and wrong aren't the same. He could have found another way."

"You act like he hadn't tried for decades, for a century," she said. "Silver was out of time. Humanity was out of time."

Vic didn't like it. He would never like it, but Silver's father had forced him to it, into stopping him. Still, Vic ground his teeth that he'd been used, that his gun had been used.

And then there was the other thing.

Because if lawful and legal were sometimes wrong, then illegal sometimes had to be right.

Vic remembered what Death had said about old tools.

But who made the call? Who decided when someone had outlived their usefulness?

Death apparently. She made the decision when your time was up.

Vic had been given no say about what had happened with Mercy. Neither had Adam, in the end. She'd pushed him to it, left him no choice. He'd been the gun, the tool.

Vic felt sick again.

If that's what being a Reaper meant, then he wanted no part of it.

He could leave all of this behind, the magic clothes, the floating cities. They were fantastic, but if the price was condoning murder, then Vic could give it up, couldn't he?

But what about Adam?

Just trying to sort out his feelings was a ball of sharp bits in his chest.

Yeah, it was definitely time to go.

He'd already decided to go home, felt like that was the right decision. Nothing hurt more than sitting on the fence, and it was time to make a choice.

"I'm ready," he said to Argent. "Please."

She held out her hands. Vic took them and they spun.

It felt like one of those games he'd played as a kid, turning and turning until you fell down, dizzy and on the edge of puking.

Then Argent let him go.

Vic was back outside his apartment, his clothes as they'd been when he'd left, his bag beside him on the ground. He checked and yes, his gun and baton were in his pockets.

"Road trip over," he muttered.

His only souvenir was the sunglasses Argent had given him. Vic pocketed them carefully, a little surprised she hadn't taken them back.

It was night. The streetlamps were on. The Denver air felt a little colder, a little more on the edge of winter. Summer was definitely winding down.

Vic's heart lay heavy in his chest.

Adam was back there, in Guthrie, dealing with whatever shit he was dealing with. Another monster. Someone else to be put down.

Vic could go upstairs. He could shower, sleep, and go to work tomorrow.

He climbed into his car instead, tossed his bag in the back seat, and drove west down Colfax.

His mom's house wasn't far. Vic hadn't been home that much before he'd been shot. He'd enjoyed moving out, being on his own.

Jesse still lived at home, probably would until he got married. If he ever got married. Vic was too nice to call his brother a mama's boy. That and Jesse still had quite a lot of muscle on him.

His mother was at the dining room table when Vic got there. Jesse was out, but Vic got an enthusiastic greeting from Chaos, Jesse's pit bull.

"Shh, girl," Vic said, scratching her between the eyes.

"Vicente," Maria said, looking up from her cup of evening tea.

She'd been getting herbal lately, developing a fondness for floral teas and scented candles. She had a little tray with a pot of hot water and a selection of mugs and packets full of tea bags.

A vase of the black roses from the backyard sat on the table. They'd bloomed that way when Vic had become a Reaper. Adam had called them a portent. Vic didn't know if they'd ever change back. His mother kept them quiet, not wanting to call attention to Adam and the way he'd saved Vic. She considered it a miracle, a blessing, but knew other people might not think so.

The dining room, with its purple wall full of photos and the low hanging fixture over the table casting a sunny glow said home to him. It said family, and Vic realized why he'd come here. He needed a bit of that at the moment. He needed his mom.

"I thought you were with Adam," Maria said, nodding for him to take a seat. "Jesse said you went to Oklahoma."

"I did," he said, pulling out a chair. "But I came back early."

"You fought?" she asked.

"Yeah, sort of," he said. "How did you know?"

"Your face," she said with a smile. She gestured to the tray. "Have some tea."

Vic did not argue. He took a mug, chose a bag of English Breakfast, kind of wishing it was coffee. He'd been drinking a lot more coffee since he'd met Adam. The guy had a serious addiction.

"Tell me about it," his mother said. "If you want, if it will help."

"I'm not sure it will," Vic said with a shrug. He shook his head. "And I never thought I'd be talking to you about boy trouble."

"Never?" she asked.

"It's still kind of new to me," Vic admitted. "You know, liking men and women."

"I did wonder sometimes," she said. "None of those girls ever stuck. They never seemed right for you. And I like Adam. I like the way you brighten when you're talking about him."

"How about Dad?" Vic asked. "Do you think he would have understood?"

"I don't know, Vicente. Your father could be very traditional, you know that. He wanted what was best for you boys, but he had his own ideas about what that meant. If he knew or had any thoughts about it, he never mentioned it to me."

Vic looked at the picture of his graduation from the academy. He stood between his parents, dressed in his uniform. His dad had been proud of him. He beamed as much as Maria.

He missed his dad so intensely that his heart seemed to pause. He'd seen Adam put a fist to his chest sometimes, rub it. Vic did that now.

If only he could talk to Eduardo. Vic loved his mother, deeply, but right then he missed his dad so much that it ached.

"Did you and Adam fight about this?" she asked. "About you being bi?"

"No," Vic said. "He kept something from me, and it's a pretty big deal."

"But he told you?" she said, taking a slow sip from her mug.

"When he had to," Vic said. "Otherwise he wasn't going to."

Maria pursed her lips.

"You love him." It wasn't a question.

"Yeah," Vic said, and it hurt like a kick in his chest because he hadn't said it out loud before, not even to Adam, too scared that Adam would think it was just the magic and run away like his hair was on fire. "I really do."

"Then you forgive him. You let him know he messed up. You give him another chance." Maria held up a single finger. "One more chance. And you forgive him."

"It's not that easy, Mom."

"I know," she said, her voice firm but a little sad. She stared into her tea for a moment, then as calmly as if she'd been imparting one of her bits of historical trivia she added, "Eduardo cheated on me once."

"Papa?" Vic asked.

"Maybe more than once," she said with a shrug. "I only knew about the one. I only wanted to know about the one."

"What?" Vic asked, still stunned. He knew he sounded like an idiot, but he didn't know what else to say.

"It was before we were married. He was young. We were young. He used to like to go out dancing. Sometimes I'd go with him. Did you know that?"

"I didn't," Vic said, trying to imagine his mother the professor at a nightclub.

"He went home with some girl. I don't even remember her name. How funny is that?" Maria laughed. "But word got out. And I was done with him."

"But you still married him?" Vic asked.

Her smile became sly. "Eventually. But I wish I'd forgiven him sooner. That old saying about carrying anger is true. It just burns you, not the person you resent."

"So what, just forgive him?" Vic asked. "Forget it?"

"*Forgive* him," she said. "No matter what, because that's what's best for you. Don't let it make you angry and bitter, Vicente. Anger is a slow poison."

"Carry water in your bucket," he said, quoting something his father used to tell him and Jesse when they were fighting. "Throw out that gasoline."

"Exactly," Maria said. "But you don't forget. Don't resent them, but don't be a doormat either."

"I can't imagine you had any trouble with that," Vic said.

His mother was smart, strong. She was warm, but she didn't take any crap.

"It can be harder than you think," she said. "I loved your

father. I love you boys. Sometimes the hardest thing is watching someone you love make a mistake that you know is going to hurt them, but you can't tell them. They have to learn for themselves."

Vic knew the look she gave him or Jesse in those moments. It said, *Go ahead. I'll get the bandages and peroxide.* He just hadn't realized she'd ever used it on Eduardo.

"Do you want to stay for dinner?" she asked, nudging him out of his thoughts.

"Please," he said. "But I still don't know what to do about Adam."

"Can you let him go?" she asked, pushing back her chair to stand. She gestured toward the kitchen.

"I don't know."

"I couldn't let your father go," she said. "I wanted to. I'm glad I didn't. I'm glad we had everything we did, especially you boys, right up to the end."

Maria stood on her toes to peer into the cupboards. She was shorter than Vic. He had her slender frame but had gotten Eduardo's height. Jesse was the opposite, shorter, but broader-shouldered.

"I don't know what I have in here," she said. "Jesse would live on pizza if I let him."

"Let me," Vic said, smiling, knowing that her invitation had been a lure, hoping he'd cook for her. He was happy to fall for it.

His mother never had been a great cook. Eduardo had been the one to make them enchiladas and sofrito. Maria's time in grad school, getting her doctorate, meant Vic had cooked for him and Jesse when Dad was working, then later, when Dad had been too sick.

They didn't talk about it much. The cancer.

"Got it," Vic said, finding a can of black beans. "Ten-minute tacos."

"If you insist," she said, smiling.

She watched him stir in garlic and onions.

"Have you cooked for Adam yet?"

"No," he said.

"You should. That boy is too skinny."

"Mom . . ."

"I know." She held up her hands. "I can't tell you what to do, but I do like him. He didn't cheat on you did he?"

"No," Vic said. "And I like him too."

There was a bag of cabbage that would make a topping and give the cooked beans a little crunch. The corn tortillas in their bag were still good but they'd go stale soon. It was good Vic was using them.

They ate in silence. Maria sipping her tea and cleaning her plate.

Vic wolfed his food down. He'd forgotten how much he needed to eat. Tilla's fried potatoes had worn off a while ago. Now Vic needed a shower, then sleep. He hoped it would calm the churn of feelings mixing in his guts.

"He's a good boy, Adam," Maria said, taking the plates to the sink. "He doesn't know it, but he is."

"I don't think he's ever had the chance to see it," Vic said.

She opened her mouth to say something and closed it. She was trying not to push, to let him sort it out. And there it was, that expression that said she'd be there if he needed her, ready with tea or first aid.

Vic leaned to kiss her on the cheek.

"Goodnight, Mama," he said.

Vic drove home, not smiling, but eased a bit.

He got his mail from the box and walked upstairs.

His apartment had that weird feeling when no one had been home for a few days. It was small, but he could imagine sharing it with someone. He imagined coming home to find Adam here, home from the garage. Vic could cook. It was a domestic picture he wasn't uncomfortable with.

"Dammit, Adam," he said aloud. He seemed to be saying that a lot lately.

"Mrow?" something said.

Vic blinked. A black cat was curled up on the couch.

"Spider?" Vic asked, knowing it couldn't be any other cat. "That's your name, right?"

The cat sprang off the couch and began rubbing against Vic's ankles.

"Why aren't you with Adam?" Vic asked.

"Who's Adam?" someone else said.

The mail fell out of Vic's hands.

"Papa?"

26

ADAM

Adam, Bobby, and Jodi were quiet as they stared at Tilla, waiting for her to speak. She trembled a bit.

Adam thought she might retreat to her bedroom to read her Bible and pray like she had whenever he and Bobby tested her patience, but she froze, cocked her head, considering.

"Your dad was your dad," she said, looking insulted. "I would know if he wasn't."

"The druid doesn't see me as a Binder," Adam said.

"Maybe he's wrong," Bobby said, moving closer, always ready to break up a fight. "Maybe it's something else."

"Yeah, probably," Adam conceded.

He rubbed his heart.

Maybe it was the warlock wound. Maybe he'd changed himself so much that he wasn't like the rest of them anymore, not even in his blood.

That wouldn't be so different. He'd never felt like he fit with his mother and brother.

Adam had to admit that there was a part of him who'd hoped he wasn't Robert Binder's son, and he realized he was mourning that, the chance for an explanation, a reason why his dad had treated Adam the way he had.

He could remember the slaps, his head rocking back. Thinking about the hatred, like hot knives digging into his chest, Adam almost reached, almost touched his own cheek out of memory.

"I'm sorry, Mom," he said. "I just don't understand what's going on."

"You are my son, Adam," she said in the tone she used when a decision was final. "And your dad was your dad."

"Okay," he said, accepting it.

"We have to tell the sheriff what we found," Bobby said.

"What about the druid?" Jodi asked. "What if he kills the cops?"

"I don't think they'll matter to him," Adam said. "He doesn't want just anyone. He wants you two."

"To eat us," Bobby said.

"Yeah," Adam said.

"But why?" Jodi asked.

"To live longer," Adam said, realizing it had to be true. "If it's great-grandpa John he's pushing a hundred, but he has way more life than somebody that old."

"You think he started with Jimmy?" Tilla asked.

"Yes," Adam said. "I think that's what Sue sensed, that John was grooming him. That's why they were so close. He wanted to keep an eye on Jimmy."

Adam looked back to the Bible.

"It says John died right after Jimmy vanished."

"So he faked his death, went underground," Bobby said.

"He went to work for Death," Adam said.

"How do we know for sure?" Jodi asked.

Tilla walked over to the phone on the wall. It was beige, with an extra-long cord, practically an antique. She dialed the sheriff's office.

"Yes," she said to whoever picked up. "I need to report a body, an old one."

"Will we be safe out there?" Bobby asked.

"We?" Adam asked.

"I'm not letting you go alone," Bobby said.

"I think so," Adam said. "The curse is broken, and the spell he was using on the snakes should be depleted. He had to build it up. If he's going to use it again, it will take him a while."

"What if he shows up?" Jodi asked.

"I'll try to get the sheriff out of there," Adam said.

Still, he wasn't sure how he could help. He was still weak, exhausted from his trick with the snakes.

"If you're coming," he said to Bobby, "do you mind driving?"

"All right, but we're taking my car."

Adam didn't mind. He loved the Cutlass but could admit that the passenger seats in Bobby's white box were more comfortable.

He lay the seat back and dozed, his hands folded atop his belly. He felt empty, kind of bloodless, despite Vran's pool and the magic it had fed him.

Adam hoped the druid didn't show. He wouldn't be up for any more duels for a while.

"You know, I've never seen you in action," Bobby said. "You held back all those snakes. Then you saved us."

Adam cracked his eyes open. He wasn't up for hero worship. He'd had too much of that from Vic.

"It's the job," Adam said.

"Would it still be the job if you went to work for the elves?"

"I don't know," Adam said. "I'll ask them when they're done saving the world."

"Early brought deputies," Bobby said, slowing the car. "Good that he's got some backup."

Adam righted his seat to see them.

"It won't help, not unless they also brought a bazooka," Adam said.

"Should we get a bazooka?" Bobby asked.

"Maybe," Adam said.

The cops stood on the road, waiting for the Binders to park and approach. At least the sun was high. Adam would not have wanted to come here or do this by night.

The brothers climbed out. Bobby's car wasn't so white anymore. Oklahoma's red clay and mud had stained its side panels and bumpers, making it look like it had been dipped in old blood.

"What brought you out here?" Early asked them.

"It was our conversation at the library," Adam said, glad he was able to tell the truth. "I talked to Mom and she mentioned that the family still owned the land, so we came to have a look."

"Strange that no one found him before," Early said.

He wasn't wearing his sunglasses this time, and his blue eyes narrowed.

"It was something she said about our great-grandpa, John," Bobby said, shuffling a little. "That he doted on Jimmy, and that Sue disapproved."

"You think John killed him?" Early asked.

"If that's Jimmy in the well," Adam said, "then yes, yes I do."

"Let's go have a look," Early said. "What made you peek in there?"

"Just wanted to see," Adam said. "It's a creepy old house. You never know what you'll find."

"Guess you found it," Early said with a shake of his head. "I've called the forensics team in Oklahoma City. They should be out tomorrow."

"You don't have anyone here?" Bobby asked.

Early laughed. "You watch too much TV."

A truck came up the road, kicking up bits of mud and gravel.

"Tommy," Adam said.

A wave of despair wafted from their cousin as he leaped out of the truck. He looked haggard, wild-haired, and rumpled like he hadn't slept.

Adam took a deep breath and called up his defenses, putting a wall between him and Tommy's live wire of feelings.

"You called, Sheriff?" Tommy demanded. "What's this about a body?"

"They think it's Jimmy," Early said, nodding to Adam and Bobby.

"I'm sorry, Tommy," Adam said, hanging his head. "We just came out to look at the place, see some family history. Then we took the cap off the well . . ."

Tommy started in that direction but Early held up a hand, holding him back.

"*If* it's a body," Early said, nodding in that direction, "we don't know who it is yet."

"But it could be him?" Tommy asked, voice torn. "It could be Jimmy?"

Adam's wards were still tattered, his magic too thin. A thread of hope, the need to know, mixed with Tommy's despair.

Adam understood it. He'd felt it often, wondering if the druid was his missing father, hoping for answers.

He'd felt it just that day, hoping that Robert Senior hadn't been his father and had some reason for hating his youngest son.

Early looked to Bobby.

"We didn't see much, just a bundle in the right shape," Bobby said. "But it's been there a while, probably long enough."

"It's like we're cursed," Tommy said.

Adam could not help but nod along. It was exactly like that, and if he was right, if it was his great-grandfather who was preying on his descendants, then Tommy had every reason to feel that way. Adam wondered about Tommy, his wife, and his girls. John had left them alone so far, likely so they'd keep the line going.

Red and black surged in Adam's chest. He scanned the grass for more snakes, trying to scan for more spells, more traps.

He'd wanted to know so badly if the druid was Jimmy. He'd rushed out here with Bobby. He shouldn't have. The druid was after them. The druid was *hunting* them.

Adam had done it again. He'd gotten cocky, and now he'd put all of them, including Early and his deputies, in danger.

"What do you know about your grandfather's relationship to Jimmy?" Early asked Tommy.

"Grandpa John?"

"Yeah," Early asked. "He died back around ninety-eight didn't he?"

Tommy nodded.

"He loved Jimmy. Spoiled him, Mom always said so. Noreen hated him for that."

"She hate him for any other reason?" Early asked. "What about John?"

"What do you mean?" Tommy asked.

"Word is that Jimmy was . . ." Pausing, Early looked to Adam.

"Gay," Adam said.

"Well, yeah," Tommy said. "I mean, Jimmy was gentle. It was Dad who tried to make him different, make him play football, always taking him hunting and fishing."

"How do you think John would have taken the news?" Early said. "That Jimmy liked men?"

"I don't think he would have cared," Tommy said, hedging. "He was quiet. He liked to read. Jimmy did too. They had that in common. What are you thinking, Sheriff?"

"At the moment, I'm thinking Jimmy came out here and something happened." Pausing, he looked at his phone, scrolled through some notes or something. "And John buried him in the well."

"You think grandpa killed Jimmy because he was gay?"

"I don't know more than you do yet," Early said. "We've got human bones at Sue's trailer. We've got a body in the well out here. Something is going on with you Binders."

He looked between the three of them and Adam realized why Early hadn't talked to Tommy in private. He wanted to see their reactions, all of their reactions.

Early was good at his job, and good enough at reading people that he'd picked up on Adam flinching at his use of the word queer.

"If it was foul play," Early continued with a nod to the well, "then forensics should let us know."

"I don't know what to think," Tommy said. He deflated. "What to feel. It's been so long. It's been almost thirty years."

"I'm so sorry," Bobby said.

Adam knew Bobby was remembering the times he'd almost lost Adam, all the times their dad had nearly killed him—until Bobby had decided enough was enough.

Adam didn't know what to say to his cousin. Tommy was watching his family vanish, one by one. A year ago, Adam might have shrugged and said it wouldn't be so bad, but that wasn't true anymore.

He considered taking Tommy aside at some point, telling him the truth, but Adam had no idea if he'd listen or think them crazy.

All Adam was certain of was that he wanted to put a stop to this before Tommy lost anyone else.

"I need to know," Tommy said. "I've always needed to know what happened to him."

The deputies lifted the well cap. Early and Tommy peered inside.

Adam and Bobby held back, not needing another whiff of that stench, not needing to see it again.

Adam watched the grass. He reached out, feeling for trouble.

Are you there, John? he asked. *Is it you?*

But all he felt was Bobby watching him.

The deputies dropped the cap, startling Adam.

"It's a body all right," Early said. "And that makes this a crime scene. You can all go. We'll tape it off and wait for forensics. We won't have any answers today."

Adam nodded to Tommy, not wanting to touch him and absorb more of his despair. Bobby hugged their cousin before they all returned to their cars.

"I need gas," Bobby said. "Let's stop on our way back."

Adam nodded. He could use a cup of coffee.

He missed Sue's coffee. The way she'd make it in an ancient, crusty percolator that she refused to ever bleach out. He'd offered to clean it and she said she liked it that way, seasoned. He'd offered to buy her a newer pot, something that wasn't from the 1950s and she'd said she liked the one she had.

She'd been set in her ways.

Adam wondered for the hundredth time why she hadn't asked him to look for Jimmy. True, Sight was often blind when you were too close to the person you were trying to read. Jimmy had been her son, but Adam hadn't known him.

All those years. He'd been missing all those years. Maybe she'd already known.

Adam would never get the chance to ask her. Maybe there would be a point when her death, when missing her, wasn't like a boulder on his back, but he wasn't there yet.

Bobby pumped gas while Adam got coffee.

He picked up a package of donuts for their mom; the yellow ones with the waxy chocolate shell. She should have something sweet on hand in case Early dropped by.

"What do you think of Mom dating?" Adam asked when they were on their way again.

"Seriously?" Bobby asked.

"Seriously."

"I think it would be good for her. I don't think she's unhappy. She's smoking less, since Annie, but I think she was telling the truth when she said she gets lonely out here."

"Me too," Adam agreed.

He hadn't missed the hitch in Bobby's voice when he'd mentioned Annie.

"And I worry about her," Bobby continued. "If she got hurt, would an ambulance even find her?"

"Yeah," Adam said, squirming a little.

This was getting dangerously close to the conversations they'd had in Denver, when Bobby had tried to manage Adam's life.

"It's about what she wants though," Adam said.

"Yeah," Bobby agreed.

He imagined that even Bobby balked at trying to tell Tilla Mae how to spend her time.

He knew there would come a day when she wouldn't be able to manage on her own, but Tilla wasn't even fifty. They had time.

Adam imagined how it would have gone if Tommy or someone had tried to uproot Sue from her trailer.

She hadn't been that alone. She'd had neighbors, her clients. People had dropped by all the time.

Out here, in the grass and scrub oak, it was just Tilla Mae.

She met them at the gate, running toward it as they pulled up.

"What is it, Mom?" Adam asked, climbing out of the car.

"It's Jodi," she said. "She's gone."

27

ADAM

"This is bad," Adam said. "What is she thinking?"

"I don't know," Bobby said. "But I might panic too, knowing an evil druid who might be my ancestor wants to eat me."

Adam gaped at his brother.

"Great," he said. "*Now* you develop a sense of humor. Super helpful, Bobby Jack."

Bobby shrugged.

"Are *you* panicking?" Adam asked.

"No," Bobby said. "I think I'm still numb."

The trailer felt a little more alive since Adam had first come here. It smelled of cooking and showers, of people and living.

"How do we find her?" Bobby asked.

"I could try a spell," Adam said. "But I'd need hair or something. Fingernails or blood."

"Plenty of her hair in the shower drain," Tilla said. "But you take that stuff outside. I don't want it in my house."

"Yes, Mom," Adam said.

It hurt a little, that she still didn't accept all of him, all of what he'd been born, but he pushed it aside when she returned with a damp ball of hair.

Adam raided the kitchen for a pinch of salt and headed for the burn barrel.

Bobby watched Adam scoop up a little mud and mix it with the hair and salt.

"So this is magic?" Bobby asked.

"One kind of it," Adam said. "Sympathetic. You use a little of something to find or affect the rest of it. But keep quiet, okay? I'm not great at this kind of thing."

Bobby nodded.

Adam had thought over the last few days that he wasn't getting stronger, but something else.

Clearer, he decided. His Sight was getting clearer.

It might be the warlock wound, or it might just be that he'd started learning to use what he'd always had a bit better, like a singer who only had a few songs, but learned to sing those tunes really well.

It only reminded him how outmatched he was.

If the dark druid *was* their great-grandpa, and he was a warlock, then he'd had decades to build up his magical reserves, to make more charms from black dust and bog iron.

Adam focused, put thoughts of the threat aside. He had to find Jodi.

He poured his will into the little ball of mud he'd made, set it atop the trash in the burn barrel, and lit it with his cigarette lighter.

The smoke rose, a tendril of black. Adam reached out, cupped it in his hand.

Jodi, he silently called. *Where are you?*

Eyes closed, arms straight, Adam opened his palms to his sides. He spread his feet a little, made sure nothing was crossed, and kept reaching.

He followed the smoke. It tasted and felt like burgundy red and the smell of carnations. There. That was Jodi.

Adam chased it until something cold slithered against his senses. He felt the canes rise around him, their thorns stretching toward him. Retreating, Adam opened his eyes with a gasp.

"What is it?" Bobby demanded.

"The druid. He's watching. I think he sensed me, almost had me."

Adam felt around inside, trying to get an idea of how much energy he had. That was something else that had changed, and it worried him.

He'd always flown under the radar, been too low in wattage for things to see him, but the druid had his number now. Like Argent had said, Adam was known.

He couldn't hide anymore.

"I'll try again later," Adam said, breathing hard. "But I need to rest first. Not enough gas in the tank."

Sometimes he hated being this weak, this powerless.

"Is there anything I can do to help?" Bobby asked.

Adam shook his head, but he smiled.

"What?" Bobby asked.

"I just appreciate you asking, that's all." Adam started back toward the trailer.

"We could try to find her the old-fashioned way," Bobby suggested.

"That might work," Adam said. "It's how I did it before. But tomorrow, okay?"

His head was still spinning. He needed food and sleep.

"Of course," Bobby said.

They ate together, the three of them. Mom made mac and cheese with bits of boiled hot dog in it.

Adam didn't complain, though he had to admit that he hadn't

eaten it since he'd been a kid. Maybe Tilla was feeling nostalgic, having her sons home again. That or she was just using what groceries Bobby had picked up. Maybe Adam's big brother was the nostalgic one.

He took his plate to the sink, rinsed it, and set it down a bit clumsily. It didn't break. His mom had used melamine plates and bowls since she'd caught on to their dad's temper tantrums. Or maybe they were just cheaper. Maybe it was both.

Too many maybes. Too many questions.

"Go crash," Bobby said. "I'll clean up."

"Thank you," Adam said.

He stumbled into their room and with a bit of tired paranoia, checked that the tarot cards were still safe in the grate.

Binder blood. Binder magic, he thought, stretching out. *Shit. That might be the way.*

Sue had left Adam the cards, gifted them to him. They'd been passed down through the family, and a little of each practitioner clung to them.

Maybe Adam couldn't use them to find Jodi, but maybe he could use them to find John.

He needed to sleep. He ached, but the idea lingered like a broken tooth he couldn't stop prodding with his tongue.

————

Adam eyed the donuts he'd bought for Early as a breakfast option but let them be. Bobby had bought cereal, some store brand Os. Adam contented himself with that. Sue had kept milk around for Spider. He'd always come begging when Adam poured some in his coffee or oatmeal.

Adam checked the shadows, half expecting a needy purr.

They piled into Bobby's car.

"Where are we going?" Bobby asked.

"Somewhere we can find Internet," Adam said. "That's how I found her last time, looking at her accounts."

"You think she'd be dumb enough to post about all of this?" Bobby asked.

"Let's hope so," Adam said.

"I wish you'd stayed behind, Mom," Bobby said.

Adam watched Tilla scoff and narrow her eyes in the rearview mirror.

"Like hell," she said. "I need some air."

Bobby winced and Adam chuckled.

He'd never doubted that he got his stubbornness from her, just like he'd never doubted that she was his mother, unless he'd been switched at birth.

Adam still liked the idea that he might not be Robert Senior's son, but he knew it was the truth. It was one more thing for later, to be put aside until Adam could wrestle with it and come to terms with the hatred and anger he'd always felt from his dad.

"She just hiked to town?" Bobby wondered absently.

"It's how I got to Sue's after Liberty House," Adam said. "It's not hard. Still, Jodi probably had someone pick her up, probably that clown Billy."

"So where do we find *him*?" Bobby asked.

"We follow the terrible band he's a roadie for," Adam said. "I'll go to the library."

"Do you want to get some lunch, Mom?" Bobby asked.

She shrugged but nodded.

Adam liked that she didn't let Bobby push her around. At the same time, he wished they were both safe behind Silver's wards.

"Be careful," Adam said, climbing out of the car. "Both of you."

The library was always quiet, but today the place was empty.

The band didn't even have a website. Still, Billy couldn't dress like a clown all the time, could he?

Adam went back to Jodi's social media accounts, started looking at who she followed and who followed her.

He gave a little shudder with how easy it all was, the amount of photos and information people put online. Social media was social.

He hoped the druid wasn't web savvy. It wouldn't take much to hunt Jodi down. Then again, there were other Binders to prey on.

If the druid were their great-grandfather, killing Jodi next didn't make much sense. Adam pushed aside the ick factor and tried to think like a farmer or a rancher.

Tommy had his daughters. They'd have kids someday.

Bobby had been trying to have kids.

If the druid were smart, he'd pick off people like Noreen, Binders done having children or unlikely to. Jodi was young. She might settle down at some point.

Unless it was about more than the blood. Maybe there needed to be magic in there too.

But Noreen hadn't had any, so why kill her?

Unless, magic being life, everyone had a little. Noreen might not have been worth much, but the druid could have snacked, if not gotten a meal.

Had Jimmy had magic? Was he like Adam in other ways?

If so, it had been a long time between Jimmy and Sue.

Why kill Noreen? Why go after Jodi?

If it was John, and he was pushing one hundred, then maybe there were diminishing returns. Maybe the trick didn't work so well when he repeated it. Or maybe he'd killed them in different ways.

Sue and Noreen had been quick, in the trailer park and the hospital, places with people around. John had killed Jimmy out at the farm. He'd been able to take his time. Perhaps there was something about that.

Adam couldn't find any Billys linked to Jodi's profiles. No Bills, Wills, or Williams either.

At this point Adam's one lead was the body. He needed more information. He needed help.

Adam wiped his browsing history and closed the tabs.

He felt in way over his head. The last time he'd felt like this Mercy had outmaneuvered him and Vic had gotten shot, starting the whole thing between them.

It was time to stop making the same mistakes over and over.

Adam left the library and walked over to the police station. It was still afternoon.

"Is Sheriff Early in?" Adam asked the deputy at the desk.

She hadn't been one of the two out at the property. A Black woman in her thirties, she didn't smile at him but looked up with curious eyes.

"He's in his office," she said. "What do you want?"

Adam pitched his voice a little higher and tried to sound respectful.

"I'm Adam Binder, ma'am," he said. "I was hoping he might have heard something about the body we found at my family's farm."

"I'll see if he wants to talk to you," she said, walking back into the office behind her.

"He's here now?" Early sort of roared. "Get him in here."

The deputy appeared and waved Adam back.

He took a breath and headed in. Early sat in his desk chair, a little red-faced. The coffee mug on his desk was half empty.

"Have a seat, Adam," he growled.

Adam obeyed.

Early took a breath, let it out, and repeated it, clearly trying to calm himself

"We think it's Jimmy all right," he said. "No reason not to. His wallet with his driver's license was in his pocket. The body's the right height and size, and it's been in there long enough for it to have happened in 1992."

Early picked up his laptop and turned it around so Adam could see the screen.

"What we don't get is this stuff."

Adam flinched.

It was what he expected, but that didn't make it easier. They'd laid the body, Jimmy, on a plastic tarp. It contrasted with the dried, desiccated skin, the ruined clothes. His chest had been ripped open, brutally, as if by an ax.

"His heart is missing," Early said. "They stuffed him with mud and sticks."

Adam didn't move. He repressed the nod of understanding. The druid would have used clay to make a poppet, something to represent the heart. He'd switched them and stolen Jimmy's life.

There would be bog iron and obsidian dust in it. The sticks would be blackberry canes.

This was how it had been different. Giving Sue and Noreen heart attacks would have been too quick for John to fully power up. Plus, they were older. The ritual he'd used on Jimmy had taken a while, hours at least. Jimmy had been young, and sacrificing him had bought John twenty or thirty years.

Adam's stomach wrenched to think of his poor cousin, bound, waiting to die by the hand of the grandfather he'd loved and trusted.

"What sick shit is this, Adam?" Early demanded. "What is your damn family into?"

So it was back to grumpy cop.

"I'm not into anything. Like I said before, Sue read people's cards. She didn't do"—Adam waved a hand at the screen—"whatever this is. And I don't either. But I think someone out there really believes in it. Have you looked my cousin up online?"

"She was trying to get in on Sue's business, you know, pick up her clients," Early said. "Word is she was at a concert the other night where more of this crap went down."

He jabbed a finger at the screen.

"But she didn't do this. Neither of you were born when Jimmy died."

"No," Adam said. "No, we weren't."

Early's eyes narrowed.

"There weren't any defensive wounds. He was struck from behind by something hard."

Just like Dad, Adam thought.

He couldn't say that Robert Binder hadn't deserved it. Adam couldn't think that. That would make Bobby a murderer.

But Jimmy, by what little he knew, hadn't deserved the fate he'd met. Adam looked at the pictures again. No one deserved that.

"And the blow was solid," Early continued. "From someone taller than Jimmy. We can rule out your great-aunt."

"I think your theory is right," Adam said, being honest. "I think it was great-grandpa John."

"He had the chance," Early said. "He was living all alone out there by then. Add homophobia and you've got motive. But he's been dead for twenty years, and I still don't see any way that kind of hate gets you this."

Early nodded back toward the screen.

Adam had to step carefully here. This was why he'd come. He needed Early on Jodi's trail, but didn't want to get Bobby or his mom into trouble.

"I think Jodi thinks this stuff is real," Adam said. "I don't know if she learned it from her mom and she learned it from John, but the last time I saw her, she was talking about a birthright. I think she blew up the trailer."

"You didn't mention this the other night," Early said.

"I thought it was nonsense, you know?" Adam asked.

"Some of the people at that bar said they saw her and some guy."

"Who?" Adam asked, trying not to grip the chair arms.

"He was wearing clown makeup, part of a shitty band." Early shook his head. "They were all wearing clown makeup."

Adam tried to find a way to slip Billy's name in, to do it in a way that wouldn't tell Early he'd been there the night of the attack. Then again, Adam hadn't found anything on Billy. It might be of no use. He decided not to take the risk.

"We're going to find her," Early asked. "And we're going to find out what she knows."

"I hope you do," Adam said. "If I hear from her, I'll tell you."

That would blow up in his face. Early would find out that Jodi had spent some time at the trailer, but Adam didn't see a way out.

The jail was pretty secure, and even John, if that's who he was, probably couldn't take several bullets. Maybe Adam could get Silver to ward the place. Maybe, if they had Jodi in a secure spot, he could figure out a way to lay a trap.

It was time to get smart.

Adam had gotten lucky twice against the druid. His luck wasn't likely to hold a third time.

"You sure you don't have anything else to tell me?" Early asked, leaning forward.

"No," Adam said. "I don't know where she is. And I'm honestly worried about her."

Early nodded, thinking hard for a moment.

"You can go," he said, dismissing Adam and seeming to forget that Adam had been the one to visit him.

Outside, the day was sunny with only a little wind. Adam hadn't missed the constant rush in his ear. He'd missed the rain. It never rained in Denver. Here, in autumn, it rained all the time. It was almost Halloween.

They'd never gotten to trick or treat as kids. Tilla had taken them into town for Truck or Treat at her church, where people had decorated their tailgates, but Adam had always wondered what it would be like to have a house in the city, to give candy to little kids.

He'd hoped to spend it with Vic. He had notions of giving out candy at Bobby's house, maybe watching a horror movie.

Of course that was if Vic had the night off. Halloween had to be a big night for cops.

Adam shook his head. His dreams and the idea that he and Vic were possible were becoming more hazy, less real by the day.

He was so absorbed in the thought of it, the misery of it, that he stepped right into someone as he left the station.

"Sorry—" Adam's heart immediately ached as the man's grief slammed into him. Tommy.

His older cousin managed a wan smile.

"The sheriff asked me to come by," he said. "I guess it's about what they found?"

Adam nodded. He didn't want to speak, be the one to deliver confirmation. It was the coward's way. How did Bobby do this, tell patients bad news?

"It's okay, Adam," Tommy said, seeming to sense what he wasn't saying. His smile remained thin, but it stayed on his face. "After all this time it will just be good to know, to put him to rest, you know?"

Adam thought of his dad, of the bones Jodi had dug up, and the whole mess surrounding that. If Early found her first, the truth of his dad's death could get dragged into the light. Maybe it was time for that too. Maybe it was time for no more Binder family secrets.

Adam was ready to try it Vic's way.

"I do," Adam said. "I really do."

"Well, I'd best get to it," Tommy said, looking at the door Adam had just exited.

Adam nodded. He really didn't know what else to say. There wasn't a card for "sorry your whole side of the family is being killed off by a malevolent ancestor who might be your grandfather."

He walked for a bit, taking in the streets, the cars. Guthrie's history made it beautiful, but it was still a town with shops and noise. It was nothing like Denver, which dwarfed it. Some instinct was whispering, trying to tell him something, but it was too quiet, too vague for Adam to pull it into the light.

Turning the corner, he saw Bobby and Tilla.

Adam could understand them better now. They'd carried a secret together for so long, and they'd had to raise him, keep it from him.

"How did it go?" Bobby asked.

Adam shook his head. "Nothing on Jodi or Billy, but I saw Early. It's definitely Jimmy."

Tilla lowered his head, pursed her lips.

"Can we go by the cemetery?" Adam asked, getting an idea.

"Why?" Tilla asked.

"I want to see it," Adam said. "Something's bugging me but I can't figure out what."

They returned to Bobby's car and drove the short distance.

Adam had to admit that the fridge on wheels rode so much smoother than the Cutlass.

He needed to check the suspension, to get it back to Jesse's garage. How would it go with Jesse if Adam and Vic broke up?

For the first time, Adam had someone and someone else's people. It wasn't just Vic. There was Jesse, and Chaos—even Maria.

Vic's family was so different than his.

They climbed out of the car and Adam led them toward the graves.

It wasn't different from any of the Oklahoma cemeteries he'd visited, and he'd visited a lot of them. They were quiet, good meeting places for supernatural beings, and some had come up far too often in his search for the druid.

Cemeteries in Oklahoma were flat. They had few tombstones. Most of them required walking and reading the plaques set into the ground.

He'd always been a little disappointed by it, especially in his goth days. He'd wanted crypts and angelic statues, not simple markers of granite and bronze with just names, dates, and phrases. Now that he had a better idea of who and what Death really was, he wasn't so keen for a closer look.

"How did great-grandpa die?" Adam asked Tilla.

"Heart attack," Tilla said. "It was a surprise. He wasn't that old."

"It's why you should give up smoking, Mom," Bobby said.

Tilla rolled her eyes.

"He's not wrong, Mom," Adam said. "I want you around awhile."

For once she didn't have a retort. They reached Sue's grave. She lay beside James Senior, in a line of Binders born and married in, but the whole thing started with John and his wife, Evelyn.

John's epitaph read: BELOVED FATHER AND GRANDFATHER.

Sue's plot was still freshly churned. They hadn't been careful with the earth they'd disturbed and it splattered the bronze markers.

Adam knelt to get a better look. Sue's plaque was shiny, unlike the others, which could use a polish.

"We should have brought them flowers," Tilla said. She looked over at Sue's grave and cut her eyes to slits. "That Noreen took all of Sue's."

Adam shook his head. He didn't want to speak ill of Noreen. They hadn't buried her yet, and she had a spot here waiting for her.

He wondered who would make the arrangements. Probably Tommy. Adam couldn't imagine Jodi being up for it.

"What do you remember about John and Evelyn?" Adam asked, nodding to his mother to get her back on track.

"I never met her, but John was at our wedding. He had a bit of a German accent. The Binders are German."

"Your family too, right?" Adam asked.

"By way of Wales," she corrected. "I'm glad it takes a monster and a murder to get you interested."

"I'm sorry, Mom," Adam said, blushing, though by the look in her eye she wasn't too annoyed. "So Evelyn died and John stayed out at the farm?"

"It was always just switchgrass and rattlesnakes out there," Tilla said. "He took work as a carpenter. Built most of that house himself."

"It's solid, still standing," Bobby said. He looked at Adam. "Do you think we need to go back out there?"

"I don't know. I wish we could find Jodi. I'm worried about her," Adam said.

Tilla scoffed.

"I didn't say I like her, Mom," Adam said.

"Well, if you go, I'm going with you," Bobby said. "He almost had you last time."

"What are you going to do, lecture him?" Adam asked. "He killed Jimmy. He's going to kill Jodi. Maybe you too if he gets the chance."

"I'll borrow Mom's shotgun," Bobby said, and Adam had to concede that yep, they were both Tilla's sons.

Beloved Father and Grandfather.

More like beloved monster, Adam thought.

28

VIC

"Who are you?" Vic asked.

Spider stopped winding between Vic's feet and went to rub up against the ghost. Vic could see through him, but the cat rubbed up against him like he was solid.

"You know who I am," the ghost of Vic's father replied. He was still smiling, but he said it with some recrimination.

"But—how are you here?" Vic asked.

"This little guy," Eduardo said, bending to scratch the cat on his chin. "He came to get me, so I followed him."

"I don't understand," Vic said.

This wasn't his father at the end, when pancreatic cancer had demolished the strong, broad-shouldered man Vic had grown up with. He looked like Jesse, or Jesse looked like him. Eduardo was big, with thick black hair that Vic had inherited.

"How?" Vic stuttered.

His heart swelled, but he couldn't trust it. How did he trust something this impossible?

"Prove it," Vic said.

Eduardo grinned.

"Yes, it's 'wondrous strange,'" he said. "'But there are more things in heaven and earth, Horatio, than are dreamt of in your philosophy.'"

And that was all he had to say for Vic to know it was really him.

His father had always liked to charm Maria with snippets of Shakespeare. She'd dragged them all to Boulder for the festival there, to see a play every year in the little outdoor amphitheater.

Maria would be cranky that her boys were rowdy and that her husband had indulged them, but Eduardo would quote lines on the way home, proving he'd been paying attention to something that only his wife cared about.

Those plays had their share of ghosts and spirits. Once, during *King Lear*, it had even rained right when the storm scene started. The audience had crowded inside the university building until it passed.

"It's really you," Vic said. "Somehow it's really you."

The dam broke a bit and Vic felt his eyes start to shine.

"It is," Eduardo said. "I think you called me back, Vicente. I think I heard you call me. Then the cat showed up and I followed her."

"Him," Vic said absently. "His name is Spider."

"That is a strange name for a cat," Eduardo said affectionately, still scratching. "But I like it."

Vic felt around inside himself. He hadn't done this, had he? There was something there, like a pull on him, different than what he felt between him and Adam. It lived in his heart, close to the love he felt for his family and yes, for Adam. This then, might be magic.

"Thank you," Vic said to Spider. "For helping. I don't know how this happened, but thank you."

He got a raspy meow in response.

Vic didn't know what else to say. He leaped forward, tried to embrace his father, but Vic's arms passed right through Eduardo.

Vic's heart seized. He *needed* that embrace, hadn't known how much until he couldn't have it.

"Not tonight," Eduardo said, reading his expression.

Sinking a bit, Vic nodded and stepped back. He didn't know what was possible. He didn't know any of the damn rules.

"Not that I believed in any of this stuff before," Eduardo said, pondering his translucent hand and how the light from the window fell through it.

Vic laughed. His father had been irreligious at best, staying home when Maria took them to mass for tradition's sake.

"What is it like?" Vic asked.

"I can't tell you," Eduardo said, dark eyes pinching in thought.

Vic opened his mouth to protest, but Eduardo interrupted.

"Literally. I don't think it's bad, where I am," he said. "It's not the hot place, but being here, I can't remember it. I know you're here, that your mother and brother are here. I think—I think that I feel loved."

Vic choked on a sob.

"And you?" Eduardo asked. "Do you feel loved?"

"I do," Vic said.

"So there's a girl?" Eduardo asked.

Vic looked to the floor. He never thought he'd have this conversation. The chance of it was a miracle.

Eduardo had always told his sons to look people in the eye. Vic lifted his eyes to his father's, even if his face wouldn't quite follow them.

"There's a boy, Papa," Vic said. "A man."

"Oh." Eduardo's eyes grew round. He didn't look angry, just surprised. "That's who Adam is?"

"Yes," Vic said. "Is that okay?"

"Vicente," Eduardo said gently. "How could you ask me that? Did you think I would love you any less?"

"I don't know," Vic said. "I don't know what to think. Everything I know about being a man I learned from you."

"That is not true," Eduardo said. "And even if it was, you have to be your own man, your own kind of man."

Vic had thought he was more comfortable with all of this. He'd told Adam he was bi without hesitation. Then the uncertainty had crept in, following Vic's doubts about Adam and the trust between them.

Vic had needed his parents, both of them. Magic had let him talk to them, talk to his dad. A few hours ago he'd been in another world, ready to throw it all away, to restore some order.

But now this.

"I've been seeing things in black and white," Vic admitted. "I thought you would disapprove."

"I think you are loved, Vicente," Eduardo said. "And while I cannot hold you, I would. You are my son. Boyfriend, girlfriend, husband, wife—just be happy. Do good."

"You make it sound so easy," Vic said.

"It *is* that easy. When you mess up, do better. Learn. Love will hold you together if he's worth it. Is he worth it?"

"I think so," Vic said.

Eduardo nodded.

He turned to the window and cocked his head as if he could hear something Vic could not.

"I think I have to go, Son."

Vic swallowed. He could feel it, not the Other Side, but someplace. It was calling Eduardo back. There was a door that Vic had cracked open, even though he hadn't meant to.

Now it was closing.

He could fight it, maybe, but he got the strong sense that he really shouldn't try, that bad things would happen if it opened too wide.

"Why did you come?" Vic asked.

"I just followed the cat," Eduardo said with a smile. "But I think maybe you needed me to."

"I did," Vic said.

Whatever else magic and Adam's crazy world might bring, it had brought this, given Vic this chance, this impossible moment.

"I love you, Papa," Vic said. "I miss you every day."

"I love you too."

And he was gone.

Vic woke with a start. The sun was high. He'd slept the day away.

He remembered falling into bed, shedding his clothes. Rising up on his elbows, Vic saw no sign of Spider or his father, no indication that the visit had been anything more than a dream.

Lying back down, Vic studied the smooth plaster of the untextured ceiling.

He'd seen too much these last few months to dismiss the visit.

He may never know if it had been a dream or a delusion, but a weight lifted when he thought of Eduardo's smile.

"Thank you," Vic said to who or whatever had let him see his father.

Maybe it had been Death. Maybe it was a perk of his second job.

Vic's eyes shone. He'd been ready to walk away from magic, but now . . . now he needed to see Adam.

29

ADAM

A gunshot jerked Adam out of a deep sleep.

"—the hell?" Bobby asked from the bunk beneath him. Another shot. A third. A fourth.

Adam was on the floor, pulling on a shirt and his boots.

Tilla was in the living room, shotgun in hand.

"Bobby! Get your ass out here!" a voice shouted. "You too, Adam!"

"Jodi," Adam growled.

"Stay here, Ma," Adam said. "Call Early."

She nodded, but shook her head when she lifted the phone.

"It's dead," she said.

The brothers exchanged a glance. Adam didn't like that Jodi was smart enough to cut the line.

"What is she up to?" Bobby asked.

"Let's go see," he said.

He went first, hands raised, nudging the trailer door open with his foot and stepping onto the little wooden porch and steps.

Jodi was there. Billy stood beside her. At least Adam thought it was Billy. It was hard to tell without the makeup but the guy had the right build. And he had a pistol. Adam didn't know the make, but he'd shot out Bobby's tires and the Cutlass's.

His car. The fucker had shot his car.

Adam swallowed the anger building in his chest. He had to stay calm. The feelings rolling off of Jodi were volatile, a green-orange grease fire of frustration and panic lit by her terror.

"I'm taking Bobby," she spat. She looked wild-eyed, high again. She clearly hadn't slept. "And Billy will shoot you if you get any closer."

"Why do you want Bobby?" Adam asked.

"To make a trade," she said, like it was obvious, like Adam was the dumbest person in the world.

"He won't take Bobby," Adam said. "He doesn't have any magic. But I do. Take me instead."

"I would. I want to," Jodi spat. "It was supposed to be you, but he can't use you, and he won't show me how to do it if I don't give him someone he can use."

"You're talking to him," Adam said, cold certainty creeping up the back of his neck. "You've been talking to him the whole time."

"In my dreams," Jodi said. "He's always there, just as soon as I close my eyes."

"You summoned him," Adam said. "You let him in."

And now she couldn't kick him out.

"I just wanted my birthright," Jodi shrieked. "Not this . . . shit!"

She waved a hand to indicate the mud and the trailer and the life Adam's mother lived.

Adam got it. He really did. Bobby probably got it even more. After all, he'd done everything he could to run away. Adam heard the crunch of shoes on the gravel behind him as Bobby moved closer.

"He doesn't have any magic," Adam repeated. "John can't use him."

"Liar," Jodi spat. "You're a damn liar, Adam Lee."

She was shaking, and Adam was glad Billy was the one holding the gun.

His face was swollen, kind of puffy, maybe a reaction to the makeup, but he was clear-eyed. Adam doubted he could wrestle the pistol away from him.

"Jodi . . ." Adam started gently. "You don't have to do this."

"I don't have a choice," she said, eyes shining. "He's already taken Mom and Grandma Sue."

"What's he going to show you?" Bobby asked.

"The magic," Jodi said wistfully. "He'll teach me the magic."

"He kills people, Jodi," Adam said. "You said it yourself. He killed your mom. You want to be like that?"

"It's better than dying!"

She flushed with rage, the fire burning brighter. Adam could see it now. She'd been working up to it, talking herself into it for a while, probably the entire time she'd been with them.

She jabbed her finger at him, and he had no doubt that he'd be dead if she were holding the gun.

"It was supposed to be you," she repeated. "You are all so stupid. They thought she was cooking. Like she could cook drugs."

"So what was with the chemicals?" Adam asked.

Black mascara ran down Jodi's face.

"We were just keeping them for Billy!" Jodi said.

"Shut up, Jodi," Billy said, eyeing her.

"I thought I could keep him out. If I'd just known what to do," Jodi said.

"The charm," Adam said. "You thought he was our dad, and you thought you could use the bones to bind him."

She really had made it for protection. Only the bones had been Robert's, not John's. He'd tricked her and the charm, made with whatever recipe she'd looked up on the Internet, hadn't held him.

"It didn't work," Jodi sobbed. "Now she's dead."

She choked, caught between crying and her high.

Even Billy looked a little worried. Adam wondered if he'd been the one to suggest that he hold the gun. If so, then Billy wasn't completely stupid. Adam couldn't decide if that was good or bad for their chances of getting out of this alive.

"I'll give him Bobby and he'll teach me," Jodi said. "That's the deal."

"Bobby doesn't have any magic," Adam repeated the lie. "But you do. What's to stop John from taking you instead?"

"He won't do that," Jodi said. "He needs me. He doesn't understand stuff like the Internet. I'll help him hide."

"He'll kill you," Adam said calmly. "He killed Jimmy, and he *loved* Jimmy."

Adam wondered if that had been part of it, the love. Maybe it wasn't just the ritual. Maybe John truly had cared about his victim and that had made for a bigger sacrifice.

"He *needs* me," Jodi repeated.

"Not as much as you think," Adam said.

He almost pointed out that Tommy had three daughters but did not want to turn Jodi's attention to their younger cousins.

Jodi turned to Billy, quick as a snake, and demanded, "Shoot him, Billy. Shoot him now."

"I don't think that's a good idea," Billy said.

"Shoot him!" Jodi shrieked.

Bobby stepped in front of Adam.

"I'll go with you," he said. "Just leave Adam alone."

"Get in the van." Jodi nodded to the beater they'd come in.

It was covered in bumper stickers for the loser clowns and a bunch of other crappy acts.

Bobby gave Adam a weak smile, a last assurance, and obeyed.

Billy shot Adam a nervous glance and followed Jodi. He slammed the door behind Bobby.

Adam was very glad he didn't have the magic to make heads explode. Then again, maybe he wished he could. If so, Jodi and Billy would meet a messy end.

Tilla emerged from the trailer after the van had peeled away.

"Why didn't you shoot Billy?" Adam asked.

"Couldn't get an angle," she said with real frustration. "This thing sprays."

Adam had no doubt that his mother knew her gun.

"I should have shot her when you first brought her out here," Tilla said.

Adam had to agree. His mother's homicidal tendencies might have been useful for once.

He couldn't feel his brother. Adam didn't have the same kind of link like he had with Vic.

"Where are they going?" Tilla asked.

"The homestead," Adam said, eyeing the Cutlass's sunken tires.

"How do you know?"

Honestly it was as much a guess as his Sight, but what Adam said was, "It's where it all started. It's where it's got to end."

"What do we do now?" his mother asked.

"We have to find them. Can you head to the neighbor's? Use their phone to call Early. I'll try to change some tires."

Adam went to check but it took a glance to see that the tires on the Cutlass and the spare on Bobby's refrigerator weren't the same size. He couldn't switch them out to get a working car.

The tires on Dad's old ATV were long flat too, not that it would have been fast enough to catch up in time.

He turned to follow Tilla to the neighbors. Maybe he could borrow their truck.

A car came down the road.

Adam knew, could already feel it.

"Vic," he said.

30

VIC

He'd felt the panic before he'd even turned onto the washboard road leading to Tilla's trailer. It was a steady thrum in his heart, leading him to Adam.

Vic pulled through the open gate and leaped out.

"What's wrong?" he asked.

"I'll explain on the way. Let me drive," Adam said, scooping up a shotgun. "I know where we're going."

They passed each other at the hood.

Vic grabbed Adam by the jacket and kissed him quickly. It wasn't much, but it was enough. The connection between them surged.

"All good?" Vic asked.

"All good," Adam said with a ragged breath and a nod.

"Call 911 as soon as you have service," he said. "Get a hold of the sheriff."

Vic had imagined a very different reunion, but there wasn't time for more.

He could feel it, the deep, full body churn of Adam's worry. He was nearly in a panic, and Adam never panicked.

Vic hurried to the passenger side.

Adam tossed the shotgun into the backseat a little too casually for Vic's comfort and climbed in.

"I thought you hated guns," Vic said.

"I do," Adam admitted, squirming. "It's my mom's."

"All right," Vic said, knowing the situation had to be bad for Adam to bring it along.

"You went back to Denver first?" Adam asked.

"Yeah," Vic said.

"What changed?" Adam asked, putting the car into reverse.

He was obviously in a hurry, but he didn't peel out. Vic spied the flat tires of the other cars and saw why.

"I did," Vic said. "Or at least, how I saw things did. We still need to talk, but first, you want to tell me where the fire is?"

"Jodi kidnapped Bobby so she can give him to the druid, to trade her life for his."

"Shit," Vic said, looking at his phone. He didn't have a signal. No service yet. "Are you okay? Maybe I should have driven."

"I'm fine," Adam said. "But she's got that Billy guy with her, the clown, and he's got a gun."

"He's the one who shot your car?" Vic asked.

"Twice," Adam said, swallowing hard. "He fired four times total. I don't know how many more bullets he has."

"What kind of gun?" Vic asked.

"I don't know," Adam admitted with a grimace. "The kind with a clip?"

Vic let out a long breath.

"When this is done, you're getting some basic firearm training," he said. "Some safety first and then I'll take you to the range."

Adam opened his mouth to say something, probably to protest or remind Vic how his father had forced all that on him at five, but then he closed it again.

"What?" Vic asked.

"So there's a later?" Adam kept his eyes on the road, like he couldn't bear to look at Vic in that moment. "You want a later, when this is done?"

"The kiss didn't tell you that?" Vic asked. "Man, I'm losing my touch."

Adam chuckled.

"Yes," Vic said. "There will be a later. There will be a lot of later, but you come clean with me and you don't keep things from me. All right?"

"Okay," Adam agreed, hands clenched to the wheel.

Vic checked his phone again. "Still no service."

"I'm not sure we'll get any," Adam said.

"So where are we going?" Vic asked.

"The old family homestead," Adam said. "It's the best place for Jodi to try and summon the druid and for him to do what he wants to do to Bobby."

"And that is?"

"Cut out his heart. Replace it with a ball of mud and nasty to consume his life and live longer."

Vic sputtered, almost wishing he didn't know.

"The worst part is that he's my great-grandpa," Adam added.

"Your family reunions really suck," Vic said.

"Yeah, they do."

"What is she even thinking, trying to reason with him?" Vic asked.

"She's pretty high," Adam said. "And scared, terrified even. I should have picked up on it, that she'd do this."

Vic scoffed.

"What?" Adam demanded.

"She kidnapped your brother and you're still trying to understand her," Vic said. Despite the situation, he couldn't help a little smile. "Argent's right about you, Adam. You're unique."

"What's that supposed to mean?" Adam asked, eyes narrowing.

He'd taken it as an insult, and how could he not? He'd been different his entire life and he'd been told it was a flaw by almost everyone he'd met.

"It means I drove all night to tell you that I love you to your face," Vic said. "Because you're you, because you're unique."

Adam took another turn onto yet another dirt road. Vic had no idea how he kept it straight. Mud and grass ran in every direction.

Vic could feel Adam making a choice. He could turn and run, or not. Vic felt the decision, felt Adam finally stop running. Like something shy, peeking its head out of its burrow despite the danger, he said, "I love you too."

They drove on for a moment, the tension still high, but not between them.

"Nice save by the way," Adam said. "But your timing sucks."

"Hey, if we're going into battle again, I'd like to have it in the open. No more secrets."

"No more secrets," Adam agreed.

Vic wanted to suggest therapy. Adam could use it, considering everything he'd been through, but it would be a touchy subject. It would have to wait. There was another topic that wouldn't.

"Speaking of later," Vic said. "You have to teach me. I need to know, to understand about this stuff."

"All right," Adam said, nodding. "But yeah, later. We're here."

He pulled to a stop.

"Should we wait for the sheriff?" Vic asked, unbuckling his seat belt because he could already guess the answer.

"No," Adam said, hefting Tilla's shotgun. "He won't be able to help with the druid."

"Will that?" Vic asked.

"It's worth trying," Adam said. "And it won't do Billy or Jodi any favors."

Vic had his gun and his baton.

"Let's try not to kill anyone," Vic said. "Only shoot if you have to."

"Okay," Adam said.

"But Adam, if you do have to shoot, don't hesitate."

Adam nodded. Vic could feel the worry take a new direction. Adam hated guns. He hated the idea of killing someone.

"Try to leave it to me," Vic said.

It wasn't much but it was the most Vic could give him in the moment.

With a nod to each other, they started for the house.

Vic could feel Adam's focus, but the worry was still at high tide.

His feelings for his brother were complicated, but Adam loved Bobby. Vic would be packing too if it were Jesse in that house.

He nearly gagged on the scent of rotten fruit. Vic realized he wasn't tasting it. Adam was.

"What is that?" he asked.

"That's him," Adam said. "He's in the barn."

It stood half-collapsed, cast in shadow, Vic could just make out some shapes inside.

Something sour and gut-churning came through their connection as Adam used his senses to feel out what lay ahead.

Vic could feel Adam's fear, and it became a ball of lead in his own guts. They were in sync. In other circumstances it could have been amazing, but for now it almost hurt to feel Adam's worry about his brother.

They raised their guns at the same time and ran for the barn.

Bobby lay sprawled inside, unconscious but breathing.

Sunlight fell in beams, filtered by the holes in the roof and the dust Jodi and the others had kicked up.

Jodi and some guy, no doubt the clown, loomed over Bobby.

Bobby! Adam thought.

He's alive, Vic thought through their connection. *Probably pistol-whipped, but alive.*

The clown had the pistol. His hands were shaking.

"Drop it," Vic said, pointing his gun. "Right now."

Adam cocked the shotgun.

"I'm not messing around, Billy," he said and Vic believed it.

So did Billy. He dropped the pistol. It fell to the dry wooden floor.

"Kick it over," Adam said.

It slid. There was blood on the pommel.

"He's not dead," Billy said. "I just hit him."

Adam lifted the shotgun, aimed.

Don't do it, Vic thought.

I won't, even though I really want to. Adam thought back. *I'm not my dad.*

Vic picked up the gun and removed the clip.

Jodi glared, wild-eyed, and probably as high as Adam had guessed. She didn't look cowed.

"He wouldn't shut up . . ." Billy stammered. "She made me."

"You are worthless, Billy," Jodi said. "But it doesn't matter. He's coming, Adam. You have to feel it. You can't stop him. Guns can't stop him."

Behind her, in the larger darkness, a form took shape. Vic narrowed his eyes. He could see the cold and smoke that circled around the figure, the druid.

Vic could feel the magic, but the sense wasn't coming from Adam. The Reaper in him was waking. Maybe, just maybe, they had this.

"You can come out, John," Adam called, turning the shotgun in that direction. "I know it's you."

The druid stepped into the light; a skull cupped in his right palm. He clutched a rusty sickle with his left hand. His ragged clothes and the leather belts completed the horror movie look. White-haired and haggard, he looked like all the years had chewed at him, like the grit and constant wind had worn him down.

"That's what you want?" Adam asked Jodi. "To be like him?"

Vic crouched and felt for Bobby's pulse. He was out, probably concussed. Vic didn't know whether to hope the sheriff got there soon or not.

Adam stepped forward, shielding Bobby. A shotgun blast at this range would be messy.

A wave of cold like a snow cloud rose from behind them.

Sounds filled the grass. Vic hadn't grown up here, but he knew the rattle. Snakes surged forward, a swarm, to block their retreat.

Adam eyed them but didn't turn away from the threat.

"You want a Binder, great-grandpa?" he asked, fixing his aim. "Take Jodi's heart."

"You don't mean that," John said. "You're too soft. I see you, boy."

"You mean like Jimmy was?" Adam asked.

"Exactly like Jimmy was."

And there was something in his eyes, something that surprised Vic. John was sad about Jimmy, truly sad about what he'd done, but here he was, ready to do it all over again.

John was right though. Adam wasn't a killer.

He didn't have it in him. If Robert Senior had lived, he'd have terrorized his wife and sons, gone on terrorizing them, probably for years, if he hadn't killed them first.

Adam would never have been able to do what Bobby had.

"Why the note?" Adam asked. "In Denver. Why did you leave me a note with the recipe?"

"Bait," John said. "To lure you back to Sue, so I could take you and it worked. Only you turned yourself into a warlock, didn't use it to make yourself stronger."

"So you killed her?" Adam asked quietly.

"Yes. She was in my way, thought she could protect you, keep you from me, like I haven't watched you your entire life. You were finally ripe, and then you had to do what you did."

Vic could feel the blow Adam took at John's answer. The gun shook in his hand.

So much for love and remorse. This man wasn't worth anyone's mercy.

Adam narrowed his eyes, and Vic thought for a moment that maybe he'd been wrong, that Adam was his father's son after all. Then Adam did what Vic wasn't certain he could have. He set aside the bubbling rage before it boiled over.

Any other time, Vic would have smiled.

Adam had so much practice putting aside other people's feelings. His own weren't much harder.

"You're running out of time, boy," John said, nodding to the snakes.

They'd swarmed closer.

"I can't use you, but your brother and cousin should be enough for now."

Jodi's eyes went wide. She looked like she might bolt.

Billy did. He turned and ran.

The snakes didn't rush him. Vic thought that maybe, just maybe, John might let him go.

Then Billy screamed as roots shot from the ground, spearing his legs. Billy dropped to all fours. Wide-eyed, crying in pain, he opened his mouth to scream again and another root shot through it, bursting from the back of his head in a bloom of blood. He slumped to the ground, gagging on the wood and dirt as the snakes swarmed closer to the barn.

Jodi pressed her hands over her mouth, stifling a scream.

"None of you are getting out of here," John said.

The barn exploded, the wood coming to life with more spikes and thorny canes. Vic was thrown off his feet. He rolled, landing near Bobby.

The shotgun went off, but Adam's aim went wide as he lost his footing.

Roots squirmed, binding hands and feet, tying all of them too tightly for Vic to rip free. He got his hand loose, tried to reach for his baton, but the thorny canes bound him tighter.

He could feel Adam straining, trying to break the spell, to focus through his own pain as the thorns twisted and pricked.

Vic couldn't help. He had no magic, no way to call the Reaper.

John grinned.

The canes tightened, pulling Vic to the ground. Bobby groaned, stirring at the attack, but he was just as bound as the rest of them.

Adam looked like a pincushion. Blood oozed from dozens of thorn pricks.

"But first," John said. "I think that's enough of you, boy."

The canes pulled back Adam's arms. They'd lassoed his neck, leaving him defenseless.

"One warlock in the family is enough," John spat.

He lifted the sickle.

"No!" Vic screamed.

Or maybe it was Adam.

Their terror and pain had mixed so deeply, so completely, that Vic wasn't certain which of them made the sound. He wasn't even certain which of them was cut as red drops slashed the air.

Adam fell back, chest soaked in blood. John stood over him, shaking his head.

He turned toward Vic, the sickle dripping.

Then Vic felt the cold. It rose deep inside, surging into him.

He looked at his hands and found white bones painted atop his skin. Black shadows crawled, swirling over him.

John's eyes widened. He looked terrified. Good.

Something inside Vic changed. All the light went out and something hungry, something ready, swirled to the surface.

He could still feel Adam, unable to move, bleeding out. Bobby was still breathing.

But Billy . . . Billy had died.

31

ADAM

He was the one dying this time. That's what it felt like. Adam might be able to apply some pressure, slow the bleeding, but his hands remained bound.

John loomed over him, the sickle ready for its next victim. He turned toward Vic, looking satisfied, looking determined.

Then cold flooded Adam's connection to Vic.

Adam felt the Reaper rise.

John saw the threat and moved as quickly as he could to slash out, but the sickle met Vic's baton.

Vic had torn free. The Reaper was free, and the baton grew, lengthening. Vic's robe of shadows unfurled like smoke.

Adam tried again to find the spell's core, the center of its web. The pain of the thorns and then the slash of the sickle had shattered his concentration, but now he felt the cold.

Inside his chest, the warlock wound pulsed. It was the strangest feeling, but it drank the pain. What remained was filled by the Reaper's cold. Numbed, Adam could think clearly again.

There. The spell. The binding.

Last time, he'd fed it a spark of his life, but now he had too little of that.

Vic and John clashed. John swept out with the sickle. Vic caught it on his scythe.

Adam had to help. He had to save Bobby, and even Jodi. He wouldn't let John hurt anyone else, especially Vic.

Adam focused on the cold, the black ice flowing through the thread. Adam took the barest hint, the smallest snowflake, and touched it to the spell.

The canes dissolved.

The snakes kept their distance. Whatever compulsion John had them under wasn't enough to bring them into the barn.

Adam shifted, and the numbness broke. His chest stung like the great-grandmother of all paper cuts. He gasped, but the hurt stopped as the warlock wound drank the pain.

John was fast. He was strong. The magic he'd stolen, the life, was giving him enough of an edge to hold Vic back.

Adam looked for a way out, an advantage.

Then something stirred, something in the frozen thread, the mix of Reaper and Warlock.

John's blue eyes went wide. He looked from Adam to Vic, and back.

Adam felt the world tilt. He fell back as Vic—no, the Reaper, seized the line, the connection to Adam's magic, and pulled.

The thread didn't snap.

For just a moment, the air broke. A hole opened. It was black and red, like looking at the sun through closed eyelids.

"You're not just a Reaper," John gasped. "What are you?"

The end, the Reaper said.

He swept out with the scythe. John leaped back, avoiding the blade, but he'd come too near the opening. Tendrils of it, like bloody veins, reached for him. They curled about his limbs.

"No!" Jodi shouted.

She hurtled forward, shoving past Vic to get to John.

Vic's hand snaked out. He grabbed her arm, tried to keep her from falling in. John was already gone.

Then the hole expanded, just once, in a burst.

Adam screamed Vic's name.

The hole closed, taking Jodi and Vic with it.

32

AFTER

He's not dead, Adam thought, over and over. It was like a mantra, a thought he repeated until it echoed through his head.

It didn't matter that he couldn't feel Vic through their connection. Wherever he'd gone was just too far. Adam would find him.

The hospital hadn't changed since Adam's last visit. At least he didn't have Noreen's old room.

Bobby had checked out with a concussion and some bruises.

Adam had gotten an insane number of stitches, a tetanus shot, and enough bandages that he could have dressed as a mummy for Halloween. Bobby had said he'd pay for it if Jesse didn't have insurance for his employees.

Adam had scoffed. Even Bobby didn't have *that* kind of money.

Early hadn't been by yet, though Bobby said there'd been drugs enough in Billy's van for the insane kidnapping to make some sort of crazy sense.

Bobby and Tilla had tried to sell Early on the idea that Jodi and Billy wanted more drugs, thinking that since Bobby was a doctor, he could get them some.

It didn't explain the barn, how Billy had died, or Adam's injuries. At least it sort of explained Jodi's disappearance, that she'd been tied up in "satanic shit," and Billy had been a sacrifice with Adam meant to follow.

Adam had asked his mother and brother to leave him alone, to let him sleep, but he couldn't. He had a deal to make.

Lying back, Adam closed his eyes. He could hardly move, so he could not assume the position, but he visualized it, pouring the tattered remains of his will into the image of an armored elf upon a snow white steed, an upraised sword in his hands.

A winter chill filled the room. Adam shivered despite himself, and even that little motion hurt.

"I'm here, Adam," Silver said.

Adam opened his eyes.

His first love looked different, and it wasn't just the crown. Silver had taken on years. Not too many, just a handful, but enough that Adam felt younger than him, felt the difference in their ages more keenly. He looked bulkier, like he'd put on muscle, though he wasn't larger. Adam was clearly out of the loop.

"I guess I'll have to call you differently next time," Adam said. His voice was raspy, dry.

Silver nodded his head in agreement.

Adam hadn't had the chance to ask Vic what had happened in Alfheimr. He assumed they'd won, though clearly there had been losses.

The story would have to wait.

"I'll do it," Adam said. "I'll take the job."

"Adam . . ." Silver said gently.

"You know what happened?" Adam asked.

"I do," Silver said.

"I'll do whatever it takes," Adam said. "Become whatever you need me to if you just give me the magic to get him back."

Silver looked paler, like more snow had settled into his skin.

"No," he said.

"What?" Adam asked. His stitches pulled as he tried to sit up. "I'm here, dammit. I'm ready. Let's make a deal."

"We don't know where he is, Adam," Silver said.

"He's not dead."

"I didn't say he was."

Gingerly, the king lowered himself onto the stool beside Adam's bed. He looked like he wanted to take Adam's hand, wanted to touch him, but thought better of it.

"But like I said, we don't know where he is."

"So I'll go find him," Adam said, though he knew without a doubt that Silver would have already looked anywhere he could. "Just give me the power and I'll find him."

"No," Silver repeated.

"Please," Adam said, feeling the tears fall. "I have to try. It's my fault. It's all my fault."

"You don't know what you're asking, my love," Silver said. "If he's in a place we cannot see, then our magic cannot go there. I could give you nine worlds of power, Adam, and I still don't think you would survive."

Adam nodded, swallowed hard, and felt the tears run from his cheeks to his neck.

What they'd been to each other had never felt like this before, like a noose, a rope around Adam's heart.

Silver wouldn't put Adam in danger, not if he thought Adam had no chance of survival. Because Silver loved him, he wouldn't risk Adam's life.

He laid a hand on Adam's wrist, finding a spot of bare skin.

Magic, cold and pure, flowed into Adam. It was like swallowing a snowstorm, so much colder than Silver's magic had ever felt before. It washed away the pain, and Adam felt his wounds knit.

He wanted to say thank you. He should say thank you. Manners meant everything among the elves. Silver had taught him that.

What came out instead was, "Please, Perak. Please."

"I will not," Silver said. And while there was love in it, there was also firmness. "I cannot."

The king was dead. Long live the king.

"Then what fucking good are you?" Adam asked.

Another little nod, more understanding. It should have pissed Adam off. He wanted to lash out again, but already the shame was settling in. The only real anger Adam had left was for himself.

"I'll take my leave," Silver said.

Adam could only let the tears fall.

Alone again, he settled back against his pillow.

He could move now, assume a position, but didn't need to.

He pictured a throne, a woman on it, an upraised sword in one hand, a pair of scales in the other. He tried to hold the image, matching it to the card, but the sword became a steel baton. The woman became a man in blue, his hair so black, his eyes so deep that their brown pierced Adam.

He opened his eyes and stood before the Hanging Tree. The crescent moon of the Other Side hung in its usual place, only tonight it had taken on a purple shade, a bit more blue. Perhaps it mourned the King of Swords. Perhaps it heralded the new age, the rule of the former knight.

"Where are we going?" a voice asked.

Vran. Adam should be surprised to see him here, to see him now, but the numbness had sunk too deep into his heart.

"I need to talk to her," Adam said, nodding to the beaten Airstream trailer resting beyond the field of sunflowers and the Reapers who scythed them. "You shouldn't come."

"Pft," Vran scoffed. "Like I'd miss this."

"Suit yourself," Adam said. He couldn't very well tell the elf to stay away, not do something stupid, not when Silver had pretty much done the same thing and Adam had thrown it back in his face.

"You told off the king," Vran said.

"Yeah, I do that sometimes," Adam said.

He started walking. He could hear Vran behind him, not quite perfectly silent.

The Reapers stopped their scything. As one, they straightened and looked to Adam.

She sat ahead, in her rocking chair, a glass of iced tea in her hand.

Death looked up and smiled.

ACKNOWLEDGMENTS

To Aaron and Jon, Ally, Bryson, Emily Ozuna, Eytan, Jake Shandy, Jayme Bean, John McDougall, Kelsey, Mya, Noor, Rachel Brittain, Rogier, Shiri, Patrick Munnelly, Trip Gailey and Robert Berg, Ben Ragunton and Keith Lane—and everyone who found *White Trash Warlock* and fell in love with Adam.

Jesse Schmitt, for the subject matter expertise.

As always, my amazing agents, Lesley Sabga, Nicole Resciniti, and everyone at the Seymour Agency.

Mandy Earles, Rick Bleiweiss, Josie Woodbridge, Deirdre Curley, Samantha Benson, Isabella Bedoya, and everyone at Blackstone who makes the magic happen.

Sean Thomas for the amazing covers. This one especially just blows me away.

Michael David Axtell for giving Adam a voice.

Todd Van Prooyen for coming up with the world's worst band name.

My mother, Paula Lee Dyess Wells, who helped with my family tree and therefore, Adam's, before she passed in July of

2021. I'll miss you. I'm so sorry we did not get more time, and I'm sorry you did not get the chance to read this one.

Mervin, James, and Judy: the gay cousins who came before me and who some of my family tried to erase. We never met, but you are not forgotten.